ARAM

BASED ON A TRUE
18TH CENTURY MURDER STORY

AMANDA TAYLOR

This story is based on fact.
All the historical events happened,
all dates and courtroom statements
are taken from official documents,
publications and press reports
of the time.

© Amanda Taylor, 2017

WEST END
PUBLICATIONS

Published by West End Publications

A CIP catalogue record for this book is available from the British Library.

ISBN 978-0-9955777-0-1 (Hardback)
ISBN 978-0-9955777-1-8 (Paperback)

Book layout and cover design by Clare Brayshaw

Cover image ©Blaseofglory Alexey Rumyantsev | dreamstime.com

Prepared and printed by:

York Publishing Services Ltd
64 Hallfield Road
Layerthorpe
York YO31 7ZQ

Tel: 01904 431213

Website: www.yps-publishing.co.uk

For all those who receive imperfect justice.

'Mankind are never corrupted at once;
villany is always progressive, and
declines from right, step after step,
till every regard of probity is lost,
and every sense of moral obligation
totally perishes.' (sic)

Eugene Aram, 1759.

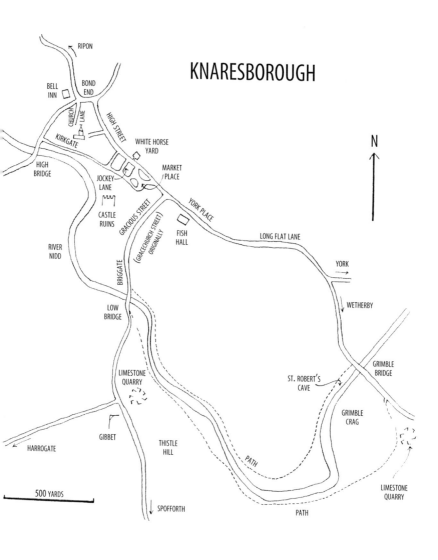

CHAPTER ONE

Yorkshire, England, Tuesday 21st August 1759.

Fox-like screeches cut through the air. My horse reared, forcing me to keep my weight balanced forward and centred against her neck, part of my luggage jamming painfully into my ribs and stomach. Ignoring us, our plight, two children stood transfixed before a towering outline several yards ahead. Still without a glance our way – their earlier hair-raising screeches exhausted – they turned and started running down the hill from where I guessed they had come. They fled as if the Devil himself was on their tail.

'Stop, wait!' I heard a woman shout. She was clearly visible now from my station on Forest Moor Road. Stout of build, each step she took appeared to be weighted with determination as she attempted to make the ascent her companions had already achieved. Far lighter of foot, the children had the sense to lift their skirts to move unencumbered over the rough ground as they made their retreat back down towards her. But they did not stop on reaching her and passed by with the speed of bracken freed by the wind.

'Seen enough, we have,' screamed the smaller girl.

''Tis a terrible thing to see,' shouted back the older girl.

'Just one look, I beg of ye,' pleaded the stout female, stopping from time to time to catch her breath before climbing upwards again. 'Please, just one look.'

The two below finally slowed down, hovered looking back, but made no reply.

'Anyhow, I'm off for a closer look,' insisted the woman. Shrugging, she turned to the challenging hill again, her burgundy dress billowing about her, an embattled man-of-war under full sail.

The two children stared after her with expressions filled with fear and dread.

'Betty! Betty come away, 'tis your natural father hanging there,' they shrilled in eerie unison.

Betty's voice bristling with spite slashed down the void between them. 'Aye, 'tis he all right.' And then with clinical detachment, 'But by now 'tis difficult to tell.'

'Miss.' I raised my hat.

'Sir,' acknowledged the woman, hardly aware of my presence. She remained focused on that terrible swinging thing elevated to a position greater than mine in his gown of pitch and tar.

My horse grew skittish again, unnerved by the smell of death. She pawed at the parcel of land, wanting to be away. The man's hanging form was silhouetted black against a moorland backdrop dressed in bishop's purple. There in the failing light of day, I saw a smile of pleasure form on the woman's lips as she looked up into the grimacing death mask.

'This is no place for a lady to be,' I told her.

'This is the very place I want to be,' she retorted more to herself.

'Was this man really known to you?'

'Was he known to you?'

'Yes, though we were not well-acquainted.'

'Not as acquainted as I was,' she scoffed.

'Is it true what those two children just said that this is your father?' Concern and incredulity fuelled my question.

'Aye, but no one would have ever noticed.'

'Is that the way down into the town?' I pointed with my riding crop down towards the field meadows reaching up from the Nidd valley.

'That is the way home.'

'Then perhaps you also had better make for it, miss. The night is drawing in.'

'There are no demons left to haunt me.' Her mouth lifted with satisfaction.

'All the same no Christian woman should linger in the gibbet's shadow.' I drew the horse's rein to the right, and we left her there, the sound of jangling chains and creaking wood tormenting me until we were out of range.

The road surface, which had degenerated near the site of the gibbet, thankfully improved again as I approached a coaching inn on the south bank before the river crossing. I decided not to put up here as I was anxious to see the town proper and examine all options.

We started to cross the bridge which was narrow but firm underfoot. For some unaccountable reason my hired nag faltered and stopped. I became exasperated, giving her hindquarters a taste of the crop – an instrument I disliked using on principle and seldom employed – still she would not budge. Looking from my lofty, if ridiculous, position into the iron coloured water cascading below and then up to the high cliff looming on the far bank, I realised that this was not a place to be thrown.

'Move you dumb creature.' I could feel the lifting northern breeze beginning to bite into my bones. The mare's nostrils flared and her eyelids peeled back as I kicked her hard with my boot heel. Finally, she responded and we slowly inched forward. For the life of me I could not understand her self-imposed boundary. Perhaps it is true, perhaps horses do possess a sixth sense.

Cottages and houses squeezed tightly together on both sides of the rise known as Gracechurch Street. I turned in the saddle to see if the three females had come down off the moor top. They were nowhere to be seen. Perhaps they knew a better way down into town. Indeed, I had not seen another living soul so far.

Even in the High Street there were few townsfolk out and about. It was as if Knaresborough had been hit by the plague. One or two men stood in shop doorways, puffing away on their pipes and contemplating the scene; a few others were gathered on a street corner and appeared to be engaged in serious conversations. I did not see one woman or child abroad. Although I visited this town on several occasions a year ago for inquests held into bones found on Thistle Hill, not far from where the corpse was now gibbeted, I had never actually stayed here. It was getting late and the darkened streets looked unfamiliar.

'Sir, can you direct me to a good inn with rooms for the night?' I shouted across the Market Place to a decently dressed bewigged fellow who was standing looking in an apothecary's window. He swung round on his walking cane in surprise.

'Aye, sir, I could if you so choose to stay in this town tonight.' His reply sounded a warning.

'I do, sir.'

'The Bell then. Keep on your road towards Bond End and the inn is there.' Using his cane he pointed up the street in a vague direction, raising his hat with the other hand in salute. 'Best of luck to you, sir.' His voice carried after me, ominous in the hushed silence.

* * * * *

'Scape Gallows, Scape Gallows Houseman,' the chant grew louder, grew momentum as it passed the Bell Inn at Bond End.

'They are making for Richard Houseman's cottage,' said the Bell's ostler. 'I wouldn't like to be him tonight.'

'Me neither.' The insurrection had started just as I arrived. Voices bounced round the yard. I had barely time to catch my breath. 'Please see to my horse and bags and tell the landlord I will take his best bedchamber,' I shouted back to the ostler as I ran from the stable after the mob.

A hard core of half a dozen men were joined by others coming out of every door they passed. Like some unwieldy monster their ranks swelled to thirty or so through the town's narrow streets.

'Knaresborough is about to riot. They'll not suffer the presence of Aram's co-accused much longer.' My Harrogate informant had not been wrong. Richard Houseman's person and premises had already been attacked once and looked as if they were about to be again.

Following Eugene Aram's trial in York, I had been enjoying a few day's respite in Harrogate's spas before decamping back to London. I had only just despatched my final report by carrier to the *Gentleman's Magazine* in St John's Gate, when I got word that this rural murder story was not yet at an end.

'Scape Gallows, Scape Gallows Houseman.' A straw effigy danced on a pole in the midst of the mob, a scarecrow harbinger like Houseman's friend dancing in chains above the town. The cry became more menacing as they pulled up in front of a modest cottage on the High Street adjoining the White Horse Inn. Their flares were reflected a hundred fold in a myriad of household and shop windows. 'Scape Gallows, Scape Gallows Houseman, show theesen.' Houseman's cottage remained in darkness. Perhaps he was not at home.

Men and even a few women were arriving now, caught up in the hysteria. I hated crowds at the best of times. I hated this one more. There was not a constable to be seen to curb the simmering threat before it rose to boiling point.

Thankfully, no Houseman materialised either. Within minutes they set about tearing at the heckler's house, brick by brick, each brick and no householder adding to their frustration. One of the supporting timbers began to rock. I shook my head in disbelief. I was here simply to report, but to stand by and do and say nothing faced with such wanton destruction – there was no justice in this.

'Someone might still be in there,' I cried out.

'Good,' said a man at my side. 'Good, it serves him right.'

'An eye for an eye,' said another.

'His wife could be in there,' I suggested.

'Widow Johnson should have chosen her second husband better,' cackled a toothless crone.

'You are without mercy.'

'They showed no mercy to poor Dan Clark,' said the biblical scholar.

A man emerged from the adjoining cottage and appealed to the mob that they were putting his own premises in jeopardy. 'You all know me well,' he screamed. 'I am an honest and innocent man and yet you are weakening the fabric of my house to rid yourselves of Dickey Houseman.'

'We have no grievance against you, Mr Shepherd,' agreed a burly looking fellow.

'Houseman is away this night, I can tell you that. Now go home, lads, and leave retribution to the Lord.'

The exasperated mob next turned their attention and anger on Houseman's effigy. One man began beating it about the head with a pickaxe before another performed a mock execution on it with a rope. Finally they set the grotesque thing on fire with their flares. If the heckler had been in his cottage and they had flushed him out, there was no doubt in my mind that the same fate would have been meted out to him. Houseman had twice cheated death: at his trial he turned King's evidence and escaped the hangman's noose; now, it seemed, he was not at home and had avoided physical retribution at the hands of his neighbours.

Burning ashes chased me up the High Street, carried by that cool late summer breeze. I watched them glow and extinguish in the darkness, spirit reminders of the awful events I had just witnessed.

* * * * *

Although the hour was late, the Bell's landlord managed to find me a bottle of wine and what was left of casseroled rabbit. Later, I settled by the hearth in the comfort of the snug little sitting-room to belch rabbit, empty the dregs of the surprisingly good Bordeaux and contemplate my day. I began to wonder if my decision to come here had been a good one. Yorkshire was so foreign to me. One of the county's better roads, the Forest Moor Road between Harrogate and Knaresborough, had been almost impassable in places with swamps and fallen trees; the landscape was untamed, impenetrable, the people the same.

The riot and near destruction of Houseman's cottage had shocked me. The truth of it was not only did I hate human crowds, I feared them too. But doubts had been gnawing away at me ever since reporting on the trial of *Rex v. Houseman, Aram and Terry*; a trial that turned out to be *Rex v. Aram* as the cases against his co-defendants seemed to simply evaporate into the ether.

I took out of my top pocket a cutting from a rival newspaper. A cutting I had kept close to my heart throughout Aram's trial. The article came from the *Whitehall Evening Post*, dated the 7th of September, 1758, a year before the assizes at York. This piece disturbed me, not so much because we had been beaten to its publication but because of its content. It purported to be part of a letter from a Yorkshire correspondent. It said there was a woman in Knaresborough who could hang several men and a husband.

Several Men in the Town agreed together
that one of them, under Specious Pretences,
should borrow Plate, Jewels etc., of all
substantial People in the Town, and then
make off with the Booty. It fell to the Lot
of one Clark to borrow, who met with the
wish'd for Success; at that time a Jew and
his Man were in the Town, they sent for him,
offered him the Goods and sold them to him
and received the Money, when done, they
murdered both the Jew and his Man, and buried
them; while they were throwing the Earth upon
them, one of the Company whose name is Aram
and who is now in York Castle, with another

Confederate, took up a Pick-Axe, and struck
Clark in the Skull and killed him, and buried
him in another Place, and so they became
Master of the Whole unsuspected: Every one
concluding Clark was quite gone off with the
Goods he had borrowed. This happened
Fourteen Years since.

No one had mentioned anything about the murder of a
Jew and his man at the trial. In light of the massacre of one
hundred and fifty York Jews, who had sought refuge within
Clifford's Tower in 1190, I could have expected uneducated
locals might still be hostile to people of difference but
for these prejudices to extend into our law courts is
unforgivable. Then again should I be surprised: look at
Henry Pelham's Jew Bill of 1753, giving Jews the chance of
naturalisation. One of my father's oldest friends, the Jewish
banker Sampson Gideon had been rewarded with that bill
by the Whigs for Jewish support of the government during
the Jacobite Rebellion 1745. Sampson had helped prop up
the country's finances raising a loan of £1,700,000 as Charles
Edward Stuart knocked on the town of Derby's door. Come
victory, come the repeal of Pelham's Bill due to public and
Tory protests the following year.

However, I thought the case against the Gentile, Aram,
was conducted in a crude and less than judicial fashion
too. Despite his credentials of good Anglican affiliations,
he had no professional representation and the arguments
he gave were scoffed at or at best ignored. I was becoming
increasingly uneasy about being here in Yorkshire. I longed
for the sophistication of Bloomsbury. Perhaps I should catch

the stage for London tomorrow but something indeterminate was holding me back.

At midnight I was resting my head on the hard flock pillow in the Bell's bedchamber. Though tired, sleep would not come.

I decided to get up and start penning my first report from Knaresborough to the *Gentleman's Magazine.*

This evening, standing outside
Richard Houseman's cottage, I
witnessed a mob assembled ...

But it was not the riot keeping me from my dreams. No, I could not rid myself of the image of father and daughter silhouetted against the twilight sky. There at the tiny writing desk in my room, I could see the beads of sweat glistening above Betty Aram's lips from her effort of climbing up the hillside, and the smile of pleasure forming on those same lips as she looked up into Aram's grimacing face. Her tongue lashed out to lick away the sweat like a satisfied cat mopping up milk. What had that man done to cause such loathing? He had originally been destined for the anatomists by the Honourable Mr Justice Noel, but this sentence had been commuted the following day. He was to be put on display as an example to the townsfolk of Knaresborough. I guessed that Eugene, sometimes known as Eugenius, would have preferred his original more private punishment.

Somehow I knew even then, as he dangled in chains from his gibbet post up the hill, it was not the end of this story but the beginning.

CHAPTER TWO

At ten o' clock, the following morning, I was enjoying a plate of freshly baked bread, cold beef and cheeses with pickle, in my room for breakfast. The Bell's brew of coffee was fair to poor. What else could I expect? Damnation, I was still in Yorkshire.

My informant in Harrogate had advised me to seek out a Knaresborough physician called Hutchinson.

'As sharp as mustard and as bright as the sun, that one,' he had told me. 'Hutchinson has a keen interest in everything going on around him. I heard he found Aram's trial absolutely fascinating. Took his mind off animals, plants and the stars for once.'

'But not off his patients, I hope,' I retorted drily.

'Them too. Joking apart, if you want a detailed insight into the goings on in that town, Hutchinson's your man.'

I knocked on Dr Hutchinson's front door. No answer. I went into the yard at the back. And there he was "my man". A duplicated, distorted Thomas Hutchinson could be seen staring down some unfortunate's throat through a multitude of bottle glass window panes. The window had been placed at the back of the building – not out of any consideration for patients' privacy – because the panes were deemed to be both a fire risk and less fashionable than the sliding sash windows fronting the High Street. Even Knaresborough was not beyond pragmatism together with architectural snobbery.

After several knocks on the back door, Hutchinson reluctantly answered. A long spoon, which I guessed had been acting as a tongue depressor, still in his hand.

'Well?' he snapped. I passed him my letter of introduction. 'So what can I do for you, Felix Kendle? As you can see I am rather busy at the moment wondering what powders to prepare for this poor fellow's quinsy.' Dr Hutchinson evidently was not over familiar with the Hippocratic Oath. 'You can close your mouth for the time being, Samuel,' he shouted back over his shoulder.

The patient's leather gaiters creaked as he relaxed and crossed his legs.

'Before returning to London after reporting on Eugene Aram's trial in York for the *Gentleman's Magazine*, I have been staying at the World's End Inn and spawing at Harrogate,' I explained. 'While there an acquaintance and fellow professional of yours informed me of trouble brewing in Knaresborough following Aram's hanging. He suggested I put up here for a few days and interview you. He said you are a gentleman who enjoys considerable respect and reputation in this community.'

'Who might this acquaintance be?'

'I never reveal my sources of information.'

'That is as it may be, however one might presume it is the same gentleman who has provided you with this letter of introduction, Doctor Thomas Short of Sheffield.'

'I never …'

'Yes, you said, you never reveal your sources. But Doctor Short is an aware and affable Scot, is he not?' asked Hutchinson, flicking the letter.

'Quite. Though he strikes me as a man who does not suffer fools gladly.'

'Indeed,' agreed Hutchinson. 'So where did you say you are staying in Knaresborough, sir?'

'I didn't. I am staying at the Bell Inn as it happens.'

'I had the good fortune to catch two good sized trout in the river Nidd this morning. If you care to share them with me for dinner, I am sure it will be no trouble for the Bell's landlady to cook them up for us.'

'Shall we say seven?'

'Seven will suit me well unless I am called to a pressing case. Meanwhile you might care to call on Vicar Collins. He knew Eugene Aram better than any man living in the town. Aram penned him some letters about his grand ancestry, poems and suchlike of a personal nature. Indeed, it was he who shared Aram's final moments. It was Collins' unenviable task to accompany Aram to the gallows.'

'And where might I find him?'

'The parish church of course.'

'Might I suggest blackcurrants.'

'Blackcurrants?'

'A cordial of crushed blackcurrants to ease your patient's throat. Failing that I have heard a mouth wash of urine is effective.'

Terrified, the old countryman sat bolt upright in his chair before being pushed back down by his lapsed physician.

* * * * *

The parish church was not hard to find. The building towered above the town second only to the castle. Its interior was more cathedral than church. My footsteps echoed in the arches on either side of the central aisle like the footsteps of a beast prowling past caves. I spied my prey towards the apse. The Reverend Collins was dressed from head to foot in black: black shoes, black spats, black tricorne hat. He was dressed in his street clothes as if newly arrived or ready to leave.

'A beautiful place of worship you have here, Reverend. Dedicated to Saint John the Baptist, I see,' was my opening line. Standing small beneath the elevated pulpit, Vicar Collins looked up in astonishment from the notes he was examining.

'Not always, sir. The church was originally named Saint Mary's before the Reformation.' Said without a smile.

'Doctor Hutchinson directed me to you.'

'Did he? And why might he have done that?'

'He said you knew Eugene Aram better than any living man.'

'And what interest have you in that poor soul lost to heaven?'

'To be honest with you, sir, I am a writer alerted to the riots taking place here following his death.'

'Oh, and what have you written?'

'I have had a few matters of interest recorded in the *Gentleman's Magazine*.'

'It is merely a few townsfolk set against Richard Houseman,' announced Collins dismissively. 'Houseman was a co-defendant at the trial until he turned King's evidence.'

'I know. I was there.'

'Then you will know what an unfortunate spectacle it proved to be, a bear pit of justice, the man's hanging was even worse.'

'You remained with the schoolmaster until the end.'

At first Thomas Collins offered no reply. He appeared to be traumatised by memories of the event on York's

Knavesmire field. He was not the only one. I knew he had been with Aram when they hanged him because I had been there too in the crowd. Something stopped me admitting this to Collins. It was as if I had participated in something shameful – hangings and whoring are not events to be boasted about.

'Eugenius was so weakened by loss of blood after slashing his arm the previous night, he was barely conscious as they hauled him beneath the gallows.'

'I am still curious to know if justice was done. I thought his defence was brilliant.'

'Brilliant and inventive. But then that was Eugenius, always too brilliant and too inventive.' Thomas Collins gave me a quizzical and searching look. 'You do not believe the verdict to be in error, do you?'

'In life as in death there is always the possibility of error. But tell me, Reverend Collins, why are the townsfolk so malevolent towards Houseman?'

'Some suspect he was culpable for Daniel Clark's murder and has escaped punishment. Some feel he is responsible for Aram's execution. After his acquittal, Houseman returned home from York to be greeted by a few friends. Anticipating trouble, two or three principals of the town shook him by the hand. They congratulated him on his freedom as if he was an innocent man. Alas, the manoeuvre was instantly seen through and the town's indignation was not averted.'

'Some of which I witnessed for myself last night.'

'They hissed, hooted and mobbed him and so furious did the multitude become his life was only preserved by a neighbour opening up his house to provide him with a refuge. The violence next escalated against the heckler's property.

That started on the Tuesday evening, a week ago, before Wednesday market and fair. Where will it all end, only God knows,' said Collins clasping his hands in agitation.

'Indeed, sir. Yesterday I was personally welcomed by the sight of Eugene Aram's body hanging from the gibbet post upon the moor as I came down into the town.'

'A terrible contraption. A terrible stain on the community.'

'And a daily reminder to the townsfolk of Knaresborough that justice might only have been partially done,' I added.

'Quite,' whispered Collins.

'I saw a girl up there on Thistle Hill. One of Aram's daughters, I believe.'

'That would be poor Betty.' Collins let out a huge sigh. 'She hated her father most of all.'

'For abandoning her mother and siblings for all those years following the shoemaker's missing?' I asked.

'We are perhaps better remaining ignorant of the girl's reasons,' replied Collins obscurely.

We both turned on hearing footsteps behind us. A lean shadowy figure crept into a corner pew. Whether man or woman, I was unsure. The bowed face was partly obscured by the lower column of one of the arches.

'Francis, what a surprise to see you in here during the working day.' Collins' voice echoed across to the seated indeterminate figure before he turned back to me. 'I cannot talk any longer.' His abruptness took me by surprise. 'You could do no better than entertain yourself at the Dropping Well after noon.' His matter-of-fact change of subject was just as sudden.

'And where might that be, Reverend Collins?'

'Turn left along the river walk after High Bridge. I am

surprised you have not already been there. It is one of the oldest and greatest curiosities in England.'

'I have heard of it of course, sir. Was it not the well visited by John Leyland, Antiquary to Henry VIII?'

''Tis the same, sir.'

I turned round after moving a yard or two away down the aisle. The mystery man and Collins were already locked in an intimate conversation.

'Forgive me, Vicar Collins,' I shouted back to him, annoyed at my ungracious dismissal. 'I would be obliged to see those final letters and poems, I understand Aram penned to you. Indeed any material that you might possess regarding him would be of immense interest to me.'

Collins' mouth fell open as my words bounced from one pillar to the next. His eyes expressed fear. He did not reply.

* * * * *

I was enjoying the finite rays of late summer sun on my skin, the direct movement of walking rather than riding. It was one of those afternoons that I felt rich for merely being alive – youthful and rich indeed – small slivers of gold leaf fluttered occasionally above my head and dropped to the ground. Several beech trees were already on the turn as I took the path along the Nidd towards the dropping well. The walk and parkland between the High and Low Bridge had been improved some twenty years before by Sir Henry Slingsby. The park had a country estate feel to it. I passed the Manor House on the Nidd's opposite bank. The building was believed to stand on the site of an old hunting lodge used by King John after a day's sport in Knaresborough Forest. The Bell's landlord had further informed me that this same house had some connection with Oliver Cromwell during the siege of the town's castle. The castle, along with its turbulent history, dominated the horizon as my path rounded a gentle bend following the course of the river.

'Good day to you, sir.' I thought I had been alone on the path but a passing woodsman raised his felt cap to me.

'And to you, sir. Pray could you tell me, am I close to the well?' I shouted after him.

He turned in his tracks, levered the axe from his shoulder before carefully hiding it behind a hornbeam trunk. His face was as weathered as Chaucer's yeoman in *The Canterbury Tales*.

'Allow me to escort you there,' he replied, leading the way down a steeper path towards the riverside. Soon our route levelled out again beneath a limestone overhang.

The Dropping Well – there it was at last – a curtain of water cascading down a huge smooth vertical slab of rock. The townsfolk of Knaresborough had not baulked at confronting Richard Houseman, but I had heard whispers that many avoided this place as if it were the bowels of hell.

'Can you tell me anything about this phenomenon?' I asked the woodsman.

'I can that, sir. There is no man better placed in England.'

'Is it true there is some witchcraft at work here where objects once immersed in these waters turn to stone?'

'I know nothing of witchcraft, sir, but it is fact should that hat of yours fall off into this water it would be petrified in months.'

I placed a hand on my new tricorne as if in a wind. I had paid good money for it only recently in Harrogate.

'Is that why the locals do not venture here?' I asked.

'Partly, they are a superstitious lot up there in town. But in the season there are plenty of others to take their place, usually visiting folk from far away seeking a cure. For them this is a magical spot rather than one of sorcery. I've seen 'em flinging their sticks to one side to either bathe under the falling water or in the cold pool beneath. I have seen some very sad sights here indeed, sir. All because of their desperation to be healed. Some even drink the stuff in a bid to cure the flux. Though I'd not be one for recommending that.'

'Why not?'

'The water is too rich in minerals for the human stomach to take.'

'Is that so? But where does it all come from, where is its source?'

'It is thought there is an underground lake on yonder moor, and that the water slowly seeps up through the limestone. Might I be so bold as to ask, are you seeking a cure for some malady yourself, sir?'

'Do I look as if I am?'

'One can never tell.' With that the woodsman went on his way leaving me to absorb his words and the scene.

I found a cave entrance further down from the tumbling water which seemed to have been formed by the same limestone deposits. I cautiously ventured inside. Though not deep it was gloomy, dank and chilling for all that. Caves are not my favourite places. There is something primeval about them and my fear of them.

I ran my fingers across the smooth rock. The sensation was tactile, pleasing. Slowly a shadow crossed the wall I was touching – a cloud across my day. The meagre light coming from the cave entrance was blocked. I turned, my exit was blocked. I was standing in near darkness.

'You the cove that's been asking all them questions about Knaresborough business?'

Business, business – words bounced off the cavern walls. Words I could not grasp. I blinked in an attempt to adjust to the diminished light.

'Yes, it's him all right.'

Right, right. Half a dozen men stood in the entrance.

'Let's get him.'

Him, him. I was trapped, hemmed in.

'Let's teach him a lesson.' The final words had not completed their echoing cycle as the wall of men moved towards me.

With the possibility of desperate flight gone, a calm spread through me – the sort of calm that besets the rabbit before the stoat. I saw the raised arm with its extension of club like a shadow show. I felt the blow on the side of my head – the dirt in my mouth – as if it was not happening to me but to a personator.

Dead, dead. You've killed, killed, killed him, him … I felt a final, good measure kick in my ribs like some dull distant pain. Partial darkness turned into total pitch nothingness. He was no longer him.

'You all right, sir?' Echoes buzzed in my head like bees. I was uncertain where I was or what was real. Two strong arms were under my shoulders lifting me. I was floating, airless, like some Lazarus. 'I thought you were gone there for a moment.'

One strong arm was now guiding me like an ice dancer out of the cave entrance. Something sticky and lukewarm was running down the side of my face. I could taste blood in my mouth. I reached up to my face and examined the reddish brown liquid cupped in my hand. The woodsman stood before me – the original tough expression of Chaucer's yeoman gone – he showed only compassion and concern. With an arm still acting as support he guided me to a natural stone basin, inset to the right of the Dropping Well, where I bathed my head wound. As I stooped over I winced at the pain in my side. My physical sensations were returning with vengeance.

'I saw them ruffians heading your way,' explained the woodsman. 'I was felling a tree high up the bank above the path. I thought they looked like trouble.'

'They were local,' I gasped. 'Their dialect was local. Did you recognise any of them?'

The woodsman shook his head. 'Too far away, sir.'

'Pity,' I said.

'I'm really sorry they did this to you, sir. Will you be all right to make it back into town alone, or shall I come with you?'

'I'll make it back.' I spat a globule of remaining blood out of my mouth like a threat.

'You nearly forgot this, sir.' The woodsman held out my filthy battered tricorne hat. Without really thinking, I threw it into the waters of the Dropping Well. 'You have to make a wish,' the woodsman shouted after me as I staggered off.

'I already have done,' I muttered without turning back.

CHAPTER THREE

'What on earth has happened to you?' asked Thomas Hutchinson. He was already waiting for me in the Bell's best room that evening. I smiled tightly. I presumed he was referring to the cut above my eye and the swelling on my left temple which had risen like a Yorkshire pudding since the afternoon. 'Allow me to examine those abrasions for you.'

'No, no.' I waved him off. 'I will be fine.'

'A tonic for my guest here,' Hutchinson shouted to the landlord. 'A jug of negus to share.'

'I see someone has taken against your friend in a big way, Doctor Hutchinson,' chuckled the landlord, with that chummy, all being part of the masculine club attitude I so despised, particularly when I was feeling so knocked about.

I scowled at him across the bar. He carelessly slopped some of the hot spicy wine onto the counter as he transferred it from jug to drinking vessels.

'Who did this to you?' For a doctor, who must have seen his fair share of terrible wounds even in a brief career, Hutchinson remained shocked. He wasn't about to let the subject drop easily either.

'Some men surrounded me in the cave along the Nidd,' I explained.

'What cave? Saint Robert's Cave?'

'No, the one near the Dropping Well.'

'Oh, Mother Shipton's Cave.'

'Mother who?'

'You've never heard of Mother Shipton?' cut in the astonished landlord.

'Fancy that,' said Hutchinson. 'Come, Mr Kendle, let us take that table in the inglenook and I will tell you all about Agatha Sontheil and her illegitimate daughter.'

'Your trout will not be long in cooking, Doctor,' assured the landlord. 'I'll have the girl bring them to your table as soon as they are out of the oven.'

'Now tell me about these rogues who attacked you,' said Hutchinson, almost before we had taken our seats.

'I did not know them. One was wielding a club.'

'Did they say anything?'

'They told me I was asking too many questions, meddling in Knaresborough business.'

'Too many difficult questions, no doubt,' muttered Hutchinson, covertly regarding an old gaitered fellow sucking peaceably on his long alderman pipe by the flaming hearth.

'I'll not be cowed,' I uttered softly into the cloud of tobacco air.

'I can see that. But Aram's conviction, Houseman's discharge, has created an explosive situation here in Knaresborough. These are dangerous times. Yorkshire is a wild and unruly place. It is best to tread carefully, Mr Kendle, you are a stranger here.'

'A stranger in search of the truth.'

'Indeed, indeed,' mused Hutchinson, looking worried.

'What camp are you in then, Doctor, the one that supports Aram or are you for Houseman?'

'I am for neither though I think Houseman is a lucky man to have gained his freedom.'

'It is Aram that I am specifically interested in.'

'I am too. I would give anything to have his skull for my museum.'

'Museum?'

'Yes, I have begun to collect for a museum of local interest. Stuffed birds, pressed flowers, objects of antiquity.'

'But to display a man's skull.'

'Yes,' pondered Hutchinson, 'I would love to measure it as well.'

'Measure his skull?'

'Yes, measure its weight and size against the skull of a normal man.'

'"A normal man", does such a thing exist? If so I have never met one.'

'Let us say then that most sane men do not murder their neighbours.'

'So what abnormalities are you expecting to find, ones which denote a murderer or a genius?'

'Both perhaps in Aram's case,' laughed Hutchinson lightly. 'Although I cannot comment personally on his intellectual prowess as I never met him. Remember he was gone from the town some thirteen years following the disappearance of the shoemaker, Daniel Clark.'

'But he left his wife and children here.'

'Most of his children.'

'Sorry, I'm not sure I catch your meaning.'

'Didn't you know, his eldest girl, Sally, was found living with her father down in Lynn when he was arrested?'

'That was never mentioned at his trial.'

'Well, it wouldn't be.' Hutchinson beamed knowingly at me over his drink.

'What are you suggesting?'

'I will not malign the reputation of a man who is no longer here to defend himself.'

'Then, I'll not press you further on the matter. But I will seek it out from another source.'

'I do not doubt that you will for a moment, Mr Kendle. There has been a lot of gossip whispered around Knaresborough and much of it has emanated from within Aram's own four walls.'

'As I said, though I will not press you personally, no stone will be left unturned in the pursuit of truth.'

'Or a good story,' threw in Hutchinson.

'Or a good story,' I repeated, unabashed by his sarcasm.

''Tis Felix Kendle the terrier then.'

'Be assured, if not from your mouth, I am determined to find out all I can about the man hanging up there on the gibbet post. How a scholar, a teacher, nay a family man came to such an end.'

'Please understand my prudency regarding this matter. Anna Aram, his widow, and her children are known to me,' said Hutchinson in justification.

The Bell's ethereal maid floated across with our trout and potatoes. She wore a plain white lawn cap pushed back at the front in the French manner. The cap's untied streamer floated loosely down her back. There was something rather exotic about this girl, a distance. She placed the dishes before Hutchinson and me as if we were two strange creatures beyond her understanding. In contrast the heavy-footed corpulent landlord, jug in hand, followed on. He edged the girl to one side with his elbow in his eagerness to refill my pot and Hutchinson's resident pewter tankard.

'I trust my wife has cooked your fish to perfection, gentlemen,' he enquired, smacking his lips together. Hutchinson gave him a dismissive nod.

'So, you were going to tell me about Agatha Sontheil,' I prompted Hutchinson as the fawning landlord bowed away into the background.

'She bore a child out of wedlock in 1488 or thereabouts.'

'That long ago?'

'Agatha, always known as a slothful idle girl, was only fifteen at the time. Her outraged neighbours, here in the town, insisted that she was prosecuted for whoring and she was hauled before the local Justice. She refused to name the father of the coming child, while reminding the Justice that two of his own servant girls were with child by him simultaneously.' Hutchinson rubbed his hands with glee. 'Uproar in court, case dismissed.'

'True, it is,' agreed the old man by the fire, who must have been listening. 'All true.'

'Ostracised from society, and the child nearing term, Agatha took to living in the cave, the same cave you were assaulted in, Felix,' continued Hutchinson between mouthfuls of earthy river trout.

I shivered at the memory in that hot, yellow tobacco stained room of the Bell. Relieved I had survived the cave and was not still lying there mortally wounded in the dark.

'It was a close July night when she began her labour. A woman, who went to help her, spoke of the smell of sulphur and a great crack of thunder as the child came into the world. It was a baby girl. Ursula, Agatha called her. She was born huge and misshapen, a horrible looking creature. The woman tending the birth reported that the creature had come into the world jeering at the storm until it was silenced. Now this is where the story gets really intriguing, Felix. Remember, Agatha had refused to name the father of her child, nevertheless the Abbot of Beverley, Beverley being some sixty miles east of Knaresborough, risked compromise by baptising Ursula who some said was the daughter of the Devil.'

'Interesting,' I said.

'Yes, either interesting or true Christian benevolence,' replied Hutchinson.

'So, what became of Agatha and Ursula?'

'When Ursula was two years old, Agatha is said to have put her with a foster mother in Knaresborough while she herself entered a convent down Nottingham way. Ursula was known to be a mischievous little girl. Though still exceedingly ugly, at the age of twenty-four she managed to entrance a carpenter, Tobias Shipton. Some folk maintained that she must have drugged the poor fellow with a magic potion into marrying her. Whether or not this was true, Ursula was becoming known around the town as a wise woman with foresight. Soon she would be known and feared by the great and the good throughout the land as Mother Shipton, the prophetess.'

'Tell me about some of these prophesies, Hutchinson. Did she predict a young London correspondent would get beaten within an inch of his life at her birthplace nearly three hundred years later?' I laughed without really laughing.

'That I cannot say but Ursula lived in one of the most turbulent periods of our history. Young Henry VIII had only just been crowned. He appointed an Ipswich merchant's son, Thomas Wolsey, as an advisor. Wolsey was soon to become

Archbishop of York in 1514. The next year, at the age of forty, Wolsey became Chancellor of England and Cardinal of Rome. He built and housed himself in Hampton Court, the finest palace in the land. "*Now shall the Mitred Peacock first begin to plume, whose Train shall make a great show in the world – for a time; but shall afterwards vanish away, and his great Honour come to nothing*," predicted Mother Shipton. Not pleasing words for Cardinal Wolsey's ears but worse was to come. Our old friend – and he must have been an old man by then – the Abbot of Beverley makes a reappearance. He paid Mother Shipton a visit, no doubt worried about Wolsey's attacks on small destitute monasteries to fund his grand schemes. "*The Mitred Peacock's lofty Pride shall to his Master be a guide.*" Her words cannot have allayed the Abbot's fears for she went on to foretell the Dissolution of the Monasteries. Soon after the Abbot's visit, a mysterious Mr Beasley arrived on Mother Shipton's doorstep with three companions: Charles Brandon the Duke of Suffolk, Lord D'Arcy of Yorkshire and the Earl of Northumberland, Lord Percy. Cardinal Wolsey had evidently heard Mother Shipton's latest prophecy of his downfall. She had predicted that Wolsey might see York as its Archbishop but never reach it.' Hutchinson took a long satisfying draught from his tankard.

'My,' I said.

'Yes, "my",' agreed Hutchinson. 'Warming himself by Mother Shipton's hearth, Brandon conveyed the Cardinal's message to her that when he did come to York he would have her burned at the stake.'

'Disapproved of by Anne Boleyn, expelled from the king's circle, did not Wolsey eventually flee to the north?'

'Yes, he arrived at Cawood Castle in 1530 from whose turrets he must have spied York on a fine evening.'

'But never reached its walls.' I gulped down my last mouthful of sweet pungent negus which had now cooled.

'Indeed. Accused of high treason, he was arrested by Lord Percy and summoned back to London by a displeased Henry. Already ill, Wolsey mercifully died at Leicester.'

'Am I not right in thinking he died of dysentery?'

'You know your history well, Felix, I am impressed.'

'I read much.'

'Not any old scribbler then,' laughed Hutchinson. '"*The northern line of Tweed The maiden Queen shall next succeed And join in one, two, mighty States – then shall Janus shut his gates.*" Mother Shipton died at the beginning of Queen Elizabeth's reign. Some say she predicted her own death in the year 1561. It is believed she was buried in unconsecrated ground outside York. A fitting end for a woman with witchlike powers, don't you think?'

'An ignominious end like that of Eugene Aram,' I proffered.

Hutchinson's smile fell. 'This is dangerous talk, Felix. You must learn to be more circumspect. You have already been warned off. The next time they might kill you.'

'I raise a toast to Mother Shipton, and all those strong enough to hold on to their beliefs.' I lifted my empty pot to Hutchinson's tankard in an attempt to deflect the mood. 'Tell me, Thomas, how did you decide upon such a strange profession?'

'It was medicine or the church.'

'And you decided it was a more straightforward proposition to care for the body rather than the soul,' I chuckled, my cheeks alight. I was beginning to feel merry.

'Something like that. I am fortunate enough to have relatives who are surgeon apothecaries. When I turned fifteen one of them allowed me to work through my apprenticeship with him. I slept in a small room behind the surgical office. It was my job to answer the night bell should it ring – it rang often – usually on the coldest of nights with a snowstorm raging outside. Pray tell me, Felix, why do womenfolk choose the most inclement conditions in which to give birth?'

'Perhaps they are punishing us,' I suggested.

'That could be so. Anyway, as a young apprentice it was my job to rouse the master and saddle his horse at all hours of the night. If the bell rang again when the master was away, I would be forced out onto the streets in search of another surgeon. After several tries, I would eventually drop into my bed wet and shivering. Early the next morning, I would be up to sweep the surgery floor, clean phials, powder and sift drugs. The one task I did enjoy, during those early days, was having the freedom to walk about the town to collect empty phials. After a year I was allowed to keep the master's accounts, bleed noncritical patients, and extract teeth. Eventually, I was allowed to treat fractures and other routine illnesses of the less privileged.'

'So your master was a prig.'

'No, he was merely pragmatic and liked to be paid.'

'Tell me more.'

'Even while indentured I knew I had more a liking for treating the inner body with potions and pills rather than the outer intervention of a surgeon's knife.'

'You have then, sir, a physician's bent.'

'I like to think so,' sighed Hutchinson. His age was difficult to gauge. His eyes had a depth of maturity to them and yet remained youthful, alive with interest at everything going on around him.

'You are my junior, I suspect, sir.'

'Am I?' Hutchinson examined the contents of his tankard as if he were still the apprentice assessing liquid to a beaker measurement.

'If you have not reached one score and five then you are.'

'So be it.' He offered no further information.

Again the toadeater of a landlord approached offering a tilted beer jug. I placed my hand over my pot risking his displeasure. I did not care, I had had enough liquor for one evening, the room was already spinning.

'Speaking of medical relatives,' resumed Hutchinson. 'You could do no better than interview John Hutchinson, surgeon apothecary and recent mayor of Ripon, as a prelude to your investigation. I believe young Eugene spent his formative years in that town.'

'Perhaps you will be kind enough to supply me with a letter of introduction.'

'It will be my pleasure,' said Hutchinson. 'Though I must warn you, Felix,' he hesitated, blowing the froth on his freshly poured draught. 'John is not entirely impartial regarding the matter of Aram's guilt.'

'Then he is in good company.'

'Tell me, Felix, who knew you were going in the direction of the Dropping Well today?'

'It was Vicar Collins who first suggested it was an interesting place to visit.'

'Could anyone else have known?'

'Well, there was another man in the church at the time who could have overheard us.'

'What man?'

'A man unseen by me, hidden behind one of the arches. A man Collins addressed only as Francis,' I told Hutchinson. He paled at this. 'But then anyone could have followed me from the town and along the river bank.'

'Do go carefully with this, Felix,' the good doctor stressed again.

CHAPTER FOUR

John Hutchinson was handing out liquorice sticks to some rosy cheeked urchins when I arrived at his premises. He was a mature man of about forty years of age. Thomas had not specified his exact relationship to this man – as it had not been offered I had not enquired – apart from their surname and their build I saw little family resemblance between the two men.

I had loved apothecary shops since early childhood. They have a universal smell to them: cinnamon, cloves and garlic imbue the air. They are clean places in which to make you feel pure and well or at least give you that possibility.

Floor to ceiling shelves lined the walls of Hutchinson's Apothecary Shop. White and blue patterned pottery jars occupied the top shelves, with blue and brown glass decanters positioned like soldiers below. On the counter a rod-shaped pestle waited to crush and grind magical ingredients into powder or pastes inside the mortar bowl. Perhaps my friend, Thomas, had practised with this very one as an apprentice.

John Hutchinson lifted down a clear glass jar containing water and numerous squirming leeches, placing it on the counter level with the children's wide eyes. They began to scream in horror and excitement. Only children scream in that particular way.

I smiled as I handed the surgeon apothecary my letter of introduction.

'How is Thomas doing these days in Knaresborough?' was his first question.

'He is well and wishes to be remembered to you.'

Hutchinson walked round his counter to usher the children out of the door before returning to me. 'It says here that you are an occasional correspondent for the *Gentleman's Magazine* and are interested in Eugenius Aram.'

'Indeed I am, sir.'

'But what interest can a dead man hold for you?'

'A story perhaps, a book even. I attended Eugene Aram's trial in York on behalf of the magazine's proprietor and editor, Mr Richard Cave.'

'I thought Sylvanus Urban was the editor.'

'A pseudonym, sir,' I could not help breaking into a smile again at this. 'Sylvanus Urban was the name used by both Edward Cave and the nephew who succeeded him.'

'You said you were at Eugenius' trial.'

'I was – a cause célèbre indeed. Afterwards, while taking the waters in Harrogate, word reached me that the townsfolk of Knaresborough were up in arms over the schoolmaster's conviction and Richard Houseman's, the heckler's acquittal.'

'If you were at Eugenius' trial, then you too must have realised the verdict was questionable.' Hutchinson's eyes roved about the empty room as if he feared a spy might somehow be lurking there. 'Molly, can you come out front and tend the shop for a while,' he turned and shouted. Almost immediately a petite woman in a white mob cap, whom I took to be a servant, darted mouse-like in through a door behind the counter. 'Come,' Hutchinson guided me through the same door into his surgical office. Sitting himself down, he beckoned me to draw a chair up to the table. 'The

Gentleman's Magazine, eh. Doctor Johnson and William Guthrie are amongst my favourite writers. I expect these two eminent gentlemen of letters are well known to you.'

'I am better acquainted with the former than the latter.'

'Really?' said Hutchinson obviously impressed.

'Now, sir, can you furnish me with any information that might improve Eugene Aram's damaged reputation, be it posthumously? Anything at all regarding that gentleman and his family's early life in Ripon?' I took out my notebook and pencil.

'Peter and Faith Aram were better acquainted with my parents, Simon and Anne, than me. Though I do remember my father telling me he found Peter Aram to be an ambitious fellow. Despite humble beginnings, his father was a fisherman I believe, Peter was not averse to moving around the country in an effort to better himself. He was born in Nottingham, moved to London where he was trained by famous gardeners such as George London and Henry Wise before working for Henry Compton, Bishop of London. He then moved north to work for Sir Edward Blackett. Sir Edward had inherited many properties throughout the North of England. Peter once told my father that his favourite landscape and gardens were those around Stockburn Hall. Around the 1690's, Sir Edward bought the manor of Newby and began building a new house there, meanwhile Peter was employed doing temporary work in the gardens of Gouthwaite Hall for Sir Thomas Yorke. Sir Thomas was Sir Edward's brother-in-law.'

'The aristocracy stick together, do they not?'

'They are buried together too. Unfortunately, Mary Blackett, née Yorke, died just before her husband's building work was completed and Peter had moved back there fulltime. As you know, Kendle, death is neither a prerogative of rich nor the poor. It walked darkly into the Aram's house as it had the Blackett's. Eugenius' parents had three or four children, two of whom I know for certain died as infants in this town. Indeed, Peter was not a young man when he married Faith. I suspect he might have enjoyed a previous marriage but that was never talked about.'

'Previous marriages rarely are,' I put in.

'Indeed,' agreed Hutchinson equally tersely, making me wonder if somehow I had committed a faux pas here. 'When Eugenius was a mere babe in arms, his parents left the high moorland reaches of the Nidd at Ramsgill to take another tithe cottage in Skelton village near Newby Hall. Peter was now Sir Edward Blackett's head gardener. Skilled in design, I believe he had considerable influence in creating the new gardens about the hall. At the age of five, Eugenius was again on the move with his family when they bought a property here at Bondgate.'

'You make them sound like Gypsies, sir.'

'If I do, Mr Kendle, then they were Gypsies with a purpose.'

'Might I say your knowledge of the Arams is encyclopaedic, sir.'

'Death was to intervene again in this story, death and cruel coincidence,' continued Hutchinson, ignoring my flattery. 'My mother, Anne, died in July, 1730. My mother was only thirty-nine years of age. Eugenius had lost his own mother only eight months before mine, although by then he was a man while I was still a youth.'

'You knew him personally then.'

'Only by sight when he came to visit his father occasionally.'

'"Occasionally", you say.' I leaped on the word like a cat.

'I can tell you this, Mr Kendle,' said Hutchinson, ignoring me again. 'Peter Aram was very respected in this town as was his son. Both originated from the labouring class but both could read and write in a fair hand. Have you ever read Peter Aram's poem *Studley-Park* published by Mr Thomas Gent of York?'

I shook my head, saying, 'I believe his son, likewise, was not averse to penning a poem or two.'

'The Arams were the most sensitive of men. Before he was married, Eugenius would write his father the most beautiful letters on flowers. They both shared a lifelong passion for botany. I still cannot believe him guilty of the terrible crime attributed to him, particularly as his main accuser was a man like Houseman.'

'Sole accuser actually. According to his trial only three men really knew what happened on that blustery February night fourteen years ago, Aram, Houseman and Daniel Clark, the murdered shoemaker.'

'Wait here a moment, I might have something of interest for you.' With that John Hutchinson disappeared. I could hear his feet mounting the steps, deliberately one by one, until they stopped. There was much scuffling in a chamber directly above my head before he reappeared and handed me a small volume. 'You will find Peter Aram's poem *Studley-Park* on page one with a dedication to William Fisher, Gardener-in-Chief to the Right Honourable John Aislabie, Esquire, of Studley.'

'Aislabie, Aislabie, that name sounds familiar.'

'It should do. The late John Aislabie was Chancellor of the Exchequer during the South Sea Bubble collapse in 1720. He was expelled from Parliament and devoted the rest of his life to his water garden in Studley Park.'

I offered the book back to Hutchinson. 'I could not possibly …'

The apothecary pressed my hand onto the marbled binding. 'Take it, take it, and when you have read it you can either deliver it back to me in person or leave it with Thomas, that way he will be forced to grace us with his presence.'

'I think you are suffering a misapprehension, sir, regarding Thomas' love and respect for you. He spoke highly of you but he is merely a young man consumed at present with setting up his medical practice.'

'All young men are the same. I was the same,' laughed Hutchinson.

'As was Aram with his *occasional* visits to his father.'

'Write your story about Eugenius, Mr Kendle, write the whole story without prejudice from beginning to end.'

'Unfortunately, we all know the end,' I pointed out.

'Yes, but few people know the beginning. Few people know how a man like Eugenius, from respectable peasant stock, finished up swinging from a gibbet post as an example to his neighbours.'

'But, I understand, Aram wrote to the Reverend Thomas Collins telling him that he was descended from grander folk.'

'I know nothing of that. He came from a line of Nottingham gardeners as far as I am aware. Eugenius' grandfather broke the mould somewhat chasing the fish rather than weeds. Tell me, Kendle, do you know the Hospital of Saint Anne?'

I shook my head. 'I am a stranger to Ripon.'

'I will give you directions for I believe you will find someone in there who can help you more than I.'

'But you have been a mine of information, sir,' I objected.

'Indeed, but this person could provide the beginning of your story. Hopefully the hospice and its inmates will have remained uncorrupted by the malady of rumour and counter rumour regarding the trial of Rex v. Aram.'

'Houseman and Terry,' I added.

'Ah, alas, the other two prisoners just melted away, did they not?'

'They did, sir.'

'Anyway, I have had occasion to treat residents at the hospital I am telling you about. An old maid living there told me that many years ago she had left her native dale to work in Ripon. She insisted that it was she who brought Eugenius Aram into the world up at Ramsgill.'

'You believe her?'

'She is worth a visit before you return to Knaresborough, don't you think? But I warn you, you must not reveal shock at her terrible physical deformity. She is sound of mind, though her body crumbles faster than the hospice that houses her. I fear she is not long for this world.'

'Then I'd best make haste.'

'I will water, feed and stable your horse for an hour or two. It will be easier to walk from here to High Saint Agnesgate.'

* * * * *

I thought I had stepped into heaven. I had stepped into Ripon Minster as the legacy of an early organ work shook the building with controlled thunder.

'A piece by Thomas Tallis?' I enquired of a passing clergyman.

'William, is practising Alleluia Post Partum again,' he sighed in apology.

'William?' I asked.

'Aye, William Ayrton, do you know him?' The clergyman took two steps back.

'No, but I wish I did. The man's a brilliant musician.'

'He's our resident organist.' This was said with a sudden flush of pride. 'Have you come here to listen or pray?'

'Neither. Actually, I wonder if it would be possible to take a look at your parish register.'

'Looking for a relative?'

'Indeed.'

'Please, follow me.' With a flourish the bowed clergyman beckoned me forward.

'What a wonderful church this is.' I stared up enthralled by the rounded Norman and pointed Gothic arches towering above us.'

'Rather a mishmash of architectural styles, I am afraid. Saint Wilfrid founded the church in the seventh century. Since then this and that has been added or rebuilt. But come in here, this crypt dates from ancient Saxon times. It is the only part of Wilfrid's original church from 672 to survive.' We walked inside a cell with a large niche in its east wall which I presumed was to display relics. 'Wilfrid may have meant this space to represent Christ's tomb,' explained the clergyman. I shivered there against the east wall. 'You're cold,' he said.

We moved on to the vestry as Ayrton began rehearsing a more reflective fugue over and over again. The vestry was thankfully warmer than "Christ's tomb". I rummaged for my notebook in the deep pockets of my greatcoat. John

Hutchinson had told me Faith Aram had died towards the end of 1729. I gently turned the vellum pages of the registry book looking for Faith under burials. There she was – Faith with two small f's.

1729 29ᵗʰ November ffaith wife of Peter Aram of Bondgate.

I visibly flinched.

'Who did you say you were looking for? – your relative?' The clergyman was back and regarding me with a degree of mistrust.

'Faith Aram, mother of Eugene Aram,' I confessed.

If I had visibly flinched, the clergyman now visibly blanched. 'Terrible business, terrible.'

'You mean Aram's crime?'

'I do wonder if Peter had done the right thing by Eugene whether any of this would have happened.'

'What do you mean by the right thing, Reverend? I have just been told Aram and his father were extremely close.'

'I am not so sure about that. I visited old Mr Aram just before he died. He told me then that he had bequeathed to his daughter, Orinda, the chamber and parlour at the north end of his Bondgate dwelling. To his younger sons, Henry and Stephen, he bequeathed the south part of his house, consisting of a parlour and chamber. The enclosed courtyard was left to Orinda. Henry and Stephen were entitled to it when they were out of apprenticeship. On reflection the most interesting aspect of Mr Aram's will was he left but one shilling to Eugene, his eldest son.'

'Good lord!'

'I seem to remember the will was extremely short and to the point. I believe it was witnessed by two Ripley yeomen and a William Coates, a tobacconist, of the same village. You are not really related to Faith Aram, are you?'

'Sorry, Reverend, I lied,' I admitted, shamefaced in the house of God. 'I am a writer interested in the Aram case.'

Perhaps he felt he had said too much. The Reverend turned on his heels and fled lest he became tainted by proximity, if not to Aram's blood, to wicked Press blood.

On cue, William Ayrton thumped down the keys on a last penetrating note.

CHAPTER FIVE

I found Thorpe Prebend House in a tight mews off Agnesgate. John Hutchinson had told me King James slept here in 1617, either from or on his way to Scotland, he was not sure. I wondered if James had slept alone in this austere house or had the comfort of one of his male flankers. I had thought better of posing this question to Hutchinson.

The Hospital of St Anne, known to some as the Maison Dieu, was situated close to Ripon Minster. The Minster's dominant walls stood before it, the river Skell flowed behind. Trees encased its position on the fertile bank – trees that must have flowered beautiful pinks in the spring.

The centre piece was an ancient 15th century chapel, adjoining the hospice in a small garden. Built when Joan of Arc was at the height of her warrior power in France, its arched windows had all the architectural grandeur of St. Wilfrid's in miniature. Under the heading of Maison Dieu in my *Travellers' Guide to Ripon*, it said that a chapel and massendew were founded in the town in honour of St Anne. The building would house one priest and eight poor folk, men and women, who in times past had been of good behaviour, and that there were also two common beds for every lone travelling man that hath no spending, and there he may be cared for one day and one night.

I knocked on the door and was part admitted – not by a priest – by a woman of middle years who looked to be too well-nourished to be one of the *poor* inmates. A bunch of keys jangled at her waist.

'Would it be possible for me to have a word with Miss Matilda Peck?' I asked, confirming the name in my notebook.

'Relative?' Her manner was officious.

I shook my head. 'Mr John Hutchinson, surgeon apothecary of this town, directed me here.'

'Come.' The harridan beckoned me further in. She appeared to have softened but not very much. 'Wait.'

She disappeared into an adjacent parlour. I could hear her calling 'Tilda, Tilda Peck,' as she moved from room to room. Left with a minute or two to absorb my surroundings, I saw this almshouse – for want of a better word – was reasonably maintained. I had seen much worse. There was a humidity in the air which I guessed came from being so near the river Skell and the river Ure was not far away.

'Here she is.' Soon the harridan reappeared. She supported a shuffling gnarled apparition bending to earth. The old woman's spine was as brittle and stooped as the branch of a dead tree. Her white wisps of hair were but cobwebs across her baldness.

"Her terrible physical deformity", Hutchinson had warned me. I struggled to keep the pity from my eyes.

'Allus cold and wet in here. Makes me bones ache something awful,' complained Matilda Peck, as if to divert the eye from her appearance.

'This young gentleman has come to visit ye,' said the harridan, ignoring her complaints.

'Really?' Matilda's disbelieving gaze lifted up to me.

The harridan lowered her down into a Windsor chair. 'I'll leave you two to talk. You'll have to shout to her, she's as deaf as an adder,' she told me and was gone.

'You're not Geoffrey, are you?'

'Geoffrey?' I shouted.

'Geoffrey, my nephew.'

'No, I am not,' I told her, feeling guilty for not being Geoffrey. 'My name is Felix Kendle.'

'Felix, that's a nice name.'

'Is it true, Miss Peck, that you brought Eugene Aram into the world at Ramsgill?'

Again scrutinisation beneath hooded lids. 'You know Ramsgill?'

I shook my head. 'Alas, I have not been there yet.'

'You should go. It is a peaceful place. Not like here, banging and slamming all day long. Usually, all there is to hear in Ramsgill is the rippling waters of Ramsgill Beck, or the bleating sheep, or the lowing from the beasts in the fields.' Matilda seemed to fall into a reverie over memories of her native dale.

'Eugene Aram,' I prompted.

'Hanged at York, I've been told. Is it true?' she asked.

'Afraid so,' I nodded.

'It was not peaceful the day he was born.'

'What time of year are we talking about?'

'It was a fine late September day. I can see it as clearly as yesterday.'

'1704, the fifth year of this century.' I began to scribble.

'Year, century, these things mean nothing to me, young man.'

'But Eugene's birth did.'

'Hard to ignore it. Faith's birth howls must have been heard by folk up in Middlesmoor and down as far as Wath. Decent everyday peace was breached right enough. Hours of labour and nothing to show for it.' Matilda rubbed her mottled hands across her own withered childless belly. 'A sense of panic began to build up in our set of houses. No one could work for her screams, we all felt so upset by them. I believe I was standing at my gate when I saw Peter hurrying up the street towards me. Not before time, I remember thinking. The Aram's cottage was only a few doors down from mine off the green.'

'The touchpaper cottage.'

'The what, sir?'

'The cottage that was igniting the village with noise.'

'The same, sir.' Matilda gave me an odd look. '"Nothing amiss, Peter?", I asked him. He was so absorbed by his own thoughts, he seemed not to hear me at first.'

'What did he look like, Peter Aram?'

'He was of generous height and bearing with the suspicion of a scholar's stoop. I'd say he had a slight curvature of the spine owing to his trade.' Matilda smiled: the irony of her own spinal deformity cannot have escaped her.

'How old were the Arams about this time?'

'Peter was already in his late thirties. She was younger. We were all much younger then.' Matilda looked a hundred but for a moment a flash of remembered youth sparkled in her blue eyes. The light had not completely gone out for her, not yet awhile. 'Peter told me his wife's time had come and he needed urgent assistance. I told him I would attend immediately, rubbing my brown-flour-palms on my apron front in preparation. I had bread in the oven and thought I must not be away too long. Funny, what you remember. I can recall that, and trying to keep up with Peter's long strides as we rushed back to his thatched cottage, yet I cannot tell you if I breakfasted this morning.'

'Thatched, you say?'

'Yes, most cottages were thatched or turfed in Ramsgill in them days. Aye, they are as clear to me as if it were yesterday. Warm little dwellings they were, not like here.'

'Always complaining of feeling cold, Tilda, yet you forget this.' On cue the harridan made a fleeting reappearance holding a cap which she placed on my interviewee's head. Not so unkind after all.

'So you entered the Aram's cottage,' I continued.

'Aye, under the evil eye.'

'The evil eye?'

'Above the cottage lintel a stone face looked out across the green, an ancient deity to ward off the evil eye. It makes my skin crawl to think of that thing staring down on me now, and in light of all that came to pass. It was not like any other day, sir, the day Eugene came into the world. I had helped with the birthing of three other bairns in the village before him but that day was memorable.'

'How so?'

'I will tell you shortly, sir.'

Another female resident of the Maison Dieu shambled by. Matilda wriggled in her shawl with irritation, lifting a finger to her lips.

'Pray go on,' I said.

'Ears everywhere,' she said.

'You entered the Aram's cottage,' I prompted again.

'Yes, and poked my head round the door of Faith's lying-in room. I could hardly catch my breath, the room's heat rushed at my face like a wall of fire. The stench of stale urine, sickness and warm blood was overpowering. I do not know if Peter Aram had intended delivering the child himself, but he had certainly called for me late in the proceedings. I blinked, the room was darkened by heavy curtains drawn across the window. Forgive me, you are a young man, I hope this tale of female suffering is not too harrowing.'

'Please, I have heard and seen much worse.'

'"Ah!" came a scream from the shadow of a four-poster. "My belly is stretched to bursting." I pulled back the window curtains and rushed to Faith's side, telling her all the while that she must bear down, bear down for her burden to be safely delivered. Her face was as white as the linen it lay on, sweat coursed off her brow like the Nidd in spate. She was in a bad way. The door of the lying-in room creaked further open and footsteps fell on the bare boards. "Is that Peter?" Faith asked me. "No, 'tis just more neighbours eager to help," I explained. Faith let out another howl, the howl of a primitive beast. I swear she lifted from the sheets like Lazarus himself. When the spasm left her she fell back helplessly and turned her attention to the four-poster's hanging drapes. The other two neighbours, who must have been encouraged by my attendance, now held back, afraid to approach. The small room had become crowded. "Caudle, one of you have Peter make up some caudle, and bring me some hog lard from the piggery," I told them. "God give me strength to bear this," Faith shouted. Just in time I held out the chamber pot for her to vomit into. The remaining neighbour, Mary Anne, who had a large wart on her cheek, turned apple green. "I wish you all would go. I am dying," Faith told us. The nausea must have filled her again. She tried to reach for the pot in my hand. Too late, the beautiful coverlet thrust back down the bed was badly soiled by her emission. Mary Anne's eyes bulged with indignation. Mary Anne was very poor and could only dream of owning such a coverlet. Meanwhile, the other neighbour, Fanny, reappeared with Peter. She offered the hog lard to me, and the caudle which had already been prepared and was cooling. Faith thrust her hand down into the sheets, down between her thighs, and withdrew her spreading fingers webbed in a blood-tinged liquor. "See," she said, "I bleed to death." Fanny and Mary Anne tumbled back squawking with shock. Faith fell silent and became strangely absorbed with the red and brown beneath her nails. My hands supporting the back of her neck, I induced her to smell and taste the caudle. She swallowed the liquid before the agony struck hard and low again. To the gathering's stunned amazement, she summoned the final vestiges of her strength and attempted to quit the bed. I suppose, on reflection, the poor soul was trying to position herself for a more natural birth. Fanny and Mary Anne fell on her, trying to pin her down …'

'Eugene's birth was something of a farce then?'

'At that point it was mayhem,' cackled Matilda. 'Birth can be like that occasionally. "Leave her be, leave her be, go easier with the lass" I told 'em. Peter stood some way off out of the affray. He had never seen his mild mannered wife so fitful and persevering.

After a little more tempered restraint on Mary Anne's part, Faith was subdued and forced to relinquish her desire to squat upon the boards. We guardians of decorum lay about her in a state of exhaustion. "I cannot bring forth the child with thee wrestling and wriggling all the while," I told her. Then I began to look to my business. If you have no stomach for more, sir, I'll stop now,' offered Matilda. I nodded for her to go on. 'Faith's lungs were filling and emptying in a shallow rhythm. I pulled away the sheets from her swollen belly right down to her thin naked ankles. I can see those poor little blue ankles now, they were so pathetic and untouched. The long nightdress she wore had become rolled up and trapped beneath her buttocks. It was sodden with warm liquid which had made her skin chafed and sore as she thrashed about. Her waters had already broken. Good, I had those three loaves of bread to consider in the oven. Faith had fallen into a stupor. With the help of my neighbours, I turned her onto her left side near the edge of the bed. We inclined her face and chest forward, pushing her knees as far up to her chest as they would go. I reached up for a pillow placing it between her thighs. Fanny remained stationed at her feet to act as a solid resistance to be pushed against. I stared into Faith's privies, a small wet crown was already visible.'

'Eugene.'

'Correct, sir, Eugene had almost entered our world. I greased my hands with the hog lard and was first to lay hands on his slippery skin. Peter jumped as his wife gave out another howl, but this was not like the others and came from somewhere deep in her throat. "Slowly, slowly, me dear," I told her. "Push, push, gently now." My voice sounded hollow in the silent and expectant room. The gardener had turned the colour of his gentlemen's lawns. Spots of blood fell on the white sheet near Faith's thigh as Eugene exploded out of his mother. She fell back in a shudder. The child seemed to slither on his hands and knees towards me. He was not like any of the other infants I had delivered. He was different. Staring up at me with those big eyes of his, as I wrapped him in a clean cloth to present him to his mother, he looked more like an adult than a baby. With outstretched arms

Faith accepted her strange living parcel, no longer weary but reborn herself. "Is all well with the child?" Peter asked me. "Have you not eyes, Peter?" scolded his wife. "Our son is perfect."'

CHAPTER SIX

The long flat ride – flat by Yorkshire standards – back to
Knaresborough on my slow hack, which John Hutchinson
had paid me the misconceived courtesy of calling a horse,
gave me time to reflect on all Matilda Peck had told me. She
was old and had lived and seen too much for guile. I believed
her. I even believed her when she said Peter Aram had
never thanked her for the safe delivery of his son but told
her instead that she should do something about her tangled
garden: Aram's father, the inveterate gardener whatever the
circumstances.

I was extremely stiff after my drizzling eight miles
rolling on the back of Bess, Bess I believe was the mare's
unimaginative name. Seated atop of her was like sailing in a
coracle on a churning sea. I settled by the flaming hearth in
my room at the Bell, my clothes still steaming, and took out
of my greatcoat pocket the book John Hutchinson had lent
me. I saw that *The Ancient and Modern History of the Loyal
Town of Rippon* had been published by Thomas Gent, in 1733,
above the Star in Stonegate, York. I had occasion to visit the
Star once or twice for my supper while covering Aram's trial,
but had remained ignorant of the fact that the respected Gent
had once had premises in the same building. I began to read
Peter Aram's poem singing the praises of Studley Park and
Fountains Abbey. There was much about woodland spirits –
"*Sylvan Beauties*" – sirens, Eve's daughters and "*beauteous*

Nymph their Lust to gratify". I decided that despite his rather ingratiating dedication to Aislabie's gardener, Peter Aram must have been a passionate man.

Lost in "*gazing Lovers, full of am'rous Fire*" – I heard a light knock, a butterfly's wing knock on the door.

'Pray enter,' I requested. Nothing happened, unwillingly I was forced to leave my book and comfortable chair by the fireside.

The inn's servant girl stood in the doorway, a bundle of papers offered in her outstretched hand. 'A gentleman has just left these for you from Vicar Collins, sir.'

'Come,' I beckoned her inside. 'Please be good enough to leave them on the writing desk over there.' She hesitated as if I was about to compromise her, but eventually taking courage she ventured in. 'What is your name, child?'

'Janet, sir, Janet Brown. And I am not a child but in my twenty-third year.'

'Umm, Janet, a pretty name. Forgive me, Miss Janet, but you do look much younger than your years.' I did my best to smile reassurance rather than threat.

'They brought him here, you know.'

'Who? Where?' I made a parody of looking round the room for the invisible man. Janet laughed a set of perfect teeth made whiter by her dark complexion.

'Mr Aram. They brought him to the Bell for the night after his arrest in Lynn,' she said, the laughter gone.

'Yes, I did know that. But tell me, Janet, how do you know of my interest in Eugene Aram?'

'Folk talk.'

'Did you see him arrive here?'

'I saw everything through the tavern window downstairs.

The crowd waiting for him outside were several rods deep. I saw him alight from the carriage with the two Knaresborough constables sent to fetch him. John Barker, who had always hated him, jerked the gyves to give him pain. "Make way!" Francis Moor stuttered ahead of them, trying to create a path. A slight man, a hatter by trade, Mr Moor looked even smaller in that mass of much larger men. "Out of the way!" growled John Barker, dragging Mr Aram behind him. "Let them through," piped up another authoritative voice. "Please, gentlemen, let the Lynn party through." Vicar Collins stood on the Bell's threshold. The Reverend Brotheric cringing behind him, skulking like the devil incarnate but also dressed in the Church.'

'You didn't like the Reverend Brotheric?'

'It was the foxy look of the man. I'd never set eyes on him before and have no wish to again.'

'It must have been a tumult,' I said, picturing the scene for myself – Hogarth, irreverent – a sea of red jeering faces parting to reveal the neck-banded clerics.

'Vicar Collins looked very solemn and worried, I could not help noticing a tic pulsating below his right eye. He looked more distressed than Mr Aram who was scrutinising him coolly from beneath his lowered lids. The mob were chanting for blood. You could tell Mr Aram was doing his best to retain some dignity, trying to remain upright.'

'All the baying dogs in the world would not make Aram bend. I saw it for myself during his trial. He was not a man to stoop before those he considered his inferiors.'

'Exactly right, sir. He was a good schoolmaster too by all accounts. If I had not been born a lass, born when he was here them fourteen years since, I would have loved to have gone to his school.'

'Do you not have any reading and writing, Janet?' I asked. She pursed her lips looking to the floor. 'You have an excellent memory for detail though.'

'I see in pictures.' She lifted her eyes now filled with enthusiasm to mine. 'I can turn those pictures into words.'

'A true and precious gift. Pray continue with your story of Aram's arrival here.'

'He casually adjusted his wrists in the gyves before he came in; his lace cuffs fluttered; the mob gasped and mewled.'

'Once inside he would be greeted by Knaresborough's more prominent citizens, no doubt.'

'Just so, sir.'

Again I pictured the scene in the fogged atmosphere of the Bell's best room. Aram spearing each man in turn with looks and hooks of fierce virtue, attempting to reel them in to his cause. He was, when all was said and done, as good as they were now, a travelled man, a man of experience, their equal in every way, at last a gentleman among gentlemen.

'Who spoke first?' I asked.

'I believe it was Vicar Collins who first made acknowledgement, sir. "Vicar Collins," Mr Aram replied. "Are you all right?" the vicar asked him. "I feel a little dizzy, the long journey," said Mr Aram. "I do hope this matter … this unpleasantness might soon be rectified, Mr Aram." "I am sure I can clear myself of the crimes imputed to me." Mr Aram slowly looked from one man to the next. "I pray you can," responded Vicar Collins. "Why, my own brother, James, suffered losses …" "Tell me, how does young Richard do these days?" asked Mr Aram, cutting him short and taking him to one side.'

'I expect the vicar's ominous shadow, the Reverend Brotheric, followed loyally on.'

Janet nodded. 'He was like Vicar Collins' limpet that afternoon. "Richard has taken up the woollen trade," the vicar told Mr Aram in lowered tones.'

'Who on earth is Richard?'

'He is a cousin, nephew, some relation of Vicar Collins' and once attended Mr Aram's school.'

'And this Richard is in trade,' I noted with interest.

'I believe he is, sir, but the Collins' are hardly of my circle. "I was wondering, Vicar Collins, if you would be good enough to intercede on my behalf and ask the constable to remove the links?" asked Mr Aram. "There is no way I can escape from this chamber full of stronger men, and these links do trouble me greatly." On compassionate grounds the vicar passed on the request. John Barker scowled, grumbled, but finally he snapped the gyves open. "I think I remember now, wasn't it you, Vicar Collins, who buried my second little Anne, my daughter who poignantly chose to celebrate her father's birthday with her own dying?" The vicar made no attempt to answer this, whether he remembered burying little Anne or not I cannot say. "When am I to be examined?" Mr Aram asked him. "The magistrate is not ready yet." The vicar eyed him steadily, trying his best to calm matters. "I am very weary," sighed Mr Aram.'

'Did the Reverend Brotheric have anything to add to this conversation?' I asked, curious as to Brotheric's role in the matter.

'I think it was he who told Mr Aram that he would be held here overnight. "But why? I have done nothing wrong, I assure all you gentlemen of that." Mr Aram flung out his arms as if to encompass the whole room. Collins and Brotheric moved away.'

'The clergy are afraid of any theatre that does not come from themselves,' I suggested. Janet smiled agreement at this.

'A bridal aisle suddenly split the middle of the room. This seemed to be a day of partings and coming together. "Well, how do you do?" asked Mr Aram. His weather-eye was not deceiving him. He bowed to his wife for the first time in thirteen years.'

'Amazing. You tell it so well.'

'It is hardly a scene I could forget. Anna Aram appeared downhearted at the occasion.'

'Reduced, would you say?'

'In her husband's absence Anna had been withered by the ticking clock and too much bread making. "And who are these young people?" he asked her. "Why, they are your daughters," she told him. Betty Aram shuffled protectively next to her mother.'

'Ah, poor Betty.'

'The same. But wild and giddy Betty is more the way of it, sir. She never liked her father, never liked being petted by him unlike her sister, Sally, who was always her father's favourite.'

'How old is Betty exactly?'

'Eighteen then, nineteen now, but she has always looked much older than her years.'

I could imagine big-breasted Betty's expression remained untouchable during that first reunion with her father.

'"Except of course Polly here, she is not family," Anna explained to her husband, her voice rising.'

'A referee to break the brawlers' stare between father and daughter.'

'"Ah, Polly Powell our neighbour." Mr Aram seemed pleased to see Polly there. Anna next pushed forward their Jane. "How are the boys, and poor Henry?" Mr Aram asked her, ignoring Jane. "They are well, apart from Henry who has grown much worse," replied his wife sharply. "If you had followed my instructions on Henry there might have been a different outcome," he told her, his lips tightening on the old sting, Henry had always caused strife between them. "Henry was born that way," she replied.'

'How sad. After many years apart it only took a minute of shared company for husband and wife to be at each other's throats once more. Tell me, as you are a contemporary of Betty Aram, are you well-acquainted with her?'

'She is known to me of course, though we are not close friends.'

'But you are not enemies either, are you?' I asked. Janet shrugged indifference. 'Do you like her?'

'I do not know her well enough to form an opinion one way or the other.'

'Do you think you would be able to arrange a meeting with her for me?'

'If I do know one thing about Betty Aram it is this, if you are against her father then she will meet you.'

'Why? Do you think I am against her late father?'

'The whole of Knaresborough believes it to be fact, sir. In this town if you are for Richard Houseman then you must believe Eugene Aram was solely accountable for the murder of Daniel Clark.'

'How on earth have I given the impression that I am for Houseman?'

'Because you expressed disapproval of the riots against him.'

'I disapprove of breaking the law against any man.'

'That might be so, sir. Folk here see it differently. To Knaresborough folk things are either black or white.'

'And are things always simply black and white for you, Janet?'

She gave a secretive smile at this. 'No, sir, they certainly are not.'

'So, who do you think was responsible for the death of the shoemaker, Clark?'

'That I cannot say.'

'What can you say?'

'I think Mr Francis Iles knew more about Daniel Clark's attempt to defraud his neighbours than he has let on.'

'Along with Houseman, Aram and Terry?'

'Aye, they were all party to it. Though the ale house keeper, Henry Terry, played but a bit part.'

'We are talking about receiving and distributing stolen goods, are we not?'

'We are, sir.'

'But was not Francis Iles one of their victims?'

'The linen draper made out he was a creditor. He was most solicitous in the recovery of the stolen property from Aram's and Houseman's dwellings after Clark went missing. Most solicitous and most loud. But I've heard tell otherwise. I've heard tell he was either after the reward for the restoration of the booty or he was concealing his own part in the plot.'

'You mean as a receiver?'

'Exactly that, sir.'

'Could he have been the brains behind Clark's scheme to defraud his neighbours?'

'He is a cunning and clever man. See how he kept his name clear of the trial in all but the most innocent sense.'

'He is an extremely shadowy figure in this whole affair, I do admit. I believe I might have seen this same Francis Iles in conversation with Vicar Collins.'

'That could well be so, sir. He enjoys considerable influence in Knaresborough. Many are afraid of him. He is a man who acquaints himself with everyone else's business, everyone else's weaknesses.'

'You sound as if you know him well.'

'He knew my mother. He is not a man to be crossed.'

'What do you mean, he knew your mother?'

'Just that.' The cap streamers shook.

I regarded her in astonishment. Her lips compressed. Her eyes said ask no more. The old eight o' clock curfew bell rang out high in the town. A bell now used to call the Knaresborough faithful to church. A bell which broke the spell between us. A cue for Janet to return to her work serving at the ale-stained tables.

'I will tell Betty Aram that you wish to speak to her,' she curtsied before leaving.

I smiled. Despite her reticence, I sensed here was an ally. She was a conundrum nonetheless. In spite of her lowly station this girl had the diplomacy and decorum of a lady. Wherever it had come from, she was the possessor of a shrewd intelligence. I was charmed by her.

Fortunately or unfortunately, I was not as enamoured by the mysterious Francis Iles. The only thraldom that gentleman held over me was I suspected he might be a key to unlocking the truth on Aram's guilt or innocence. Speaking of keys – the key question for me was why had a provincial schoolmaster, a man of learning like Aram, ever got involved in such an amateurish plot to defraud his neighbours in the first place? Debt, desperation perhaps. The plot had been fraught with the likelihood of exposure, admittedly less so with the supposedly runaway Clark dead. Then there was that suggestion from a mysterious Yorkshire correspondent in the *Whitehall Evening Post* that this criminal gang – I can think of no better term – had previously killed a Jew and his servant after taking payment for the "loaned" goods. Had the gang got greedy or had the murder of the two Jews been their intention all along? The little mentioned Jews, I might add.

I picked up Thomas Collins' documents from the writing desk. He had enclosed a covering letter saying that I would find herewith the final words penned by Eugenius Aram in York Castle on the eve of his execution. The vicar assured me that he was always eager to help a gentleman in search of the truth. He ended by saying he would appreciate the return of the documents in their original state of care.

One document particularly caught my interest: it was a brief autobiography which Aram appeared to have written at the behest of Collins. He said he was born at Ramsgill, a small Netherdale village in 1704. Aram dismissed his mother's side of the family in a few words, Faith's relations were "substantial and reputable in that dale". Peter, his father, enjoyed considerably more attention.

My father was of Nottinghamshire, a gardener of great abilities in botany, and an excellent draftsman. He served the right rev. the bishop of London, Dr. Compton with great approbation: which occasioned his being recommended to Newby, in this county, to Sir Edward Blackett, whom he served in the capacity of a gardener, with much credit to himself and satisfaction to that family, for above 30 years. Upon the decease of that baronet, he went and was retained in the service of Sir John Ingilby, of Ripley, bart, where he died; respected when living, and lamented when dead.

My father's ancestors were of great antiquity and consideration in this county, and originally british. Their surname is local; for they were formerly lords of the town of Haram, or Aram, on the southern banks of the Tees, and opposite to Stockburn, in Bishoprick; and appear in the records of St. Mary's, at York, among many charitable names, early and considerable benefactors to that abbey. They, many centuries ago, removed from these parts, and were settled, under the fee of the lords Mowbray in Nottinghamshire, at Aram, or Aram-Park, in the neighbourhood of Newark-upon-Trent; where they were possessed of no less than three knights fees, in the reign of Edward III. Their lands, I find not whether by purchase or marriage, came into the hands of the present lord Lexington. While the name existed in this county, some of them were several times high-sheriffs for this county; and one was professor of divinity, if I remember right, at Oxford, and died at York. The last of the chief of this family, was Thomas Aram, esq; sometime of Grey's Inn, and one of the commissioners of the salt-office, under the late queen Anne. He married one of the co-heiresses *of Sir John Coningsby, of North-Mims, in Hertfordshire. His seat which was his own estate, was at the Wild, near Shenley, in Hertfordshire, where I saw him, and where he died, without issue.*

Many more anecdotes are contained in my papers, which are not present; yet these may be thought more than enough, as they may be considered rather as ostentatious than pertinent: but the first was always far from me.

"Stockburn". The place-name was familiar to me. Eugene Aram said his ancestors were formerly lords of the town of Haram, or Aram, on the southern banks of the Tees, opposite to Stockburn. That was it, I remembered now, John Hutchinson had told me that Aram's father loved the landscape round Stockburn – a small estate owned by the Blackett family, the head of which was Sir Edward Blackett, Peter Aram's employer. A chance occurrence? – Peter's and Eugene's grand ancestors' lordship happened to lay across the river from land known to the gardener, land perhaps he had occasionally tilled and toiled for his crust.

Eugene Aram's hand was scrolling and flamboyant, in spite of his professed disdain for ostentation. Perhaps there was some truth in his aristocratic connections, or perhaps he had inherited his father's ambition to better himself against all the odds. What harm was there in a little imaginative play anyway? – when you had to bend a leg for a master who was considered your social superior but whom you knew to be your intellectual inferior. While the father tamed and prettied the wild landscape for the gentry to look out on, his son attempted to tame and educate their spoilt children. But if blue blood had run through Peter's and Eugene's veins, it had become somewhat diluted and pastel through generations of artisans. What fascinated me was that Aram considered fine lineage important enough to give it mention prior to the day of his execution. Obviously less important was his and his father's achievement in educating themselves to a degree of scholarship way beyond that of most of their peers – titled or otherwise.

Peter had even christened his son "Eugenius" – the Latin form from the Greek name *Ευγενιος* – meaning well born. Had he filled his son's head with ideas of grandeur and ownership of landscapes where one could "*Beneath cool Shades*" listen to Eve's daughters "*rehearse their am'rous Tales*". Shades made and created by your own sweat and ingenuity rather than Sir Edward Blackett's inherited money.

CHAPTER SEVEN

Thomas Collins was not in the parish church the next morning. His sexton directed me to his family home, a modest rectory not far from the church.

Collins' fastidious insistence that I return Aram's final musings to him in their original condition had offended and annoyed me. What did the "reverend sir" think I would do with them, stamp them beneath my muddy boots?

I lifted the brass door knocker. After a minute or two the door opened. My agitated state was somewhat mollified with the appearance of Collins himself framed in the doorway. Hatless and in daylight, I got a better look at Knaresborough's vicar than I had in the gloom of his church or from my distant view towards York's Tyburn. His face was lined and he looked to be about the same age as Aram himself. His build was not dissimilar to that of the executed man either.

'The maid is out on an errand with my wife,' he explained. 'Mary will be disappointed to have missed you, Kendle. We do not have a glut of cultured company to entertain us here in Knaresborough. Come, come, man, and warm yourself by my sitting-room fire. There is a chill in the air this morning, is there not?'

I smiled at his theatrical shiver. I was young and my circulation was good. Sometimes, as with my ride back from Ripon, I could feel stiff from too much dampness in the air but rarely did I feel cold.

'Thank you for allowing me to take a look at these,' I passed him back the Aram letters.

'What did you think of them?'

'Interesting,' I said, guarded.

'Only that?' Collins sounded disappointed.

'They are the ramblings of a man found guilty of a most heinous crime. Despite that he is still bent on proving his grandiose lineage to the end.'

'But did you believe him?'

'I suspect that social connections and background had become a way of life for Aram during his exile in the south of England. And possibly before that, possibly he had learnt from an early age that the only way to advancement in our society was to curry favour with your "betters". But, I suspect, deep in his heart he never felt anyone was better than him.'

'Perhaps you are right.' Collins fell silent.

'Did I not see Francis Iles in your church the other day?'

'Aye, Francis, what of it?'

'Aram implicated him as a participant in the crime to defraud his neighbours, did he not?'

'I believe he did.' It was Collins' turn to be guarded.

'Do you believe he was?'

'What I believe and what is provable are two different matters. It seemed at both the hearings and the trial everyone was blaming everyone else to save their own necks. A cup of tea, Mr Kendle?' offered the Reverend.

'That would be nice. Tell me, sir, how did you cope accompanying a man to Tyburn?' I called after him; remembering the scene of Aram's hanging with a literary eye, remembering Collins' part in it.

The Reverend hesitated. 'Tea first,' he murmured without turning.

The crowd, on the green field that day, greeting the tatty procession had been immense. Several children perched on their fathers' shoulders to ensure they got a good view, an early lesson in the wages of sin. Arresting officers, Constables Barker and Moor, had spoken at Aram's trial of his perturbation on passing the gibbet at the Lynn crossroads as they travelled back with him to Yorkshire. On that final death cart journey along Micklegate – his coffin riding fellow passenger at his back, the crowd buzzing round him – Aram must have been reminded of those late summer flies around the Lynn gibbet post. Hundreds of flies rubbing their front legs together like hands in anticipation of a feast. But the people waiting without Micklegate Bar were to be disappointed: it was a poor Monday morning offering between the two high-wheels and escorting beefy giants.

Strangers held him up beneath the three posted gallows, known with cynical affection as the three-legged mare. But no one was laughing, not even cynically, as Aram's once robust hiking legs buckled and gave way. The crowd had fallen eerily silent. They took in the old frilled shirt drenched in blood, the pathetic half-dead schoolmaster. They sighed their compassion and indignation – something wasn't quite as it should be about this – there was no jeering, no bloodlust cry for retribution to be heard on the field that day.

'Sugar?' Collins was back, tea tray in hand. I nodded. 'I didn't,' he said unexpectedly.

'Sorry,' I asked; my thoughts still there on the Tyburn field.

'I didn't, haven't really coped over the days and weeks following Eugenius' manner of death,' he admitted. '"Take this, Eugene," I told him, handing him a clean white shirt to die in. Shaking his head, he refused to wear it. "Fear not, all will be quick and well," the hangman reassured him: the hangman, a recently convicted felon himself reprieved to executioner. "Thank you." Aram was taken aback, moved, and although feeble he seemed to have some vestige of empathy with this man who was about to kill him. It was then that he smiled. I imagined he saw Sally, his beloved daughter's face down there among the rest – all sunshine – as the slack rope played against his neck, the bulky knot a lump at his ear. I started praying out loud. "Have you anything to say?" Aram was asked. "No," he mimed to the forest of faces. The cart jerked forward and the knot fell hard.'

'A cruel death for a proud man.'

'Indeed.'

'But should he have died like that, a common criminal? Should others have died alongside him? Should others have died instead of him?' I asked, clearing my throat.

'It is not for me to say. Nevertheless the man was regarded as a wonderful teacher in these parts. Look, might I be so bold as to suggest you interview my kinsman, Richard Collins, who was educated by Aram in his schoolhouse up the White Horse Yard.'

'Where shall I find him?'

'He is rarely at home. Business interests in Leeds. Often out here and there abroad. You know young people, you are a young man yourself with all the restlessness that entails. I do envy you your energy, Mr Kendle, perhaps it will help bring closure to this matter once and for all.' With a trembling hand, to the refrain of my own tinkling cup, Thomas Collins kindly wrote me a note of introduction.

* * * * *

A man crossed and recrossed from one building to the next in the White Horse Yard. I watched him going to and fro for some minutes. He carried sacks of what I took to be flax over his shoulders. He was a burly sort of chap, sullen and stooped. I recognised him straight away from the York Assizes.

'Mr Houseman! Mr Houseman! Pray, might I trouble you for a word?'

Without a word, the heckler scuttled up an external stone staircase to his workshop abutting Aram's old thatched schoolhouse. On reflection, I cannot say Houseman exactly scuttled back to his hole like a mouse, more like a swaying plump rat was the way of it. My heart thumping with trepidation, I pursued him. There was a tame raven on the wooden handrail at the top of the steps, it never moved as Houseman passed. But as I mounted the staircase, the raven squawked with indignation. Black feathers fluttered alarmingly in my face like a dowager's fan. The bird was attacking me. A guard dog of a raven then. I swiped my left arm at it before moving on quickly.

The heckling floor was of a but and ben design, the but end stored bundles of flax, the ben end was the working space where the flax was dressed. Linen is made from common flax stems which are retted, soaked in water-filled pits for a week or two, then scrunched with a hinged batten to separate the individual fibres from any outer bark or central woody stem. Hecklers, like Houseman, removed any remaining non-fibrous material by drawing the stems through a big comb which was a bed of nails on a wooden board. It was this – the main tool of his trade – that Houseman stood before, appearing to guard it defensively at my approach.

The room was dim. The only illumination came from the open door. I squinted to see Houseman's expression more clearly. He exhibited neither fear nor boldness. There was an acceptance, a dull melancholy about the man.

I introduced myself, telling him I was a correspondent for the *Gentleman's Magazine* and was interested in *Rex v. Aram*.

'I've nowt to say. Nowt to say on t' matter.'

The flax dust was suffocating, the smell in the windowless room made my guts churn. I was forced to place my kerchief over my nose and mouth lest I disgrace myself.

'What, you have nothing to say in your defence when your fellow townsfolk bear you such malice? Surely, you might express some sentiment to appease them,' I mumbled.

'I was forced to it. That is all I will say.'

'You were forced to give testimony that resulted in your good friend, Aram, hanging up there on Thistle Hill, or you were forced into a fraudulent conspiracy that led to murder?'

'I was forced to testify against him,' muttered Houseman to the floor.

'Forced? How forced?' I lifted the kerchief from my face, daring my senses to adjust to the stench of the room.

'Look, Mister, you would be as well served asking him a swinging up there as trying to get summat out of me.'

'If you do not wish to put your case forward for posterity, Houseman, so be it.' I made as if to leave.

'Wait,' he said. 'London you said?'

'I did.'

'*Gentleman's Magazine*, you said?'

I was unsure whether this was a genuine enquiry or a sneer. Without turning round, I hesitated in the doorway.

'Yes, that is who I write for,' I reaffirmed.

'And you will print nothing detrimental to my position?'

'Unless you are about to admit to murder, you have my word on it.' He had – although I could not stomach shaking his hand on the bargain.

'You do understand, Mister, that I could still be appealed by Clark's heir-at-law?'

'I do,' I said with little sympathy. 'That being Mr Philip Coates, brother-in-law to the late Daniel Clark, is it not?'

'Aye, 'tis him.'

'Then there remain the charges of theft and fraud.'

'Both capital offences,' grunted Houseman.

'I understand your position perfectly. So, although this is a personal interview, you will not be publically diverted from the depositions you made and the testimony you gave to the court.'

'No, sir, I will not. Not for the printed word.'

'And for the confidential word?' I asked. Houseman made no reply. 'Shall we proceed then?'

'Might I enquire first, what is in this for me?'

'As I have told you, Mr Houseman, posterity, your version for posterity.'

'I think I will need some greater incentive than that, Mister.'

I wrote out Richard Houseman a note of hand for a few shillings there and then.

'It all started some thirteen years since,' began Houseman.

'Fourteen now, is it not so?' I took out my notebook and pencil as if it was a gun.

'Aye, thereabouts.'

'Complicated by the change from the Julian to Gregorian Calendar in 1752.'

'Coroner, justices, lawyers all got befuddled wi' it. Settled on calling it '44, '45.'

'Yes, I remember them doing that at the assizes.'

'You were there?' gauped Houseman.

'Yes, I told you, I work for the *Gentleman's Magazine*. The magazine reported on the trial. The whole of England was interested in it.'

'Umm,' pondered Houseman. 'Folks is always too interested in others' business.'

'"Business", Mr Houseman, we are talking about the business of fraud and murder here.' Houseman blinked at me before lowering his eyes. 'You were a contemporary of Eugene Aram, were you not?' I asked, deciding to lull him onto safer ground for the moment.

'I believe I was a few months older than he. I was born in Marton in May, 1704, and he was born in the September of the same year up in Netherdale.'

'So you are both in your mid-fifties?'

'Aye, should Aram have lived,' muttered Houseman. Marton – I had his complex East Riding dialect placed now.

'And Daniel Clark, how old was he?'

'Dan was in his early twenties, about twenty-three when he went missing.'

'"Went missing",' I was incredulous. 'It has been proved that the young shoemaker is dead and gone, has it not, at the hands of your friend Eugene Aram?' Houseman merely shrugged at this. 'Tell me, how did such a disparate band of men ever get together in friendship.' Houseman looked at me blankly. 'What had you, a flax-dresser, Clark, a shoemaker, and Aram, a schoolmaster with an interest in languages and learning, have in common?'

'Ah, that's easy,' said Houseman. 'Anna Aram did a little spinning for me. Eugene and Dan shared a great interest in gardening.'

'Such an interest that they would lay traps for any stray neighbourhood cats, I've heard rumoured.'

'All true,' Houseman grinned. 'Eugene had this contrivance, took poor Dan to see it one night. Dan told me he nearly jumped out of his skin, there was such a screeching and shrieking coming from the bottom of Aram's garden. Under the wall, on a flower bed, Eugene had set a bar of spikes, set 'em like sharpened teeth in an old man's jaw. Still alive and impaled on part of the trap, the latest victim of the night struggled for its life amid flying fur. Dan said he was both paralysed and awestruck: standing over the fast fading Tom, side by side, with its grinning tormentor. "He only twitches now. Shouldn't we put a quick end to him out of common decency," he whined to Eugene. Decency – Dan Clark and his bloody decency – Eugene should have seen him then for the weakling he turned out to be. "Nay, we'll leave him till morning," Eugene told him. "He has enough fight in him yet to scratch a man's eyes out."' Houseman began to laugh manically at the tale.

'You did not have much time for Clark then?'

'The little whelp owed me money, twenty pounds,' Houseman sniffed his indignation.

'And his death nearly cost you your life.'

'True enough.'

'It has cost Aram his.'

'Yes.'

I turned to the front of my notebook to check my trial notes. 'But Clark paid you back during that Thursday night,

Friday morning, the seventh and eighth of February, '45, did he not? He paid you back in leather and lining cloth.'

'You know them dates you have just quoted to me, I was never too sure of 'em. It all started with that coroner, John Theakston, I think he was called. He insisted on them times and dates. Then the justice, William Thornton, following on. Can you tell me, Mister, what you were doing on any given day at the beginning of February thirteen years ago?'

'I think not.'

'That's right.'

'Unless you keep a daily journal.' Houseman stared at me as if I was suggesting he should fly to the moon. 'But we are talking of murder here, Mr Houseman,' I reminded him.

'Don't make no difference,' said Houseman.

'However, I think I would have some recollection of the time I killed a man.'

'Not the exact date though. Not after all them years.' Again Houseman cackled like an inmate of Bedlam. He cackled until he realised his mistake.

'This is beginning to sound like a confession, Mr Houseman.'

'You are trying to trick me with your clever words.'

'Not at all. But if you wish to unburden yourself, consider me your man. Although, that being the case, I could no longer guarantee your immunity.'

'Listen, Mister, I was in prison with Benjamin Windle and Henry Nelson, both hanged before Eugene. Windle for burglary and stealing one hundred gold coins, Nelson alongside him for perjury and forgery. Then there was Benjamin Hoult executed for stealing a horse. Last month I stood at the bar next to George Mason accused of stealing two pecks of malt and three of wheat for which he was condemned to be burnt in the hand. Most of these men were poor men, poor men like me, hungry men. What sort of a deterrent is it when a tradesman is maimed by the law for two pecks of malt? What sort of justice is it when two men are strung from the Tyburn tree for stealing a few coins or telling a lie?'

'You might as well be hanged for stealing a sheep as a lamb, is that what you are saying, Houseman? You, Clark and Aram defrauded your neighbours of so much valuable property should you have been caught you would have hanged for it anyway.'

'No, I am not saying that at all. I am telling you that men who have done little wrong in their lives apart from find themselves impoverished and desperate to feed their families, these are the men who are forced to endure that death cart ride onto the Knavesmire.'

'So you turned King's evidence lest the same fate befell you?'

'The drop is not always clean, the neck not always broken. Men piss and shit their breeches at the thought of it on the death cart ride.'

'By the way, have you been to see your friend Eugene swinging up there from his gibbet post?' I asked, unmoved.

Houseman was speechless. His head lolled from side to side. The little colour he had drained from his face.

'I never thought they would find him down there in Lynn,' he finally whispered. 'I thought he was safe, thought it was safe to say it was him.'

'You told the court that you went to Aram's house on account of some leather about Candlemas, 1745. Nineteen skins and more were mentioned, I believe.' Houseman nodded. 'Between two and three in the morning, Aram and Clark went out of the house and asked you to join them for a walk. You said there was another unknown man across the way. Was that the Jewish pedlar from York who went missing about the same time as Clark?'

'I don't know who he was,' snapped Houseman quickly.

'But other Knaresborough folk said they had seen you, Clark and Aram sitting with a Jew in Mr Carter's public house that evening.'

'I know nowt about a Jew,' snapped Houseman.

'So Aram and Clark alone went over a hedge into Saint Robert's Cave?' Again Houseman nodded. 'You saw the two men quarrelling. This is when you saw Aram strike Daniel Clark down. You said you saw Aram strike Clark several times on the breast and head.'

'I did.'

'That would suggest Aram was striking Clark face to face. But Aaron Locock, the Knaresborough surgeon, testified that a fatal blow from a blunt instrument could be seen on the back of the skull.' Houseman made no answer. 'Surgeon William Higgins' previously made deposition is likewise. Why, if it is as you said, did you not stop these two men fighting?'

'I was some way off.'

'According to your court testimony from your position at the bridge end you saw Aram leaving the cave side carrying some bundle in his hand. How could you be so sure of such detail if you were "some way off"?'

'There was moonlight and snow on the ground.'

'I take it we are talking about the Grimble Bridge end as Low Bridge is miles away?' Houseman stared at me, his head motionless now. 'By my reckoning the moon was but two days after the full. I agree the reflecting snow on the ground would aid visibility further. However, you cannot see the cave side from Grimble Bridge, I've checked.' This was a lie on my part and an instinctive gamble. I had not checked. After my experience at Mother Shipton's Cave – caves had become anathema to me – nevertheless, I knew then I would have to check in the near future.

'I tell you I saw Eugene carrying a bundle.'

'And what do you think this bundle consisted of?'

'Clothing.'

'Clark's clothing?' Houseman nodded. 'I thought you couldn't remember much detail about the given dates.'

'I remembered that much.'

'Following your remand in York's Castle Prison, did you tell Constable Barker that Clark's body had been buried in the turn of the cave's entrance?'

'I might have done.' Houseman's full bottom lip pouted. 'If he said I did then perhaps it is so.'

'How could you be so precise about its position if you were viewing this scene from far away?'

'I've nowt to say about that.'

'Did Francis Iles play any part in Clark's plot to defraud his neighbours?'

'I've nowt to say about him.' Houseman looked alarmed.

'Did you kill or were you party to the killing of Daniel Clark?' I asked him as he swayed from side to side. 'Did you kill or were you party to the killing of a Jewish merchant or his servant or both?' Houseman fell taciturn. 'If you have any further thoughts on the matter, I can be found at the Bell. Remember posterity, Mr Houseman, this might be your final chance to put forward your case.'

'Tis not posterity that worries me, Mister, 'tis more the hangman's noose.'

CHAPTER EIGHT

The sky had turned grey, the temperature dropped, as I walked down the steps from Richard Houseman's heckling shop. A north easterly wind was blowing across the Plain of York and penetrating my light clothing. Could autumn be on the way already? Even the tame raven on the wooden handrail ignored me, frozen and disinterested now I was leaving.

Like a grenadier facing the ignominy of the cat-o'-nine-tails, I decided it would not be long before I would have to chew the bullet and investigate St Robert's Cave myself – the place the gang had beaten out more than the silver plate – the final resting place of the twenty-three year old shoemaker, Daniel Clark.

The heckler had left me with a lot to think about. He had been right: the theft and fraud he and his fellow conspirators had indulged in was a capital offence. Nay, as he had pointed out, we hang men for merely telling lies. How had Houseman got away with it? How had they *all* got way with it? – at the expense of Aram of course. I was sure there had been other Knaresborough men involved in this complex crime. Nevertheless, Richard Houseman was the luckiest man alive.

I took out my notebook to refresh myself on the facts of the case. Jammed between the pages was a thin newspaper cutting – the *York Courant*, I think it came from. The newspaper had listed many of the items taken by Clark from his neighbours through one bizarre pretence or another. Either the townsfolk of Knaresborough were extremely gullible or Clark's credit had been irreproachable. He took up great quantities of linen and woollen drapery with the excuse that he was lately married and wanted clothes to appear in. He wanted good table linen to eat over and excellent bed linen in which to woo his late December sweetheart and bride, Hannah Oldham, daughter of Oxley Oldham, exciseman, of Newell Hall near Otley. He borrowed from several innkeepers in the town, one would have thought they would have known better. A silver tankard from one, a pint from another, ales and other assortments of liquors from anyone generous enough to give.

Clark told all and sundry that he would be glad of the supplies for supper. He amassed three more silver tankards; four silver pints; one silver pot; one ring set with an emerald, and two brilliant diamonds. Another ring was set with three rose diamonds; a third with an amethyst in the shape of a heart, and six plain rings. A ring for his beloved's every finger. He finally obtained eight watches to tell the time with; two snuff boxes; two volumes of Chambers' Dictionary; six bound volumes of Pope's Homer. Clark promised all the benefactors that they would all be reimbursed once his new, already rich wife came into her fortune.

But Clark's eight watches must have failed him because he missed a 9 o' clock appointment at his brother-in-law's, Philip Coates' house. Coates was married to Hannah Oldham's sister. Rumours began to breed in the alleys and snickelways of Knaresborough. Clark had gone off. A search started for the goods and plate. True enough some skins were found under flax in Houseman's warehouse and velvets were dug up in Aram's garden, but no plate and no Clark. The strictest enquiry was made about him, men dispatched hither and thither, his disappearance was advertised in many papers. The getaway of the pock-broken cordwainer was becoming a mystery for he had not taken his horse, the horse he stabled at Bryan Hardcastle's livery, the horse it was believed he loved more than Hannah Oldham.

A day or two later, on the Sunday, Aram, who was already suspected of being an accomplice of Clark's, was arrested on the pretext of debt to a Mr William Norton. Before a Justice of the Peace's warrant could be obtained relating to the fraud charges, Aram paid off his debt to Mr Norton. Soon after being released he left Knaresborough and was not heard from again with any certainty until the month of June, last year, when he was spotted in a country park in Norfolk.

Once Aram had left Knaresborough, it seemed to stop any further speculation or examination regarding Clark's disappearance along with most of his neighbours' property. Even Francis Iles fell silent regarding his professed interest in the return of the conspirators' ill-gotten gains.

Then on a hot August day, thirteen years later, all hell broke loose.

It was a Tuesday, the first day of the month, when William Thompson started to dig for stone on Thistle Hill to supply a lime kiln. William Thompson smeared dirt across his sweating brow. The casual Knaresborough sweep was finding this manual labour heavier and hotter than even the chimneys. Although only a slight man, he was forced to discard his waistcoat in the midday heat. He had dug to a depth of just over half a yard in one particular place, when he heard a scrape on his spade. Judging that he had gone deep enough, he stopped and blinked through stinging sweat towards his handiwork. Seeing what he took to be another stone, he reached down and enthusiastically dug it up. The weight on his spade was too light for stone. He smeared more dirt across his sweating brow as he pondered his find.

''Tis definitely no splinter bone o' a dog that.' He carefully placed what he took to be the leg bone of some larger animal on the grassy lip of his excavation. Next he pulled out another bone silhouetted black against the sun – a broken bone – a human arm bone, it could be nothing else.

Blinking again in the sun's glare, he felt dizzy with it all. Swearing loudly he put both bones gently back and covered them with a thin layer of soil. The God-fearing countryman was horrified to have disturbed the final resting place of some dear departed soul. Perhaps he would be punished for it.

Quickly gathering his thoughts and things, he abandoned the stone already collected and, trembling, rushed away from the quarry. For the next two days, he felt his discovery was such a curse on him that he dared not mention it to another living soul.

By the third day, Thompson's secret find had really begun to prey on his mind. What if it was not some pagan grave or the site of a soldier's last fall in some far off war? What if instead it was the site of some heinous crime? Thompson forced himself back up Thistle Hill to the place at the edge of the cliff, and digging forward he discovered the rest of the bones. Unless disturbed by a fox, which he doubted, from the layout of the bones the body must have been buried doubled up. During his first excavation he had damaged the original arm and small leg bone. This second time he proceeded with greater care and kept the skeleton entire as best he could. He found several teeth still in the jaw but there was no remaining identifiable clothing, not so much as a button.

On his way back through Knaresborough, in need of some fortification after the grisly task, the sweep called at his local alehouse. Glass in soiled hand, he blurted out his find to the landlord there. *My landlord at the Bell swears he was the man and is now full of the tale.* Whatever the truth of this, Thompson's publican immediately raised the alarm and summoned the main authorities of the town to investigate his troubled customer's claim.

On the fourth day of August, as back in Lynn Aram struggled with end of term schoolboys, the two Knaresborough surgeons, Higgins and Locock, were setting out up Thistle Hill to view the human remains in situ for themselves. Before a waiting and silent crowd they broke a thigh bone, consulted, and judged it reasonably fresh. The crowd sighed at their professionalism. They both looked official; they both felt very officious. This was the scene of a possible murder – something had to be done – a culprit or culprits found.

On the fifth, sixth and seventh day, the rumble of rumours picked up momentum throughout the town. Nobody had forgotten Daniel Clark and with good reason. Even his wife Hannah, mother Dorothy and friend and brother-in-law Philip Coates had become convinced that the cordwainer must have absconded with the dowry and booty, now they too began to question again. When told of the sweep's gruesome find only Anna Aram remained smug and composed. Well, why shouldn't she clasp her hands beneath her bosom? – this was her moment for revenge – here at last was confirmation of the things she had hinted at for years about the town.

This is when the story gets extremely interesting: a travelling servant of a Jew was reported missing with his stock-in-trade about the same time as Daniel Clark. His employer could trace him no further than Knaresborough. It was feared he had been murdered. There was an eerie similarity here with the *Whitehall Evening Post* article, purporting to be from a Yorkshire correspondent, that said a Knaresborough woman (surely Anna Aram) could hang several men and a husband in the town who had been involved with the murder of a Jew and his man. But Thompson had found only one skeleton on Thistle Hill. These bones must be the bones of Daniel Clark as nobody else had been known to be missing thereabouts for sixty years. The missing servant of the Jew was not taken into consideration, he was of no consequence.

It was not until twelve days after the Thompson find that an inquest was opened by the West Riding of Yorkshire Coroner, John Theakston, already mentioned to me by Richard Houseman. This is when I got involved in the case. My father had granted me a small annuity after leaving university, and I had decided to experience the spas of England. Harrogate pleased me more than most, and while there I first learned of the bones found on Thistle Hill. Though I longed to be a writer of books like Swift and Defoe, my achievements thus far had been published correspondence in one or two London magazines. Richard Cave had suggested that an inquest into a possible murder in the rural wastelands of Yorkshire would be a good test for an aspiring writer and no harm done. If I sent my piece to the *Gentleman's Magazine,* he offered to give it the benefit of his editorial expertise.

Things began to fall my way. I was later given the opportunity to examine at leisure many of the inquest papers through the kind offices, and a little liquid persuasion, of one of Theakston's clerks in Leeds. These documents proved invaluable to my memory of the rustic legal proceeding that took place at Henry Mellor's Knaresborough house.

'Thomas Payley, John Mountain, Jonathan Wilks, Barwick Clapham ...' Each juror's name, thirteen in all, floated a unique magic into the air, each name held its own spell for those who had come to gaup.

At the back of the packed room, barely visible through clouds of swirling pipe smoke, a glum and shrinking Houseman was first pointed out to me. He had been ordered to attend the inquest because insinuations were circulating about the town concerning his relationship to the missing Clark.

By the time thin-faced John Theakston, coroner and gentleman, opened the proceedings proper any standing space left had been taken up.

Thompson confirmed his discovery. John Yeats, a barber, said he had gone over the spot where the remains had been found, nigh Candlemas thirteen or fourteen years before, and had seen a place fresh dug up. Barbara Leetham, a widow, told a similar story. She said she had seen a place dug up, during the same period as Yeats, which had not been so dug when she had passed the spot the previous night. She said the earth at this excavation had been filled up in a careless manner.

Bryan Hardcastle told the court about Clark's horse left at livery.

Stolid Stephen Latham, Aram's arresting officer around the time Clark was first reported missing, next stood up to be counted. He addressed himself with deference to Mr Theakston rather than the jury, telling him that while a prisoner for debt Aram had a large quantity of money on him.

'How much money?' asked Theakston.

'I could not say precisely, sir, but there looked to be a hundred pounds or more in guineas and coins. I've never seen the like of it in one man's hand then or since.'

'And had you expected Eugenius Aram to have such a sum in his possession?'

'No, sir, he was very poor.'

'And that was his general character?'

'Yes, sir.' Those in court who remembered the schoolmaster mumbled their agreement as Latham cleared his nervous throat. 'And Eugenius Aram had very great quantities of goods of different sorts o' Clark's in his custody.' Latham paused and peered round the room. 'Richard Houseman had likewise several sorts of goods o' Clark's,' he said, shaking his finger towards Houseman.

'Thump! Thump!' A few members of the public started stamping appreciative feet in New World lynch mob fashion.

'Silence!' shouted Theakston. This was English justice, God damn it.

The slumped Houseman's face turned the yellow-grey of the smoke about him. He sensed the court, nay the whole town against him now.

'How much were the goods at Houseman's appraised at?' asked Theakston, seemingly having a special interest in the sum total of things.

'Forty-five pounds, sir,' replied Latham, looking to a dog-eared page of the book shaking in his hand.

All the witnesses so far had been important enough to be bound over. John Theakston was having a busy Saturday but then he had known it would be from the outset. There was another man present that day of the first inquest who had always shown an interest in the sum total of things, but who now had a vested interest in keeping his name from being mangled in the mechanics of law or even the press. Francis Iles, sitting towards the front of the room, kept his vision firmly fixed on John Theakston as witness followed witness.

A very worried looking William Tuton followed to take the oath. Throughout his evidence he tried to avoid the hostile eyes of his two relatives on the jury, particularly those of Thomas Tuton the Elder whose staring eyes put the fear of God into him. For the first time in his life, Tuton realised that our relatives can be our harshest critics.

The mason had decided it was better to admit his transaction with Clark over the leather. He gave a vivid and damaging description of Houseman and Aram in Clark's company on the night in question around Candlemas.

'Never saw him more, sir,' said Tuton.

The public fizzed. The wooden floor beneath them groaned.

'Anything to add, Mr Tuton?' asked Theakston, well-pleased.

'Aye,' said Tuton, sucking his tense lips harder together. 'I found a pick o' mine in Aram's house.' Tuton felt obliged to make a clean breast of the pick business, too, in case Anna had reported the incident or someone else had seen it that day against the wall – the day of Aram's arrest. But Tuton never confessed that he had lent Daniel Clark, with a good heart, the tools that might have eventually been used to murder and bury him. That was too much involvement for Tuton to take upon himself. No, the tools must have been stolen or so he led the court to believe.

A hush fell across the court as Anna stood up to tell what she knew concerning her young friend Clark. She had waited nearly fourteen years for this stage, this audience. She was not going to hold back anymore, not for her brother Abraham, not for her mainly grown-up children, and especially not for the husband who had deserted her years ago. Anna told how it was on that cold night back in February, 1744, '45 by the new calendar. She told of the comings and goings; the missing Clark; a proposal to kill her; newly burnt ashes out in the yard; a handkerchief lent to Houseman to bind about his wigless head found discarded the next morning with a blood spot on it the size of a shilling.

'I believe Daniel Clark to have been murdered by my husband and Richard Houseman,' she shouted; finally, bitterly and out loud to the memory of dear supportive Daniel. The whole theatre – now a theatre of war – gasped. Houseman sank deeper into his chair.

Next to stand was a rather sheepish Philip Coates. Coates admitted he had been suspicious at first about the young cordwainer's disappearance, but suspicion had turned to anger when he remembered that he was instrumental in Clark's introduction to Hannah Oldham and her subsequent missing fortune. Not long after Clark's disappearance, Coates' loadstone for truth had swung further against his one time friend: he had him outlawed at the Castle of York through what was aptly called a writ of vengeance. Mr Coates, man of business, soon warmed to the business of the court. He told them how in the early days of Daniel's missing the family had widely advertised for information of his whereabouts. On the Thursday of the skeleton being uncovered he, Coates, had been informed and had examined part of it. As nobody else in Knaresborough or its neighbourhood had ever disappeared during his time, he told the court with jutting chin that the bones found on Thistle Hill must be those of his brother-in-law.

The surgeons, Higgins and Locock, spoke like Gemini twins saying they believed the bones found on Thistle Hill were those of Daniel Clark.

In view of all the evidence and accusations against him, Theakston beckoned Richard Houseman forward. The background murmur, which had been playing for most of the trial, stopped abruptly. The courtroom fell mortuary silent as the squeaking leather boots of Houseman fumbled their way across the wooden floor to come to a standstill before Theakston and the jury.

'Now, sir, what have you to say of this matter?' Theakston asked him abruptly, watching in fascination the beads of sweat festooned and dripping from the stooping witness.

There came an inaudible mumble from the bulk of clothing. Although the day was warm, Houseman had sought fit to muffle himself up from prying eyes.

'What was that he said? What did he say?' The general murmur rose and fell again.

'What did you say?' Theakston voiced the public question. 'Speak up, man.'

'I can give no account o' t' matter,' came the sullen and husky reply, as if the whole atmosphere of the smoky room had caught in his throat.

'And what of the question of murder and your part in it as put forward by Mrs Aram say?'

'Wicked lies. I … I deny everything she said,' faltered Houseman, turning even paler.

John Theakston looked down from his temporary dais in disbelief onto the stubborn flax-dresser's head. Houseman had now given way to a fit of coughing.

'Are you *really* sure you have no answer for your accusers?' Theakston's fingers turned white against his pen. The flax-dresser below slowly shook his bowed head. It was now that the coroner resolved to break his man, now that Richard Houseman would admit that he, and possibly others, had murdered and buried Daniel Clark. Theakston instructed Houseman to take hold of one of the bones from the Thistle Hill skeleton. A skeleton that had been removed from its grave and displayed before the court for that very purpose.

'See if the bone bleeds,' whispered a rustic next to me.

'Hush,' said another, who I guessed could not spell his own name but knew how things should be.

Houseman held up the bone tentatively at first and then his grasp tightened. The jury gaped; the crowd gaped; Theakston waited patiently. An animal rage suddenly gripped the once cowed Houseman as he looked defiantly at his drooling persecutors. He had felt trapped all morning, now he felt only scorn for the fools about him.

'This is no more Dan Clark's bone than 'tis mine,' he sneered, shaking the bone like a weapon. He felt good: he had broken the yoke, broken free, regained his self-esteem.

Disconcerting as Houseman's sudden outburst was, Theakston was the first to realise that the flax-dresser had snared himself by his own arrogance. 'How are you so sure this is not a bone of Daniel Clark?'

'Err …'

'Yes?'

'I can produce a witness who saw Dan Clark upon t' road two or three days after he was missing at Knaresborough,' palliated Houseman.

'Who is this surprise witness, Mr Houseman, whom you have not thought fit to mention before?' Theakston no longer made any attempt to conceal his disbelief.

'Parkinson.'

'Is Mr Parkinson a Knaresborough man?' Houseman nodded. 'Then we will send for him,' instructed Theakston.

Accordingly Parkinson was sent for. He admitted that he himself had never seen Daniel Clark after the 8[th.] of February, 1744/45.

'So why are you here, sir?' asked Theakston.

'A friend o' mine, sir, told me he had met a person like Daniel Clark,' said Parkinson, rubbing his stubble and shifting from one foot to the other with obvious awkwardness at having been summoned.

'A friend of yours?' smiled Theakston. Adding a scathing, 'And not a friend of Houseman's, I suppose.'

'No, sir. Mine, sir,' replied the bewildered Parkinson, looking helplessly over to where Houseman sat. 'But it were a snowy day, and the person had the cape of his greatcoat up. He could not say, mi friend, wi' the least degree of certainty who he was.'

'I see,' sighed Theakston, waving Parkinson down. Weary of Houseman and his prevaricating cronies, he turned to address the jury. 'As there is considerable doubt regarding the identity of the bones found on Thistle Hill, I feel there is no alternative but to hold a second inquest there.'

The rowdies in the public gave a raucous cheer.

With renewed determination, Theakston swore in another jury of sixteen this time: three of whom could not write. In the afternoon he, followed by his literate and illiterate retinue, climbed to the place above the Rock on Thistle Hill. They returned a verdict of murder of a person unknown by persons unknown.

That night the court constable, John Barker, who had earlier barred the throng from the doorway to Henry Mellor's house, went round to the house of William Thornton armed with the incriminating depositions and applied for a warrant to apprehend Richard Houseman.

CHAPTER NINE

The residence of the local magistrate was on the road between Knaresborough and York at Kirk Hammerton. I sent word to him by a boy – the best runner in town I was assured – before I breakfasted. Mr William Thornton, Esquire, replied by return. He would receive me that day at 12.30 p.m. precisely.

Thornville was a square box of house, a sombre house without fun, the small red bricks an example of an architecture popular in the previous century. Looking upwards I could not help admire the gauged brickwork and the curving Dutch gabled end. That was it, Thornville had a brooding Rembrandt feel to it.

However, sterility was the word that hit me as soon as I stepped inside – cool sterility. The panelled drawing room was a room devoid of warmth. I shivered, there is nothing as emotionally chilling as a large room without fire in the grate.

There I stood – the child before the father in a house that somehow had banished children – a much maligned hackney writer seeking understanding (and information) from the Justice of the Peace. A footman stood at attention behind us. From time to time he coughed nervously. I was on edge and the man's sporadic cough began to irritate me.

On the other side of a large table the seated Thornton was studiously examining an array of documents, moving them this way and that like Marlborough planning his next campaign. Thornton was pink, fresh-faced and looked to be in his late forties. His nails were manicured as well as any noble woman's but, although his hair was thinning, he had not troubled himself with a wig for his morning audience with the likes of me. Indeed, as yet, he had hardly acknowledged my presence.

'Charles, you may leave us,' he told the footman.

There was an ink stain a foot from my foot – a quill, a pot, a dip and lazy flick a long time ago – an unseen historical ink stain spreading out and sinking fast through the wooden floor of Thornville. Here at last was something imperfect, almost human, to absorb my disquiet. The stain, preserved by years of polish, was at odds with its surroundings: a warm bruise of character on a house with none, a comforting blot on the characterless.

'So, Mr …' Thornton finally looked up from his papers to address me.

'Kendle, sir. Felix Kendle.' I stuck out my arm like a stick – a stick Thornton seemed unprepared to embrace – I jerked it back.

'Your note introduced you as some form of writer,' snorted Thornton, preening like a peacock. 'I expect you've come to record my exploits in the Second Jacobite Rebellion.'

'Well, actually, sir …'

'And Blind Jack Metcalf's of course?' interrupted Thornton.

'Blind Jack? Is he not the gentleman who walked from London to Harrogate for a wager?'

'The same. Hardly a gentleman though, a wonderful character nonetheless. Born in a modest cottage abutting Knaresborough churchyard, he lost his eyesight to smallpox at the age of six. That did not hold back our Jack from any of his manly pursuits. He can run, swim, hunt, play a fiddle better than any man alive. Used to entertain us all here at Thornville at Christmas-tide. When he was still a young man, Colonel George Liddell invited Jack down to London to play his fiddle for his Covent Garden houseguests. With the London winter season over and the Harrogate season about to open, his patron offered Jack a ride back on his coach. Jack replied that he could complete the journey north faster on foot. Starting on the Monday morning, he beat George to nearly every staging post along the way. He eventually arrived back in Harrogate on the Saturday, two whole days before old George's coach rumbled into town,' guffawed Thornton.

'Wonderful though Blind Jack might be, it is not he who captures my interest, sir.'

'Not Jack, so who?'

'Why Eugene Aram, sir. I am writing a piece on Eugene Aram.'

'Eugene Aram?' Thornton wrinkled his noble nose in disgust. 'Why Eugene Aram? – fella was a waster, a blaggard.'

'I covered his cause célèbre at York, sir.'

'Did you really?' Said with indifference.

'I believe you are connected by marriage to two other eminent gentlemen mentioned in the case, Mr Norton and Sir Edward Blackett.'

'Indeed, indeed, what of it?' sniffed Thornton. 'The two gentlemen you have just mentioned were only associated with Eugene Aram in the loosest sense, as I myself was.'

'Of course, sir, but were you not the Justice of the Peace who took down the witnesses' and the accused's depositions?'

'A tedious affair, I must say. When Clark went missing, I was more concerned with the possibility of the Young Pretender, Charles Edward Stuart, renewing his attempt to land an army on English soil. Though the county agreed to raise funds to rebuff him, they refused to raise an army to go out and meet him. The majority of gentlemen preferred a defensive stand, shall we say,' Thornton sniffed his distaste once more.

'But not you, sir. I understand you raised sixty-four volunteers from Knaresborough alone,' I flattered.

'Aye, Jack along with a sergeant recruited most of 'em for me and I dressed 'em.'

'A grand sight they must have presented. The Blue and Buffs marching down the High Street with Blind Jack at their head, wearing his large gold laced hat, playing a rousing tune on his oboe to meet General Wade at Boroughbridge,' I enthused.

'You are well informed for a Londoner, Kendle.'

'The Bell's landlord is a great admirer of yours, sir.'

Thornton remained frowning. Obviously he did not feel the landlord's admiration was worthy of comment. 'I was afraid the Frenchies were about to join the Pretender's invasion.'

'Many gentlemen in the country shared your misgivings, I'll warrant.'

'Have you ever fought on a battlefield, Kendle?' I shook my head, immediately reduced. 'The Yorkshire Blues were right in the centre of things at Falkirk. We lost that first battle. Our bloody guns got stuck in the mud. Gunpowder smoke stuck in our nostrils from the few rounds we did manage to get off. The smell of fear, sweat, blood mingled with wet field are not things I am liable to forget. Led by that incompetent, Lieutenant General Henry Hawley, we were forced to drop back into the town. Did you know we called him "Hangman Hawley" because of his harsh treatment of both friend or foe? A rigid disciplinarian, furious at our defeat, he would hang any poor soldier suspected of desertion without a second thought. With Hawley on our side, we didn't need the Scots to reduce our numbers. Keeping my head down for a while, I lodged with a local woman who took me in. I heard no news of Blind Jack, thought he was dead. Afraid I had been taken prisoner in the chaos, the cheeky bastard attempted to get a job playing his fiddle for Bonnie Prince Charlie's troops in an effort to locate me. Someone from Harrogate, with allegiance to the rebel cause, recognised him and he came under suspicion of spying. After a summary court martial from the Stuart cause, amazingly Jack escaped with his life. We were reunited in Edinburgh.'

'Then there was Culloden,' I offered. I could see Thornton loved to be indulged in this military theme.

'Ah, Culloden,' sighed Thornton. 'The same stench but English and Scottish fortunes were reversed.'

There was the sound of scuffling behind Thornton's drawing room door and a competent knock.

'Enter,' commanded the old captain of Culloden.

With rather ridiculous pomposity, I thought, a footman announced, 'Master Thomas Thornton, Esquire'.

I was wrong about children and Thornville. Thomas Thornton, Esquire, looked to be a boy of no more than eleven or twelve. A tutor pattered behind him. A long thin tutor who could have been the embodiment of Aram. I always felt sorry for tutors, their positions usually difficult if not untenable. This man already looked cowed by Thornton the son, let alone Thornton the father.

'My son,' Thornton told me with obvious pride. Thomas Thornton was pink cheeked like his father with a fine head of black curls.

'What a fine young chap,' I said.

'A late gift from my wife Mary. Doesn't like schooling very much though do you, Thomas?'

'Hate Charterhouse, sir. Can't deny it,' the boy announced emphatically.

'Are you married, Kendle?' asked his father.

'No, unfortunately …'

'Time enough,' he interrupted. 'Time enough to play the field.'

Obviously provoked by the mention of "the field", the tutor piped up 'Master Thomas is more eager to test his goshawk in the park than attend to his studies.'

'Do let me, Papa, mathematics is such dull stuff.' The black curls danced as Thornton junior stamped his feet with impatience.

'See,' said the tutor in justification.

'The park might be good for the boy during his present bout of ill health,' suggested Thornton.

'But, sir, you wished to take this opportunity of improving Master Thomas' education during his long absence from school.'

'The hawk was Papa's birthday present.' Thomas' pretty face pouted.

'None of this wishy-washy, French salon nonsense for the boy. See his pallor. Nothing like fresh air for an up and coming Englishman, eh, Kendle?'

I did not answer. Thornton obviously doted on the boy. This was one dispute I had no desire to become involved in.

'Thank you, Papa.' Pout turned to beam of achievement.

'But,' gaped the tutor.

'It's a fine day. Let the lad have his head this once and make sport with the hawk,' said Thornton, dismissing the pair with an abrupt wave of his hand. 'Love seeing him training a bird,' he whispered to me in confidence. 'He has a gift for it. More an empathy with horses, dogs and birds than people, I fear. Now where were we?' Thornton began to delve in his desk drawer, eventually lifting out some papers. 'See, here, these might interest you, Kendle. After the trial I kept most of the original witness depositions I'd taken. Would you like to see 'em?' I nodded speechless. I had merely indulged this man and his late gift son for a few minutes and he had come up with this priceless offer. Thornton began rolling out the documents on his leather desk top. 'Lots of erasures in both Houseman's and Aram's depositions as you will see. Neither seemed able to get his story straight. They were lying through their teeth, kept changing things. Much of what they said didn't make any sense to me.'

William Thornton had nothing like the neat coroner's hand of Theakston. He was right about the erasures. These depositions, which in fairness had been taken at the time and not transcribed later, were something of a mess. But that only served to add to their interest and immediacy – much can be learnt from erasures.

'I wonder if you would be kind enough to allow me to make a copy of one or two of these depositions to study in greater detail at leisure, sir,' I dared to ask.

'Better let you get on with it then. Expect it will take up the rest of the day,' laughed Thornton, shaking the bell on his desk. 'Charles, here, will escort you to one of the guest rooms with a writing desk. You'll be able to work there on the papers in peace.' With that he stood up and bowed. I was dismissed.

* * * * *

It was evening when I reached the Long Flat on the outskirts of Knaresborough, perched up on ridiculous Bess, a leather satchel containing my precious copies swinging at the hip. The satchel was a present from William Thornton. He had sent it – via a footman up the sweeping staircase before I left – as if it was nothing. The wigless, once Whig member for York was obviously an extremely rich man.

Reaching the outskirts of Knaresborough, I passed at an ungainly trot some new and imposing mansions being built for the town's rich. But it was not until I was well up the High Street at its junction with Finkle Street that I saw something that really arrested my attention.

A hatless Janet Brown – her free flowing hair as dark as Houseman's raven – was spinning a top with a much younger child. The child was as dark skinned as she was. Neither of them would have stood out round a fire in an Egyptian encampment or begging on Florence's Ponte Vecchio. Yes, this scene was more appropriate for a Mediterranean setting. Janet and the child stood in the cobbled shadow of a building. The spinning top was not. It span in a final splash of pavement light. I glimpsed Janet appearing to enjoy the swirl of colour more than the child. She laughed as the child struggled and cried to pull the whip from her. Janet Brown was indeed a child herself. She would not relinquish her joy at a moment soon to be gone.

'I saw you earlier in Finkle Street,' I told her over dinner. 'You were spinning a top with a little boy.'

'My little brother,' she said.

'Really,' I said, tucking into my thick mutton chop. They seemed to have a propensity for mutton in this part of the world.

'I have news …' she began.

The landlord arrived and as usual edged her roughly aside to deliver a jug of ale upon my table.

'Please don't do that.' I rebuked him as gently as I could.

'Eh?' he growled.

'Don't push the maid about like that.'

'Maid is it?' chuckled the landlord, hands on hips. 'Don't be so gullible to a pretty wench's smile, sir. This maid's maiden head has been broken a good while.'

Conditioned Janet hardly reacted to the landlord's taunts. With a lift of her dark head, she flounced away as if "what did it matter anyway, one way or the other she was doomed".

'Expect during all those little tête-à-têtes you had with her in your bedchamber, she failed to mention the existence of her base child,' resumed the landlord.

'Yours perhaps?'

'Now look here, sir, I'll not be insulted in my own house.' Hands on hips, moved to hands across chest.

Sensing a confrontation, or alerted by Janet, the landlady cook rushed out of the kitchen to make one of her infrequent appearances. 'How are your chops, sir?' she asked, forcing a smile.

CHAPTER TEN

The clouds hung low, motionless, the colour of lead as I stood in the Bell's beery front doorway. I was about to make the same journey Aram, Houseman and Clark had made on that cold February night in 1745. But mine was being taken in muggy daytime August, fourteen years later, and I was starting from the cusp of the High Street, whereas they would have joined Bond End from Aram's humble Church Lane cottage in the lower town.

I had not seen Janet Brown since the previous night's incident in the Bell's best room. My rather grey looking bedding had not been turned down and she had not appeared that morning to serve at breakfast. If she was so upset, I feared my last chance of an introduction to Betty Aram had gone too.

Checking my silver Millington pocket watch, I stepped out onto the High Street. There had been much toing and froing on that Thursday night, Friday morning, the 7th and 8th of February, 1745. But the plot to defraud seemed to have gathered momentum a fortnight before with the awaited arrival of Clark to Aram's cottage with his wife's dowry. According to the eye-witness statement of Clark's own servant, Peter Moor, that small cottage parlour must have been a little crowded with Aram, Houseman and himself there to greet the cordwainer.

'You are welcome home, Mr Clark, have you got the money?' Aram asked him; no doubt a false smile crossing the pedagogue's face more like a cloud than the sun.

'I have r … r … received mi wife's fortune, and have it in mi pocket, though it was with d … d … difficulty I got it,' stammered a fidgeting Clark. Though Moor made no mention of it, I can imagine his young employer kept casting antagonistic side glances in his direction, unhappy to be talking of such personal matters before a servant. Moor also failed to explain what his own business had been that day at the Church Lane cottage. No doubt he too must have been involved with the movement of fraudulently obtained goods from one premises to another.

Aram would have been quick to assess the situation and suggest, 'We need more privacy, gentlemen.' Whereupon Moor was given leave and Clark, Houseman and Aram disappeared upstairs.

Back to the Thursday before Clark disappeared. He had told his mother, Dorothy, that he was going off to see his wife who was away with her family at Newell Hall. That was the last time she ever saw him. The poor woman believed that had her son still been living he would surely have written to her.

Another sighting of Clark alive had been at 8 o' clock at the house of Jonathan Locock where he had called to borrow a tankard. He had been accompanied by Houseman who remained in the entry. Locock was found not to be at home and his servant, Mary Bransby, sent the pair on their way empty handed.

It had taken me only a few minutes from the Bell to reach the turn into the alleyway that was Jockey Lane, so called because of the horse dealers' stabling that abounds here.

At 9 o' clock, fourteen years before, Mrs Bransby was making her way to the Assembly Room along this same lane and saw Clark and Houseman again with Eugene Aram. They passed the lane end walking along Kirkgate.

I could not help looking left and right and over my shoulder. This was a perfect place for an ambush with its narrow walls and courts. Thankfully, no one was about. I was alone and unthreatened. A deep breath and out into Kirkgate. One end of this street looks up into town, the other dips away later to rise to the distant vista of wild moorland and hills of the North Riding. I turned towards the town.

In Houseman's first examination, he told Thornton that he had been in Clark's company that night collecting goods in lieu of twenty pounds previously lent by him to the cordwainer. He eventually left Clark at Aram's house. There was another man present at the Church Lane property who was unknown to him. Houseman further said that Aram, Clark and the unknown person immediately followed him out of the house and went up into the Market Place. He could clearly discern them by the light of the moon but does not know what happened to them after that.

Houseman was being clearly evasive here to the point of lying. But why did Houseman bother to mention this mystery man at all? The presence of a shadowy Jew hangs over this whole affair like a Saracen in the mystery plays.

One part of Clark's murder deeply troubled me. If the body on Thistle Hill was not Daniel Clark's then whose was it? I saw from the depositions taken by William Thornton at Thornville that he had closely interrogated Aram about being seen at Mr Carter's public house with Houseman, Clark and a Jew at about midnight on the evening in question. Aram denied any memory of such an occasion. Houseman had vehemently denied to me any knowledge of a Jew. And no witnesses had been called to testify that these three men had been seen and heard conspiring with the unfortunate Israelite over a jug of beer. Witnesses drinking in Mr Carter's on the night in question were not called, although I have been assured there were many of them with the acute hearing of bats. They were not called because shamefully the coroner's inquest had only been interested in identifying the bones of Daniel Clark, a local man.

'Of course I will have to see these pretty things you talk of before we talk of buying,' the swarthy, usually abstemious young man told them, as the other three drank on greedily after their evening of sweaty fetching and carrying.

This Jew was a servant of a Jew and travelled the markets for his master. He usually dealt in baubles, trifles of little value. But this night was to be different. He had been contacted in the market, the previous day, by a gentleman who offered to sell him watches, rings and small objects of great value. This same gentleman, Clark, now sat opposite him.

"Pretty things" – those two words arched from my mind round the square. Market Place is one of the few open spaces in Knaresborough. Only on Wednesdays is it cluttered with stall holders selling everything from leeks to linen to Nottingham lace. During normal weekdays, it still remains the hub of the town. It cannot have changed in centuries, let alone years, with its enclosure of shops and small businesses. The Jewish pedlar had been known to many of the market traders. He had nothing of the strong foreign accent of Levi, his master, who had worked the markets before him. Perhaps roaming the country as he did, carrying the trinket box upon his back, he had become susceptible to the accent of Gentiles rather than his fellow Jews. The young are always so much more impressionable.

* * * * *

Sniffing and testing his prey, pugilistic Houseman was nervous before the pounce. Despite the pedlar's command of good English there was an unfamiliar smell to him which was perplexing to the flax-dresser. Lifting his nose higher, he tried to place it amidst ale and smoke. Oil, that was it. Not the oil from sheep's wool – no, a different oil oozed from this man's pores – foreign eastern oil.

With a sudden flood of overpowering resentment, Houseman thought of grasping this young Shylock's neck with his bare hands; thought of taking his own pound of flesh; thought of how poor men like him had been bled dry by the Hebrews. Everything seemed foreign now to Houseman, like this man, like his own dreams of solvency. He turned from the man in disgust. What he had to do from now on was going to be easier.

'Thee will see 'em soon enough, these pretty things as thee calls 'em. Now sup up,' Houseman told the young pedlar.

The boy regarded Houseman with dull suspicion, then his dark eyes rolled up under his hooded lids as if he was about to faint. It did not take long for his three drinking companions to realise that though he was accustomed to wheedle and barter, he wasn't accustomed to strong ale. Shouting abruptly across to Mr Carter, Houseman ordered a final jug of the same.

On first meeting, the four at the corner table had sat back on their chairs content to observe each other. Over this their last drink they sat with heads bunched together whispering. Those around them could hear nothing now.

Raising his eyes briefly from the ale-slopped table, Aram became aware that their conspiratorial attitude had not escaped the keen attention of the landlord. To Mr Carter they must have looked like some sinister jungle flower that at first had been open to the light and then had closed its petals round some dark wrong doing. Aram comforted himself with the knowledge that one of the first requirements of an inn-keeper's trade was discretion, and, as long as his customers were supping up and paying for the privilege, they could huddle and plot as much as they pleased. Nevertheless, with his large hands covering his takings, Aram saw that Mr Carter visibly breathed a little easier as the four of them got to their feet and made for the door.

* * * * *

A fellow correspondent at Aram's trial suggested to me that this supposed Jew might not have been the missing pedlar at all but Abraham Spence, brother to Anna Aram, née Spence. I had seen both brother and sister in York, and had to agree both were of a rather dark Semitic countenance. It also became apparent that Abraham had played some part in the plot. In his deposition to William Thornton, Aram accused his brother-in-law of disposing of some of Clark's booty in the Dales, which he alleged Mr Iles later availed himself of. This same Iles accusation was alluded to by Henry Terry. Somehow cunning Mr Iles had managed to supress the allegation. It did not appear in one newspaper or journal, nor did any mention of it surface at the York trial.

The hour was late, had Aram, Clark and Houseman somehow cajoled the pedlar into concluding their business out of view on Thistle Hill? – or did they continue their transactions about the town? – clinging to the buildings in fear of exposure on what Houseman described as a moonlit night.

From the evidence of the dyer, Thomas Barnett, some attempt was made at concealment. Barnett testified that between 12 o'clock and 2 o'clock, before Clark went missing, he and his wife were going home from the Crown Inn in the High Street. Reaching Church Lane end he saw a man come out of Eugenius Aram's passageway. The man was wrapped up in a wide greatcoat with the hood pulled over his head. When Barnett approached him, the man attempted to shun him. It was Richard Houseman.

Was the mystery man, possibly the Jewish pedlar, alive or dead then?

I began down Gracechurch Street towards Low Bridge and up to the Woodsman's Cottage where I turned off to take the circuitous route along the south bank of the river Nidd. So far the path was not too difficult and soon I reached the obvious limestone workings of Thistle Hill on my right. I climbed a steep embankment and looked across towards Aram's gibbet. The area directly below me was pitted with quarrying and kilns. The perfect isolated place to quickly dispose of a body. Witnesses John Yeats and Barbara Leetham had testified to Theakston that they had seen ground "fresh dug up" here around the time of the suspected offence. Like them I saw a similar spot in the full clarity of daylight.

* * * * *

Houseman, Aram, Clark and the Jew stepped out into Mr Carter's yard. The stable boy was snoring away on his sack in the shadows. Clark and Aram took up the two spades they had secreted in a corner earlier.

Although the four of them had drunk hard and fast and not stayed haggling in the inn long, and the Jew's servant had about him a long woollen coat, still the lad's narrow frail face was blue with cold and unaccustomed alcohol.

'Can't take your drink like a man yet,' laughed the twenty-three year old, pock-broken Clark, cuffing the servant boy's ear.

'Ouch!' cried the lad.

'Leave 'im be, Dan,' muttered Houseman.

The air cut fresh across all their faces as they set off at a brisk pace up the road to Thistle Hill. Clark led the way, followed by the boy, with Houseman and Aram bringing up the rear.

''Tis good the night is clear and we have no need of lanterns for our footing,' puffed Houseman; his beery breath stale and hot in Aram's face.

'Aye, 'tis good all right,' scoffed Aram. 'Your eyes must be more accustomed than mine.'

Houseman chose to ignore his pessimistic companion's view, asking instead, 'Has Dan told thee yet where 'tis hidden?'

'No, his trust has not stretched that far. Apart from telling him to hide it wide and deep, I know only as much as you.'

'See t' change in 'im? Look, he leads on like a strutting captain.'

'For the moment.'

'Aye, for the moment,' agreed Houseman. And a little later … 'Do you think Dan might have forgotten where he's buried it?'

'I think not,' answered Eugene dryly.

'More will be t' pity for 'im,' said Houseman, spitting into the night.

The Jewish pedlar must have sobered up a little because as well as carrying his trinket box he took one of the spades from Aram, who had begun to struggle over the rough ground of Thistle Hill. For a thin lad he appeared to be immensely strong. Aram gave him a thankful half-smile. A nerve started twitching in the schoolmaster's face – the first jolt of conscience perhaps – the Jew wasn't supposed to be kind.

Clark led them closer to the edge of the Rock, a looming black fortress over the town.

'So this is t' place,' whispered Houseman.

They stopped – an incomplete ring – the pedlar, still obviously unsteady on his feet, leaned for support on the spade.

'Are you sure you have all the money before I start?' demanded Clark, snatching the spade from him.

'Yes, the money. I have the money.' The nodding boy appeared disconcerted by the loss of his crutch, by Clark's sudden physical abruptness.

Clark handed Houseman the extra spade and they began to dig quickly at a spot designated by Clark. Employing an existing hollowed out lime working, Clark had used some large stones to help fill in the recent burial. He had realised that when the time was ripe, stones would be quicker and easier to remove than soil. These he now flung to one side.

Houseman was huffing and blowing and having a rest when Clark shouted, 'Ah! Here is summat at last.'

The rest of the party tottered forward to have a look. The pedlar swayed uneasily on the brink, Aram grabbed his shoulders from behind to steady him. Clark had buried his treasure well: he was standing in the excavation. The pedlar looked on wide-eyed. He wasn't sure he liked these men; he did not like this situation; he did not like anything that resembled his deceased mother's workhouse grave.

Unaware of the constraints around him, a victorious Clark pulled himself out onto the snow covered turf and held up a large leather wallet. 'Give me the money now and you can be on your way to Wetherby and the Great North Road,' he told the pedlar.

'See inside first,' said the boy, straining to see as a stooping Clark freed the bag's outer surface of soil. Clark made as if to pass him the wallet. From then on events seemed to move like a slow macabre dance.

Aram slunk back into the shadows. Houseman moved in, circling behind his unsuspecting victim. There was the explosive snap of breaking bone. In one swift twist and pull, Houseman's strong muscled arms had broken the boy's thin neck as if he were a rabbit.

Clark stared with disbelief at the twitching pedlar at his feet, then looked at Houseman and then at Aram. 'You've killed him. You've dispatched him like those bloody cats,' he screamed.

'Not me, not me this time, Daniel, 'twas Dickey who put him down,' corrected Aram impassively. Aram, who had always had more time for boys than men.

'You told me robbery not murder was our business this night.'

''Tis done, Dan, and there's an end to it,' said Houseman.

'For God's sake!' cried the still dazed Clark.

'Pull yourself together,' Aram told him, picking up the wallet and slinging it across his shoulder. 'We have to dispose of the corpse.'

Clark vomited as a desolate horse out on Thistle Hill whinnied its condolence.

The ever practical Houseman looked about deep in thought. Peeling off the boy's coat and rags, he dragged his naked body forward, lowering it carefully into Clark's waiting pit. The boy's corpse was left in a grotesque sitting position. The once blue face, now as white as the snow around it, lolled to one side as if in sleep. Houseman kicked the body over with as much respect as if it had been a sack of flax. The face folded onto the knees with a sigh.

Clark jumped, thinking the boy was still alive.

'See, it'll double in like so,' said Houseman, well-pleased with his arrangement.

How soon a *he* can become an *it*.

Clark still whimpering kept asking, 'Why? Why?'

In answer Aram delved into the pedlar's trinket box, lifting out a soft, brown leather purse. He held it up to the moonlight by its drawstrings. 'Jewish gold and silver, gold and silver.'

'And we've given nowt for it see, Dan lad,' laughed Houseman. 'Now stop thee snivelling and pick up yon spade.'

Out of his eye-corner Aram, the purse holder, watched Houseman and the trembling Clark attempt to fold the surrounding earth into the boy's grave. The peripheral surface soil was difficult to dig and break, and the final result looked disappointingly sunken and cloddy. They all agreed that unless they made some improvements by morning their murdered victim would soon be discovered. Aram reasoned that the bigger stones needed to be broken up into fragments, and a deeper layer of topsoil put on the grave to deter those seeking stone in summer months.

'We must leave the spades here and return with a pickaxe to finish the job,' he told them wearily.

'Now who'd possess one o' them?' asked Houseman, putting the jumble of discarded clothes in the trinket box and hauling it across his broad shoulders.

'I know someone,' said Clark, who seemed to have recovered a little composure through labour.

On the way back into Knaresborough, Houseman took the victim's clothes out of the box and flung them off Low Bridge. They ballooned out eerily as if still occupied before speeding away on the spate waters of the winter Nidd. The three men next examined the box. Judging the baubles inside to be both worthless and incriminating to sell on, box and contents followed the clothing but this time with a splash.

'Hope it all sinks,' muttered Houseman into his coat.

'I'll take that.' In Gracechurch Street, Clark suddenly insisted on relieving Aram of the wallet. Aram easily acquiesced but told him he was being childish.

'What's in the damn thing anyway?' asked Aram.

'Pretty things,' sibilated Houseman, trying to mimic the dead Jew.

CHAPTER ELEVEN

Happy to leave the Thistle Hill pits to the ghosts of that far off night, I walked on. The path narrowed between riverside bushes and trees. To the uninitiated this path with its roots and branches would have been hazardous at night, but then Aram, Houseman and Clark were local to the area and they had snow and reflecting moonlight. The bank of the Nidd was steep in places and I was aware how easy it would be to slip down into the freezing water. An even more alarming prospect was that one could just as easily be pushed into the river with no witnesses. But wasn't that just the point? If in daylight hours there is no one to see, who would have been abroad to witness the goings-on during the early hours of a Friday morning?

Whatever had been said of her – and her husband had plenty to say, including his suspicions that she enjoyed an adulterous affair with young Clark – Anna Aram was the only principal in this case whose testimony remained consistent.

* * * * *

'It was just before two o' clock in the morning,' she said, 'when Clark, Houseman and her husband arrived back at Church Lane.'

They were met in the room above stairs by a fire and a mute, rather anxious looking Anna. She must have guessed from all the evening's comings and goings that something big and illegal was afoot. She had been waiting there alone, the children safely abed, wondering, no doubt, if the next knock on her door would be the constable's. As the men huddled by the warm hearth muttering between themselves, Anna tried to busy herself with her knitting. Although she could not have appreciated the exact nature of their business, she must have noticed that both Houseman and Clark looked particularly dirty and Houseman was without his wig. Indeed, it was this missing wig that was causing Houseman and her husband most concern. In the excitement on Thistle Hill, Houseman was uncertain where he had actually lost it. Could it have fallen in the grave as he dug? Aram now voiced the disagreeable possibility that Houseman's "hair" could be under the partially buried Jew.

'And there it will have to stay,' he told the flax-dresser, blinking into the flickering fire. 'Decaying with the body.'

'How can I be seen without mi wig?' objected Houseman.

'Anna,' shouted Aram to his wife. 'Would you be so good as to fetch a handkerchief for Dickey to tie about his head?'

Clark laughed hysterically: Houseman had murdered a boy that night and all he was concerned about was his vanity.

'Dickey will next see that old brown mat of his hanging from a rook's nest,' the young cordwainer joked. But his smile up to Anna was troubled as she passed Houseman the handkerchief. With a flash of pique, Aram did not miss the quick empathic smile his wife returned Clark either. Innocent or not, there was obviously an ingratiating warmth between the two of them. This alliance could eventually prove troublesome.

'Now to more serious matters,' Aram announced coldly.

Clark opened up the wallet and pulled out some of the watches, rings and small things of value he had made a pretence of selling to the Jew. They agreed that Houseman would pocket these to sell by and by. Most of the silver plate that had not already been sold but delivered to Aram's house earlier, was now transferred to the wallet. First they must finish their business on Thistle Hill, then Aram and Houseman agreed to accompany Clark to St. Robert's Cave in the Long Flat to help beat out the plate and hide it there. They had previously arranged with Clark that he would remain in the cave until the following night. He would be supplied with food and his share of the money during the day by Henry Terry – a shooter with an excuse to be out in the countryside – before absconding for good.

'We now need that pickaxe for Thistle Hill as well as a hammer for beating out the plate,' whispered Aram, careful to be out of Anna's earshot.

'William Tuton has already promised me the hammer. I'm sure he'll lend us an axe as well,' said Clark, rising and moving nervously to the window. 'See, it will soon be morning and we must get off.'

Anna followed them down the stairs. Her eyes never left Clark as he heaved up the wallet and swung it across his stooping shoulders. Houseman was first up and out of the passage only to be confronted with a further stroke of misfortune on reaching Church Lane end – the slightly inebriated Thomas Barnett and his wife. Barnett was not a man to be shunned when in drink, but finding it was only Richard Houseman who had done him this disservice he just laughed and wished the flax-dresser "good-night".

'Damn!' cursed Houseman, turning to Aram and Clark who had quickly caught him up.

'Best keep moving before we are seen more,' muttered Aram irritably.

* * * * *

Grimble Bridge. I took out my pocket watch. It had taken me a good hour from Bond End to reach the bridge via the south bank of the Nidd. Somehow I knew this bridge held the clue to the mystery. Eugene Aram had vigorously denied being on the bridge at all. Whereas Richard Houseman testified that "Aram and Clark stopped a little, and in their way thither stopped a while at the Grimble Bridge, and there he saw Aram strike Clark several times over the breast and head and killed (*sic*) him." There were many erasures to this statement. According to the surgeons, Locock and Higgins, Daniel Clark died from one blow to the back of the head. Houseman was clearly lying here. But why did he mention Grimble Bridge? The men would not cross over Grimble Bridge to St Robert's Cave unless like me they had come from Thistle Hill along the south side of the river. If they had been going directly to St Robert's Cave, they would have taken Long Flat Lane or the Abbey path along the northern bank. This suggests to me that when they left Church Lane a second time, in the early hours of Friday morning, they had unfinished business on Thistle Hill.

Once across Grimble Bridge, like Aram, Clark and Houseman, I risked the trespass one hundred yards on and climbed over a fence. Not knowing the ground, it was with some difficulty that I eventually found the overgrown path down the northern river bank to the hermit's cave. The path was steep, the cave hidden beneath a rock formation – the perfect place to conceal a crime. The river rushed past fierce here. I stood watching it on a rock stage, reluctant to stoop into the dark backdrop of the play.

I did not attend Theakston's St Robert's Cave inquest. What a macabre affair it must have been though. Daniel Clark's bones freshly dug from the earth in the exact position described by Houseman with his head to the right in the turn of the cave entrance.

The voices of witnesses echo forth. Witnesses like Philip Coates who said he believed the skeleton to be that of Daniel Clark. William Tuton, the mason, who testified that he saw Clark at between 11 p.m. and 12 p.m. on account of taking some leather into his house, and then again the cordwainer called him out of bed a 3 a.m. the following morning. Tuton later changed his story, telling William Thornton that it was just the once at about 2 a.m. that Clark visited him. Not only the leading players but the supporting actors – everyone was beginning to distance himself from the performance.

I heard a noise – a rustle of leaves, the breaking of a twig – was it an animal, a bird perhaps? I listened rooted to the spot where Clark met his end.

* * * * *

It took several handfuls of small stones to bring night-shirted William Tuton to his bedchamber window again. Clark engaged the yawning mason in conversation, requesting the loan of a pick as well as the hammer, as Aram and Houseman waited apprehensively a little way off in Clark's cellar doorway.

Tuton was not long in giving his permission for Clark to take both tools from his yard at the back. With two calls from the shoemaker at unreasonable times, Tuton was beginning to fear that the whole neighbourhood might become privy to his illegal leather.

On that cold early Friday morning, Aram, in his light-coloured riding coat, and Houseman, in his darker one, tried to huddle deeper into the cellar doorway away from the keen-eyed mason. Despite their best efforts, gallingly they soon realised from Tuton's nods and glances in their direction that he had spotted them.

Tuton continued to watch on suspiciously as they ambled to the corner of the street, soon to be joined by Clark carrying a wallet along with the pickaxe and hammer. Clark gave Houseman the hammer to carry as they moved off towards the Castle Yard. With the three men out of sight, the mason thankfully moved back to his bed and guileless dreams.

Aram, Clark and Houseman walked and ran to their fresh cemetery on Thistle Hill, knowing they had much work to do and complete before daybreak.

Clark retrieved the two glinting spades left hidden in the bushes. This time they all participated: Richard Houseman broke up the soil around the shallow grave, while the two proficient gardeners shovelled it in and did their best to turf the surface and cream over the snow.

'Does it look respectable enough for thee now?' asked Houseman, patting flat the top of the Jew's grave with the end of his pick.

'Aye, it will have to do,' replied Aram. 'We must have been nigh on twenty minutes at the task.'

While Houseman took a piss over the grave, his companions collected up all the tools. Soon they were on the move again along the bank of the Nidd towards Grimble Bridge and St. Robert's Cave.

Whether or not Clark had become tired or apprehensive at the thought of a coming day and night spent alone out in the Long Flat, it was at Grimble Bridge that he became more vocal and dissatisfied with his lot. Houseman, who had already mastered the art of selective deafness against a new and nagging woman in his life, kept his own counsel. Aram, on the other hand, began to seethe.

'There were no need to kill that Jew boy,' Clark started shouting. 'We could have robbed him and he would have been too afraid to tell. You both planned to kill him from the start, didn't ye? And, God forgive thee, tha's now made an accomplice out o' me.'

'May the devil cut out your tongue,' hissed Aram. 'Your accusations will travel the river to Knaresborough unless you keep your noise down.'

'I'll do as I please and not be bossed by the likes of ye, schoolmaster.'

'Quiet,' snarled Aram between clenched teeth, looking uncomfortably about him.

But Clark, like a man determined to push his fate to the extreme, would not be silenced. Poking Houseman in the ribs, he continued screaming, 'Tha should be tethered up in a field like a beast away from decent folk.'

After climbing the fence, the three men wavered at the top of the difficult and overgrown steps leading down to the cave and river. Clark seemed reluctant to begin the descent. He started shouting again, protesting at having to spend the night alone in such a black accursed place.

'You'll be right enough, Dan lad,' reassured Houseman scornfully. 'Saint Robert's Christian soul will not trouble itself with thee.'

'You agreed to the plan, Daniel,' Aram reminded him sharply.

'And what's an a … a … agreement to you, Eugene Aram?' retorted Clark.

'Enough,' warned Aram, shoving Clark so hard in the back that he slipped and missed the first two steps.

'Leave off, Aram. Don't think Anna hasn't told me all about you,' sneered Clark; until another push, this time from Houseman, sent him slithering further into the abyss.

Aram paused briefly to reflect on the shoemaker's words before he too followed on. Houseman, heavy-footed, brought up the rear. Still, Clark's vociferous complaints and insults flew up to meet them.

Soon they all stood together before the cave's gloomy mouth – undecided how to act out the next scene with only the river for an audience – Houseman looked to Aram and Aram looked to Clark.

'We'd best start beating out the plate,' suggested Houseman quietly.

'Why k … k … kill?' Clark's stammer echoed piping and revived. Still he did not seem to fully appreciate the company he was keeping.

'We'd best start beating out the plate,' growled Houseman a second time.

'If I'm caught, I swear I'll not h … h … hang alone.' Clark's voice rose hysterically. 'I'll not swing to save the necks of a vulgar killer and gutless pedant.'

Aram slapped Clark across the face, leaving the red imprints of his fingers on the shoemaker's putty skin. Clark began to blubber.

'Shut up,' Houseman told him, looking across to Aram.

A dangerous unspoken speculation passed between them: a speculation that said if Clark were allowed to go free he might break and tell.

In that moment, that intercepted look between Houseman and Aram, Daniel Clark froze with the sudden realisation that he had been set up to play the second victim. He searched his companions' faces for a glimmer of mercy – he saw none. In that moment, that look, Daniel Clark must have seen his coming fate.

Aram nodded and Houseman coiled behind Clark like a snake, holding the mason's hammer aloft.

Clump! He brought it down hard. *Clump*! It was as simple as that, as simply done as that. Clark's breaking skull made the sound of wood splintered by metal, the sound of an axe felling a tree. Houseman struck the blow with all his usual control. He did it as if it was something he was used to doing, had always wanted to do. He struck the blow not so much in anger, greed or fear of Clark talking, he struck him down with all the cool satisfaction of a professional squaring his account.

For a second Clark remained on his feet; then, in almost disbelief, he keeled backwards. Houseman hovered over his victim at first curious and then perplexed.

'Is he dead?' Aram asked him, forcing himself into a kneeling position next to the prostrate shoemaker.

'This is a pretty pickle if I'm not mistaken,' rasped Houseman, ignoring Aram's too apparent question. 'Should we strip him like t' other, there's plenty abroad who would recognise Dan's garments should they get caught on a branch or summat. Plenty too who knows he kept regular company wi' thee and me. Plenty to point t' finger towards the three-legged mare.'

'Once he started panicking at Grimble Bridge like that we had to get rid of him,' rationalised Aram; eager not to upset Houseman the killer further. 'We'll just have to burn his clothing.'

* * * * *

This is what I believed happened after vigilantly following Aram's trial in York. My conjecture neither complied with the schoolmaster's account nor the heckler's – it fell somewhere in between – it made both Aram and Houseman equally culpable – it was comfortable. But did Clark's murder simply happen this way? Did these two men share the guilt alone?

Once satisfied there was no one else around, and that I was not about to be assaulted a second time in a cave by Knaresborough ruffians, I began to assess St Robert's Cave in greater detail. Taking out my kerchief, I tied it round a bush outside the entrance. Then I bounded back up the bank and along to Grimble Bridge. I looked for my white kerchief. It was nowhere to be seen, totally lost from view in the undergrowth. I had satisfied myself that Houseman had been lying about seeing Aram striking Clark face to face from a distance, and later seeing him emerge from the cave with a bundle of clothing. From Grimble Bridge end it was impossible to see the rock promontory let alone the cave mouth.

* * * * *

Like the Jewish boy they stripped the cordwainer naked, leaving his emaciated looking body stretched out on its own rock slab, pathetic in the moonlight. Aram found this task distasteful. Clark, if not always liked by him, was known to him in life. He and Houseman gingerly stepped across the mossy promontory, cluttered in places with debris and brushwood, and crawled into the cavern beyond.

The work of digging Clark's grave was much easier and quicker than the similar task had been on Thistle Hill. The cavern floor was thickened with soft silt from the river. It was not long before they were pulling Clark's body through the narrow entrance to its final resting place.

'It'll soon be dawn. It's not safe to start beating out the plate now. We'll have to get rid of it as it is,' Aram told Houseman.

Stuffing Clark's clothes with the plate into the wallet, and collecting up their tools again, they made a hasty retreat along the bank of the Nidd towards Knaresborough.

'Trunks and trees and blocks of ice catch at yon Grimble Bridge and flood t' banks wi' water,' grumbled Houseman. 'Suppose river was to wash Dan out?'

'You've seen as well as I, Dickey, given high-water the cave's more likely to be filled up with more river dross than lose it.' Houseman's sudden outpouring over the demise of Clark had begun to annoy Aram. They walked on through the town's empty streets in silence. Realising his accomplice was in no mood to be reassured, Aram let him be.

It must have been after five o' clock when they returned to the relative safety of Church Lane. This time Aram went up alone to the room above stairs, and was surprised to find Anna still awake and more agitated than when they had left her a few hours before. She sat shuddering by the fire although it still glowed hot with life. In an attempt to counter her alarm, her husband remained his calm indifferent self and requested a candle to make a fire below.

'There is no occasion for two fires,' she objected. 'There already is a good one here.'

'Dickey is below and does not choose to come upstairs,' shrugged Aram.

'Where is Daniel?' she asked. Aram looked away. 'What have you done with Daniel?' she wailed, wringing her hands in frustration. She waited longer, still her husband made no answer.

'Go to bed,' he finally told her.

'No,' she said, determined to stand her ground. 'You've been doing something bad.'

'To hear you talk I'm always doing something bad.' Leaving it at that Aram snatched up a lighted candle and went back down to Houseman who must have heard their raised voices.

'She follows, she's coming,' whispered Houseman.

'We'll not let her,' Aram retorted firmly.

'If she does, she'll tell.' Houseman for once seemed close to panic.

'What can she tell? Poor simple thing, she knows nothing.'

'If she tells that I am here, 'twill be enough.'

Another sound of movement on the staircase.

'I will hold the door to prevent her from coming,' Aram offered lamely.

'Summat must be done to prevent her telling. She's thy responsibility, Eugene, tha must put an end to any chance of her wagging her tongue. If she does not tell now, she may at some other time.'

'No. We will coax her a little until her passion be off, and then take an opportunity to shoot her.'

'What must be done with her clothes?'

'We'll let her lie where she is shot in her clothes, Dickey.'

This seemed to do the trick: the soft tip, tip, of Anna's shoes could be heard retreating swiftly back upstairs.

They set about laboriously burning Clark's clothing item by item, continuously bellowing the fire for greater heat, before scattering the hot ashes over the cottage's dunghill outside. After bidding the schoolmaster a surly "goodbye", Houseman took himself off home. Careless Houseman had lost a wig that night, now, unknowingly, he left behind the handkerchief loaned to him by Anna bearing its telltale spot of blood.

A few minutes later, wallet of plate slung across his shoulder, Aram was hammering on Henry Terry's door.

The ale-draper was still in his nightshirt and looked either drunk or sleepy. Terry was famed throughout Knaresborough for keeping a late house. His wife, Elizabeth, was fussing over some cooking ham on the stove. Terry asked Aram if he would share some breakfast with them. It smelt and looked good. Realising he hadn't eaten since about six o' clock the previous night, Aram gladly accepted.

'Would you be good enough to get rid of this for me?' he asked, passing the wallet full of clinking silver plate under the table towards Terry.

Terry stared with a mixture of unease and bewilderment down into the wallet. 'I thought Dan was taking this with him?'

'No, no, he found the plate too heavy. He's been fully paid out and has already made good his escape. So he'll not be needing you to deliver the victuals to the cave today after all.' Aram tried to make the statement sound casual.

'But I thought … I have them prepared.'

'Well, as I've just said he's already gone off.'

'"Gone off"?' exclaimed Terry. His gaping mouth revealing the chewed remains of breakfast.

'Aye, gone off.' The fastidious Aram winced, not troubling to sound convincing a second time.

CHAPTER TWELVE

Safely back in the doorway of the Bell, I checked my pocket watch again.

'Nice watch, sir,' said the ostler, rubbing past with a kitchen maid.

I nodded, preoccupied. I had completed the entire walk, a slow walk in well under two hours. It took me thirty-five minutes to walk from St Robert's Cave, passing the Abbey to Low Bridge, and climb back into town. It was possible, the timing was just possible that the events of that February night had happened this way.

I had not been followed. Apart from my disquiet in confining Jockey Lane, I had had no sense of being in jeopardy. Perhaps my adversaries had lost interest.

There was a knock on my bedchamber door only minutes following my arrival there. The same light knock as before. It must be her.

'Come in,' I said, trying my best to sound welcoming. Nothing happened so I went to open the door. I was not mistaken, Janet Brown stood waiting in the hall. I took a step back, she took a step into my room.

'I hope I am not disturbing you, sir.'

'Not at all. I am just back from a long walk. A one hour and forty minute walk to be precise.' Again I produced my Millington but this time to emphasis my point.

'I have arranged for you to meet Betty Aram, sir. Will a quarter past the hour of ten tomorrow morning suit?' I nodded. 'She will be waiting near her mother's house and shop in Hilton Lane.'

'Do the Arams no longer live in Church Lane then?'

'No, Anna Aram removed with Polly Powell to open a pie and black pudding shop in bigger premises.'

'Has she abandoned her bread making then?'

'No, she still sells bread there too.'

'So Mrs Aram fares well.'

'She is doing better than she did with her husband.'

'Thank you for arranging this,' I said, taking her hand to kiss it.

'No!' She snatched her hand back as if burnt before my lips could make contact.

'What's wrong, Janet?'

'I am no rich man's plaything.'

'Who said you were?' Then I remembered. 'I took no notice of the landlord and his offensive comments yesterday evening.'

'No, sir, you might not have done but I did.'

'He is ill-disposed to you because he desires you.'

'Yes, and I am dependent on his wages to put food on the table to feed me and my child. You have no notion of the difficulties of my situation. Tomorrow morning then in Hilton Lane,' she reminded me, reaching for the door handle.

* * * * *

The church clock struck ten. I sought my silver pocket watch to verify it was keeping good time. I remembered I had left it on a bedside table the previous evening before I went down to supper. It was not there. I searched the room high and low but could not find it. My heart sank. It must have been stolen while I was out. It was emotionally irreplaceable – a present from a sweetheart who died of winter fever in her twenty-first year. Pressed for time, I was reluctantly forced to abandon my search. Any further investigation would have to wait.

Hilton Lane was a rather steep lane running from the High Street down towards the river and Kirkgate.

I recognised her straight away. Betty Aram lounged against the wall of a building. Dressed in a floral patterned dress, intermittently she hopped from one fat leg to the other – the actions of an impatient child rather than a young woman. I had not seen her since she had been viewing her father's remains on the gibbet. She glowered, her mouth turned down, there was not even a curl of macabre satisfaction that morning.

'Thank you for meeting me,' I told her.

'I've not long,' she mumbled. 'Mam doesn't know I am talking to you. She is busy baking in the back at present.' Betty nodded to a house across the way. I could just make out what appeared to be a few meagre food items displayed in the window.

'Does the family cope, Betty?' I decided to conduct this interview from memory rather than using my intimidating notebook.

'We do our best. We sell a lot of pies, particularly in winter. Mam is not always well and my sister Jane is away in service. Henry is an idiot and spends most of his time with our Joseph who is a saddler over in Green Hammerton.

Michael, ah well, our Michael is Michael. There is only me left here to help out.'

'Does your eldest sister ever visit?'

'Oh, her. I've not seen her in years.'

'Didn't she live with your father down in Lynn for a time?'

'I know nothing of that.' Betty's mouth clamped shut.

'How did you get on with Sally?'

'All right.'

'Did you like her?'

'Not as much as my father did. He never had time for Jane, me and the boys, only our Sally.'

'She was academically clever, was she not?'

'Schooling you mean?' she asked. I nodded. 'Our Sally thought she knew everything but she knew nowt o' life.'

'I heard your father took her to his school up the White Horse Yard to demonstrate her academic scholarship before his male pupils.'

'That would be before my time, Mister, but it sounds like my father. He enjoyed humiliating folk.'

'What of your aunt and uncles over in Ripon? Do they not visit?'

'Oh, them,' sighed Betty. 'We do not see them from one year till the next either.'

'I understand your grandfather, Peter Aram, left them his Bondgate cottage and your father only a shilling. Do you know anything about that? Did your father resent it?'

'No, no, grandfather felt my father was settled with his school. That Bondgate cottage was mortgaged to the hilt anyway. Before he went away to the south of England, my father paid it off for his two brothers and sister to live in.'

'So, there was no bad feeling over that?'

'None that I knew of.'

'Perhaps they held your mother responsible for all the difficulties that befell your father.'

'That could be so. Whenever anything went wrong, he told everyone that Mam was to blame.'

'Would you say your mother was a loyal wife, Betty?'

'She didn't have the chance to be anything else, did she? He was always at her. 'Twas he that was born with a perverse nature.'

'What do you mean by "perverse"?' My ears physically pricked up at this.

'He once gave money to a young local lad to dress up as a woman, and then paid court to him about town as if he was his ladylove, all in a pathetic attempt to make our mother jealous.'

'So you don't believe your father's confession, purportedly made to two clergymen after his trial, that he killed Daniel Clark because he was over familiar with your mother?'

'Fiddle-faddle.'

'Why fiddle-faddle?'

'Janet Brown told me you would pay me for my talk,' corner-mouthed Betty petulantly. I handed her a shilling. She stared at it as if she was holding stardust but with the guile to keep her hand there for more. I dropped a penny or two in the waiting palm. At last a smile. 'You have to understand, Mister, I was a mere child of five when Dan disappeared. But from what my mother always said, although she was some fifteen years Dan's senior, he was one of the few friends she had in Knaresborough at the time.'

'So nothing improper ever took place between them?'

'That's as it has been told to me.'

'More a mother and son relationship?'

'I believe that to be the case.'

'Have you not a good word for your dead father then, the man who reared you?'

'The man who left us all virtually penniless.'

'But not Sally. He sent for her.'

'He had to. She had a bairn in her belly.'

'Whose child was she expecting?'

'That I could not say.' Again the clamped mouth as Betty Aram kicked out at a piece of dried horse dung close to her booted foot.

* * * * *

Then he saw her reading by a solitary candle in the cottage window down Church Lane – a lone figure waiting up for him – his child-woman. She was beautiful. Full of self-loathing, he made for her like a lizard makes for shade. Stroking her hair, he begged forgiveness.

'Forgive you for what, Father?' Sally asked in alarm, turning away from his ale fetid breath with transparent disgust.

'Do not take on at my words, lass, for I wish never to give you away.'

'Give me away? What have you done, Father?' Aram sensed Sally's highly-strung, adolescent fears and thoughts flying wildly about her. Somehow he felt inadequate, incapable of catching them, allaying them. 'I never want to leave you, Papa. I never want to be wife to another man.' Her hysterical screams muffled in his waistcoat as she clung to him with match-stick arms.

That was it, under the influence of drink she thought he had made some unwelcome marriage settlement for her with a stranger. It happened sometimes, it had happened in the Crown. "Never be another man's wife", she had said that though, hadn't she? – he had not misheard her?

He began to fondle the swan neck in the chair below. His fingers seemed to have a will of their own, were unconnected to him. At last Sally allowed herself to be comforted. He felt her relax. She lolled her head back against his thigh – his thigh, her head – he could hear his own breathing becoming deeper and more even. She gently sobbed as he searched down her bodice, tugging at the laces for those two elusive breasts. Her sobs and his breathing hypnotic in the silence.

'Whatever was all t' commotion about?'

With his back to the door that led to the upper chamber he had not seen Anna slip into the room. He remained transfixed at the sound of her voice, his thumb and forefinger locked on Sally's awakening nipple.

'I'm talking to ye, Eugene,' came Anna's insistent sobriety again; came insistent and frightening normality.

Aram swung round – a thief caught in the act.

* * * * *

Back in my room at the Bell, I examined the bedside table half expecting to see my Millington watch returned there. I stroked the wood surface as if I could magically conjure it out from between the grains. I might as well have believed in fairies. The only thing to be seen was a smear in the dust where it had once lain. The Bell's less than thorough housekeeping had left an irrefutable impression. Regardless, I searched high and low for that watch before accusing anybody.

I found the landlord wiping down the bar. He did not look best pleased to see me and I hadn't opened my mouth yet.

'Yes, Mr Kendle?' he sighed.

'My pocket watch is missing from my room.'

'Are you sure?'

'I am.'

'Nevertheless …'

'Nevertheless, I am just drawing your attention to the fact that you might have a thief in your house.'

'I thank you for that,' said the landlord disingenuously.

'And any process you might be able to put into place for the return of my property would be much appreciated.'

'I expect it would.'

'The watch had sentimental value,' I added, in the vain hope that "sentimental" would appeal to a smidgen of sympathy in an otherwise bellicose personality.

The landlord hesitated over his work, discarded his bar cloth, and stared somewhere above my head.

'JANET BROWN.' He spelt out her name like a curse.

'Not necessarily,' I said, foreseeing the awful consequences of this arbitrary judgement.

'Why not? She is the only one who goes into your room to clean.'

'There are no locks on the door, no key, anyone could have seen me leave and walked in.'

'You will not have it because you are sweet on the girl.'

'There is no proof that she is to blame.'

'You have indulged her and she has taken advantage. Her kind always do.'

'Rather than an innocent be accused, I would have the guilty go free. Best drop the matter,' I told him, finally appreciating that I should never have raised it in the first place.

'But you have made a serious allegation, sir.' I could see that the landlord was determined to milk this situation for all it was worth.

'Forget I mentioned it,' I said, walking away.

* * * * *

As I prepared to go down for the evening meal – I'll not grace the Bell's basic fare with the status dinner – I heard a furore coming from outside. Leaning out of my chamber window, I looked up and down the street but could see nothing.

'No, no. Help! In the name of God, don't!' A high female voice. From the echoing quality of the pleading, I realised it was being amplified through the archway from the stable yard. Then a bloodcurdling scream. I rushed out and down the stairway in my bare feet.

First I saw the leering ostler standing next to the landlord. The landlord was lashing out with a bullwhip at a foetal contortion curled for protection in the corner of the yard. The whip cracked before sounding a dull percussion as it met its target. So tightly balled was this figure, I hardly recognised it as human. Then I saw the skirt of the brown dress fanned out and smeared in dirt and dust. The brown dress that only she could wear and look fetching in.

'What the hell are you doing?' I yelled.

The landlord hesitated, whip handle raised above his head.

'Here's your thief,' he exclaimed.

'What proof have you?'

'You told me to forget it, sir. I'll forget nothing with this Jezebel in my employment,' bellowed the landlord.

'She's only a girl.'

'She's a Jewess, a whore, I tell you.' The red faced landlord launched another attack against the prone body of Janet Brown who was whimpering now. Even the ostler began to look uncomfortable.

'For God's sake, man, stop at once!'

'Mind your own business.' The landlord cracked the whip in my direction.

That was his one big mistake. Catching the leather thong in my hand, I dragged him towards me and wrapped it round his neck.

'Please, sir, this isn't worth murder.' If the ostler hadn't physically intervened, I am sure I would have choked the landlord to death with his own whip.

Between us the ostler and I lifted a sobbing and broken Janet Brown to her feet.

'Get off my premises,' coughed and spluttered the landlord at Janet and me, a hand cradling his crushed throat.

'It will be my pleasure.' My spittle was well-aimed landing on the puffed shirt sleeve emerging from his fancy waistcoat to point our expulsion.

I quickly gathered my things from the Bell. Janet was waiting for me round the corner in Timber Yard and I escorted her up the High Street towards her home in Finkle Street.

'Is it true that you are Jewish?' I asked.

'Would that trouble you?'

'No, only unjust prejudice bothers me. You do know that a Jewish servant boy went missing around the time of Daniel Clark's murder?'

She nodded saying: 'No one in these parts would concern themselves with that.'

'Exactly so. One could almost expect as much from rough and ready folk, folk who are uneducated, but I regret to tell you I have come across the same anti-Jewish sentiment from my fellow professionals who should know better.'

'I have suffered all my life from the prejudice you talk of. You have to live it to know it. My mother came from a family of early Jewish settlers to Leeds. She told me my father was a Scottish soldier whom she met in Knaresborough while working in the linen trade. He deserted her soon after learning she was with child. I am of impure blood because my father was a Gentile and I no longer observe the Torah.'

'And where is your mother now?'

'My mother died many years ago of a broken heart, I suspect. Her family back in Leeds never forgave her, forcing us to remain in Knaresborough. I never knew my real father. And now, see, I am abandoned all over again and without employment. What shall I do? What on earth shall I do, sir? There's my boy.'

'Your boy who is your "little brother",' I laughed. She did not laugh but leaned heavier on my arm. 'Something will turn up,' I reassured her. 'I will see that something turns up.'

* * * * *

There had been no rewarding kiss for me on Janet Brown's doorstep. It was only after I turned away that I realised I had left Bess at the Bell's stabling. Deciding my priority was a bed for the night and somewhere to house my bags and document satchel provided by William Thornton, I settled on collecting the mare in the morning.

But where to stay locally that was the vexing question. Night was coming on. I was already wilting from the effort of transporting my luggage. I decided to consult the only man

I felt I could rely on in Knaresborough. Judging he would no longer be engaged in his surgery, I beat desperately on the front door of Thomas Hutchinson's house until my knuckles felt sore.

Eventually, the doctor opened the door himself.

'You,' he said. 'What in heaven's name is the matter?'

'I thought you would never answer,' I replied, resting my bags on his step.

'Sorry, the maid is off tonight and I had settled in the back room with a series of illustrations of exotic birds from the Portuguese Amazon.'

'Pray, how did you come by them, sir?'

'A friend. A friend has lent them to me for one night only.' He looked perplexed as he regarded my luggage. 'Leaving already?' he asked.

'No, no. I have been ejected from the Bell.'

'Ejected? What for?'

'Too long a story to relate here and now.'

'I don't know why you chose to stay there in the first place.'

'So, where would you recommend?'

'The Royal Oak in the Market Place, not a stone's throw from here.'

'I hope they have a room.'

'That will not be a problem this time of year. But you are very welcome to stay here for the night, Kendle,' he offered.

'No, no, I wouldn't presume on your kind hospitality at such short notice. Anyway, you have your Amazonian wildlife to study.'

'Speaking of wildlife, I must admit they do a wonderful pigeon pie at the Oak. Indeed, might I join you there tomorrow night, and bring a friend along if he is available?'

'You can bring along whom you like.'

'A surprise friend,' smiled Hutchinson. 'Someone who has heard about you and is anxious to meet you, Felix.'

'One last thing, Thomas, would you be good enough to accompany me to the Bell in the morning to collect my horse otherwise I fear for my safety?'

'I'll meet you before breakfast at eight o' clock by the cross.'

Bowing, I left Hutchinson to his evening of exotic birds and made my way to the Market Place.

CHAPTER THIRTEEN

The bed was comfortable, the linen clean and my sleep heavy at the Royal Oak. I had pushed the turbulent events of the previous evening out of my mind but now with morning it had to be faced.

My greatcoat wrapped around me against the cool air, I sat waiting for Thomas Hutchinson on one of the four concentric steps beneath the Butter Cross. I could feel the cold rising up from the millstone grit into my rump. I shivered possibly more from the thought of the difficult task ahead than my arctic seat – I sensed that my previously maligned Bess would not be easy to retrieve.

I looked across the Market Place to the large timber-framed Royal Oak, where I had received such a warm welcome the night before from a lady whom I took to be the landlord's wife. My room there, the entire atmosphere had a better feel to it than the Bell. The realisation that I should have chosen to stay there originally and so avoid my present vexations was galling.

'Penny for 'em?' asked Hutchinson, suddenly standing before me with his boot on my step.

'Don't rely on strangers to recommend a fitting hostelry.'

'I would have immediately directed you to the Oak rather than the Bell but you said you were already lodged there. But the Oak's pigeon pie is better than anything the Bell can offer, you'll have to agree.'

'You seem to be something of a culinary expert, Thomas.'

'If you are implying that I like my food, sir, then you are correct.'

'And exotic birds from the Portuguese Amazon.'

'I like them too though not to eat,' laughed Hutchinson. 'They are too beautiful to eat. The artist's illustration of the scarlet macaw is a thing of wonder, the colours, the cobalt blue of the bird's remiges.'

'"Remiges"?'

'Quill feathers to you. Though the plainest of Amazonian birds the flightless greater rhea took my fancy last night too. They are something akin to the ostriches of Africa though I have never seen anything quite like them before. They are said to be polygamous.'

'Have you ever seen an ostrich, Thomas?'

'No, have you?'

'But you like the idea of polygamy?'

'No, the great rhea captivates me because it is unusual.'

'Unlike warts and quinsies?'

'Unlike warts and quinsies,' agreed Hutchinson. 'If I could choose I would give up my profession tomorrow and open a museum of extraordinary things, things people have never seen before. I would open their eyes and amaze them.' He gestured to a world well outside the reaches of Knaresborough.

'I will enjoy exploring your passion for the extraordinary further, Thomas. But first I suggest we recover my horse.'

We walked into the High Street at a sharp pace. Hutchinson pointed to a plain undistinguished house on our right incorporating the arch leading through to the White Horse Yard, once the site of Aram's schoolhouse and still the location of Houseman's heckling shop.

'Oliver Cromwell stayed there, in 1648, while having our beautiful castle torn down,' he explained.

'But the Bell's landlord told me he stayed in the Manor House following a siege and that the property had previously been a hunting lodge used by King John.'

'There you are, you see, the man's nothing but a fool.'

'The complications of getting accurate historical information,' I grimaced.

There was no one to be seen in the yard of my previous lodging. Forthright Hutchinson rang the livery bell not once but twice. Eventually the ostler appeared out of one of the stables. He was red-faced and flustered. The kitchen maid, whom I had already seen sharing his company, hid like a lean cat behind his back before sliding slyly away into the inn.

'Bit early for that sort of thing,' coughed my companion; a physician immune to any form of embarrassment.

With his clothing still in disarray, his waistcoat unbuttoned, the ostler did not realise that my watch was clearly visible poking out of his pocket. I held back: deciding not to confront him with the theft for the moment.

'My horse,' I insisted instead. 'I want my horse.'

'It will cost you,' he retorted insolently. 'The nag has already been several days in livery.'

'How much?'

'That's for the landlord to decide.'

'How much?' I repeated.

'And there is the rest of your bill to settle, Mr Kendle, don't forget that.' Obviously alerted by the kitchen maid the landlord had sidled out into the yard from the inn. 'You have already enjoyed our hospitality for nine days.'

'Have I?' I said.

'Indeed, your entire bill for food, lodging and stabling comes to …' he hesitated, obviously plucking some imaginary figure out of the air. 'Thirteen shillings,' he finally came up with. 'Nine shillings for you, four for the horse.'

'A shilling a night for a place like this. Outrageous,' objected Hutchinson.

'And you've charged me for last night, Wednesday night, when you well know I did not sleep here or take supper.'

'I can vouch for that,' agreed Hutchinson.

'Doctor Hutchinson, I am really surprised that you are willing to interfere in a matter of business between this gentleman and me,' berated the landlord, hands on apron hips. 'You are taking sides on behalf of a stranger against a fellow townsman.'

'"Townsman"? Scoundrel is more the way of it,' said Hutchinson, puffing out his chest contemptuously.

'Scoundrels both,' I added.

'How do you mean?' sneered the landlord.

'My stolen watch is dangling out of your man's waistcoat pocket.'

This was obviously news to the landlord. He stared at the ostler in horror and disbelief.

'Is what he says true?' he asked him.

The ostler turned puce by way of reply.

'Give it back to him right now. You could hang for this, you fool.'

The ostler appeared to be in a state of shock and shook his head like one of the paper dolls my sister used to play with.

'Give him it back, I tell you.'

'No, mine,' insisted the ostler like a petulant child.

'No, it is mine,' I asserted becoming increasingly vexed.

'Has it any distinguishing features?' Hutchinson asked me calmly.

'It is a silver Millington watch,' I began. 'The casing on the back is inscribed with the words "To Felix with all my love, Bella".'

'Ah!' exclaimed Hutchinson with a wry smile and a wink. 'Bella, as in beautiful.'

'Bella, as in Isabel. Although she was certainly beautiful too.'

'Best let us see that watch, if you know what is good for you,' Hutchinson told the ostler. Again the ostler did his paper doll imitation. Hutchinson pounced and was behind the ostler in a fraction of a second. His arm wrapped round the man's throat.

'There's no need for …' Before the landlord had finished his sentence, I had fished the watch out from the ostler's pocket. Hutchinson still held him fast.

Grabbing the landlord by his apron strings, I held the inscription an inch from his face.

For once he was mute, his stare squinting and fixed, only his Adam's apple worked away in his throat. I realised after last night this bully was cowed, he had no stomach for further fisticuffs.

'It's that lass he's been knocking about with,' he snarled, racking his brains to somehow distance himself and his establishment from what was now a criminal act. 'The kitchen maid. She sometimes helps out Brown cleaning the rooms. I saw her working in your room only the other day. She must have helped herself to your watch then.'

'No,' gasped the ostler.

'But yesterday you accused Janet Brown of being the only one with access to my valuables, and you whipped her harshly for the theft,' I pointed out.

Ignoring this unpalatable truth, the landlord screamed at the ostler instead, 'Both you and the girl get out. Collect all your personal belongings and leave the Bell and Knaresborough before I set the constable onto you.'

'Now wait a minute,' I said. 'If there is any calling of the constable to be done it will be done by me.'

'Go ahead then,' said the landlord wearily.

'What about the wrong you have done to Janet Brown?'

'She can have her job back,' snapped the landlord.

'I doubt she would work here again with you.'

'So what do you want me to do?'

'Make a note of reference regarding her suitability for future employment.'

'That might persuade her not to bring a charge of common assault against you,' added Hutchinson.

'I'll have one made up before you leave,' replied the landlord.

'And Mr Kendle would like his bill halved for all this undue distress, I shouldn't wonder,' said Hutchinson, releasing the ostler with a little push in the back towards his master.

'Done,' grudgingly consented the landlord.

'Sorry, sir,' muttered the ostler, reduced to an uncertain future. 'Your watch is truly a splendid piece.'

* * * * *

'That ostler was a really strange chap,' said Hutchinson that evening in the Royal Oak. 'All he could say was how he coveted your watch, Felix.'

'Sadly, because owning such a timepiece was beyond his dreams,' I retorted.

'Unless, he stole it,' proposed a cynical Richard Collins. This was Hutchinson's surprise friend, and he had obviously acquainted him with that morning's events at the Bell.

The three of us sat with a bottle of claret in the centre of the table, each with a generous helping of the inn's famous pigeon pie and beetroot.

'Good, is it not?' asked Hutchinson, obviously dressed for the occasion in dove grey from top to toe.

I nodded. This was to be my treat for the doctor's help in getting my horse back and as luck would have it my watch too. This was an expense I was willing to meet for any information Richard Collins provided which might help me to understand his one time teacher better.

'Wonderful man, wonderful teacher, I can hardly believe what has befallen Mr Aram.' Collins gestured upwards with a finger – whether it was meant to be towards Thistle Hill or Heaven I could not tell. He lifted his glass and took a deep swig of wine as if to fortify himself against his old schoolteacher's disastrous fate.

'Did you know any of Aram's children?' I asked.

'Only Sally but I did not know her well.'

'You had occasion to meet her once or twice,' prompted Hutchinson.

'Indeed that is so,' agreed Collins.

'In what capacity?' I asked him.

'Mr Aram would bring her to sit in our schoolroom flouncing with petticoats and bursting with knowledge. Her devotion to study was held up as an example for us to follow. Her father boasted that soon she would beat the brightest boys in the kingdom, and given the chance I would not doubt it.'

'How did Sally react to all this public flattery?'

'She would blush and bore it modestly.'

'Yet Aram shunned his wife in the street, I've been told,' said Hutchinson.

Again Betty Aram's smile of pleasure looking up into her dead father's face flashed into my imagination. Betty Aram, who hadn't a good word for him. And suddenly I realised how some men's professional face could be totally opposed to their domestic one.

'How's the woollen trade, Richard?' asked Hutchinson, changing the subject.

'It fares quite well.'

'"Fares quite well", but Yorkshire is the wool capital of the world.'

'We prefer not to draw attention to the fact lest it moves elsewhere,' replied Collins dryly.

'I fear you are spending too much time in the cloth halls, Richard,' joked Hutchinson.

'And you peering into the fundaments.'

'But you must allow that we Englishmen are living in the most exciting period of history.'

'If you call the barbarity of a great linguistic scholar's corpse left to swing and decay from the gibbet before his neighbours exciting, then it is certainly that.'

'Ah, you're referring to Aram's incomplete lexicon, which would have proved that the Celtic language had more influence on European languages than Greek or Latin.' I interrupted. Collins nodded.

'But wasn't Edward Lhuyd first to champion that theory?' asked Hutchinson.

'No, the Welshman never went that far,' pointed out Collins.

'I thought he did,' said Hutchinson.

'No, he merely differentiated between various forms of the Celtic language but concluded they originate from the same source and the people who spoke them were therefore Celts.'

'You believe Aram was a great philologist then?' I asked Collins, interested.

'He was a great nobody,' snorted Hutchinson.

'I believe, Doctor, you would deny slavery despite having your nose pushed down a ship's hold,' retorted Collins.

'Now just a minute, I abhor the trade, I've seen those sailors in the Port of Liverpool unloading their cargo of darkies,' objected Hutchinson reddening. 'Half-naked men, women and children, I consider it a degrading abomination.'

'Thank the Lord for that,' clapped Collins. 'We agree on something.'

'I am sure we agree on many things, Richard. What I am saying to you is that there is much to commend about this country too. Why, only last April we lost one of our greatest composers, George Frideric Handel, but we are left to enjoy his legacy.'

'He was German.'

'Yes, but he chose to be English,' replied Hutchinson gamely.

'Tell me about Francis Iles.' I began to sense that I might learn something to my benefit from these two informed men once their passion had abated a little. I ordered a second bottle of claret and refilled their glasses.

'Oh, Francis is a good man,' said Collins.

'But both Aram and Henry Terry accused Iles of possessing himself of much of the booty,' I pointed out.

'Nonsense, as your fellow correspondents have reported, Iles was as much a victim of this fraudulent plot as anyone else in Knaresborough,' said Collins.

'But why was his name never mentioned at the trial following Aram's and Terry's allegations during their examinations?'

'Hearsay,' scoffed Collins.

'Or perhaps both the press and the law were bought off,' suggested Hutchinson.

'Thomas, that is outrageous,' exclaimed Collins. 'Francis is an upstanding member of our community.'

'He is that,' agreed Hutchinson sarcastically. 'And in the October, before the conspiracy was completed, he married Dorothy I'ans in York Minster.'

'What has that to do with anything?'

'Well, it was rather a coincidence: marriage in October, murder in February.'

'You're not suggesting that Dorothy had anything to do with it?' asked a horrified Collins.

'No, I am not, but Dorothy was the daughter of Thomas I'ans of Instow in Devon. They are a prominent West Country family, are they not?'

'Indeed, what of it?'

'Ah, the Devon coast, smuggling and piracy,' I put in wickedly, mimicking a West Country accent.

'Quite,' replied Hutchinson unimpressed. 'But despite any outlandish speculation on that front, Dorothy would have had high expectations following her marriage. She was after all used to certain standards.'

'As was Clark's wife,' countered Collins.

'True, but not to the same standard.'

'Are you saying that there has been a miscarriage of justice, Thomas?' asked Collins.

'I am not sure, Richard. But I will say that you are perhaps overgenerous regarding Iles' respectability.'

'And Houseman's?' I enquired.

'Houseman is just a mule,' replied Hutchinson.

'Aram told William Thornton that Iles later possessed himself of goods taken away into the Dales by his brother-in-law, Abraham Spence,' I informed Hutchinson when Collins had taken himself off for a piss.

'Then, Mr Kendle, I think a trip up Netherdale is called for,' chuckled the doctor, merry again. 'And you'd better take this with you.' He took from his pocket a beautiful French flintlock pistol and pushed it across the table to me.

'No, no, I couldn't possibly take it.' I moved the pistol back to him.

'Why not? For your protection, old fellow.'

'I refuse to carry arms under any circumstances. My pen is my protection.'

CHAPTER FOURTEEN

The next morning I sent the same boy – the good runner I had used to go to Thornville – with a note for Abraham Spence up in Netherdale saying I would like to meet him.

Thomas Hutchinson told me the Spence family now farmed a good acreage at Stean on the high fells.

Hutchinson was a man who knew everything about everybody hereabouts but he knew very little about Janet Brown, I had asked him. Since pushing the note of reference made out by the Bell's landlord under her Finkle Street door, I had heard nothing from her, not one word of thanks.

However my messenger to Stean returned in the late evening with some positive news. Abraham Spence had agreed to a meeting the next day, saying he was eager to redress the wicked rumours surrounding his maligned sister, Anna.

Saturday morning – Saturday mornings always felt special to me wherever I was. I emptied the satchel of the depositions, replacing them with my notebook, pencil and an old but accurate John Speede map of the West Riding. Happily reunited with my freshly shod "steed", we started out on my quest to follow the brilliant river Nidd to its upper reaches.

I was glad to leave Knaresborough for more rural vistas, feeling in my heart that this would be a pleasant and interesting journey.

'I bet priest holes and plain dresses is all you'll find up there, Kendle,' Hutchinson had teased me.

I was well aware that Netherdale, sometimes known as Nidderdale, had a long reputation as a stronghold for Catholic recusants and Quaker dissent.

'We'll see, Thomas, we'll see,' I had smiled back. What had I to lose?

To my astonishment I felt comfortable bumping along on Bess' broad backside. Dare I admit it, I had grown a fondness for the old girl. Yet she did not avoid shaming me by fouling the pavement in the orderly village of Ripley. It was as if she had saved it all up for the right moment. Obviously the background grandeur of the Inglebys' castle, where Peter Aram once worked as head gardener, served to stimulate her more basic function. Then again, maybe she was a Protestant horse and it was a comment on the castle's chequered history.

Richard Collins had told me that his family were intimates of the castle owner, the unmarried Sir John Ingleby. Two hundred years before, his ancestor Sir William Ingleby married the staunchly Catholic Ann Mallory. Two of their sons were known as "the most dangerous papists in the North". Preaching in York, Francis was one of the priests harboured by Margaret Clitherow. He was hanged, drawn and quartered on the Knavesmire on 3rd June, 1586. If this sounds to be a neat end to a man's life, it is anything but. Francis was towed through the street on a hurdle to his hanging. He was suspended and half-strangled before the halter round his neck was cut; while he lived he was disembowelled and his heart was ripped from his body before his eyes; next he was quartered, parboiled in a cauldron and his body parts impaled on the city gates.

His brother, David – known as "the Fox" because of his ability to evade capture – avoided the same fate, dying in exile in Belgium. Queen Elizabeth took pity on David's widow and awarded her a pension subject to good behaviour. Sir William's daughter, Elizabeth, married Peter Yorke of Gouthwaite Hall. Further proof that not only the poor but many of the grand houses in Yorkshire stubbornly stuck together – clung to the old faith like blowing cotton grasses rooted in their native peat bogs – however, there is risk in failure to adapt to the prevailing wind which many Netherdale martyrs found to their cost.

Starting with the popular rising in York against Henry VIII's separation from the Catholic Church, known as the Pilgrimage of Grace, I have great sympathy for those brave adherents of Rome: why should they have been forced to abandon their manner of worship to suit the lusts of a king?

In the background of these difficult thoughts of mine, the Nidd remained somnolent. In the small village of Burnt Yates, Bess took her fill from a communal water trough placed at the side of the track. We rode through the Monks Wall, built by the brothers of Fountains Abbey to protect themselves and their granges from the evil contamination of Knaresborough Forest, and on and up to safer ground splitting acutely away from the river. I could see the rolling away hills across the valley were gently gaining height too.

Bess stopped abruptly. My heart missed a beat. We suddenly found ourselves in the midst of the most amazing tors I had ever seen. Huge millstone boulders balanced precariously on thinner columns some rising to a hundred feet high. Each one formed a unique shape to challenge the imagination. As we weaved our way between them I wondered how these sculptures came to be. Towards the end of my evening with Collins and Hutchinson in the Royal Oak, Collins had told me that the rocks at Brimham were the subject of keen debate. Some men believed them to be the remnants of a Druid temple, others that they were formed at the time of Genesis. Looking up at these towering shapes, I myself felt that they were the result of some great natural force not yet understood. Whatever they were, I was reluctant to leave their grandeur but we had to move on.

In the manor of Bishopside – so called because it was given by the warrior king, Athelstan, to the Archbishop of York in the first half of the 10th century – we were still forced to keep to higher ground because of perpetual marsh. Luckily for us the weather had remained clement and soon we reached hilly Pateley Bridge. There had been few people to be seen on our journey so far, now there were many on either side of the narrow pavements of this bustling market town. I feared they might step out into Bess' path at any moment as her new shoes sparked and slipped on the cobblestones. My nervousness finally abated as we completed the steep descent and crossed the bridge out of Pateley.

Thankfully alone again, we clipped along Low Wath Road in the township of Stonebeck Down which is part of the ancient parish of Kirkby-Malzeard. The hills dwarfed us now and were heavily wooded. Rounding a bend the valley opened out once more, but Bess became uneasy beneath me on passing the gates to Gouthwaite Hall. The coursed squared stone hall had a slate roof and looked to be in the style of the 17th century. It was a long building with gables and mullioned windows. According to my knowledgeable source on the Catholic gentry, Richard Collins, this remote hall had its own story to tell. Like Sir William Ingleby, Sir John Yorke married a staunch Catholic, Juliana Hansby. How Catholic at heart the husbands of these women remained is open to conjecture – but Catholic or Protestant they were about to embark on one of the bloodiest periods of our history – father against son, brother against brother.

During the Christmas festivities of 1609, early in the reign of James I, the Yorkes invited some travelling players from Whitby to entertain them. Christopher and Robert Simpson performed the play, *Saint Christopher*, which ended with a Protestant being dragged into hell and a Catholic rising to heaven. Most of the guests seemed to enjoy the performance apart from one disaffected former servant, Elizabeth Stubbs, who reported the Yorkes to the local Justice of the Peace.

Sir John and Lady Juliana continued to support the Simpson players while awaiting trial. Eventually they stood before the infamous Court of Star Chamber for sedition. They were fined £1,000 each and imprisoned in the Fleet Debtors' Prison for three years, until February, 1617, when they were able to pay off part of the fine and were released to "sin" no more. I cannot help wondering what happened to their informer, Elizabeth Stubbs.

At Ramsgill – the gill or valley of wild garlic – the unspoken capital of the parish of Stonebeck Down, I noticed a smithy and an inn abutting the green on the opposite side of the road. Other less substantial dwellings were scattered about higgledy-piggledy as if they had fallen at random from the heavens.

One of these thatched cottages caught my eye. It was singled out by a Celtic stone head framed in carved ram's horns set above the doorway. There was no doubt that this was the dwelling in which Aram was born from the description given to me by Matilda Peck in the Maison Dieu at Ripon. My muse, Doctor Hutchinson, had already informed me that the Brigante tribe in this area worshipped horned gods, similar to the Gaulish Cernunnos, the stag god found on a pillar in the foundations of the Cathedral of Notre Dame earlier this century. Later generations would reproduce these heads and incorporate them into the fabric of their houses to ward off the evil eye. Alas, in Aram's case this ram god had not been successful. I stared in awe for a minute or two at the primitive depiction. For all its crudity it lost nothing. It had been handed down through folk memory from a people and beliefs beyond my comprehension. When Aram came back to Ramsgill – taught in his schoolroom at Gouthwaite Hall – wouldn't this head, signalling his birthplace, have been a constant reminder of those mystical Celts who had once roamed his native dale? Was this head the spur for his interest in these ancient people and their language? This was the aspect of the man that most intrigued me: like his father, Peter Aram, he had a love of poetry and scholarship – every flourish of his pen stroke revealed his disposition – yet in Knaresborough he threw himself into low life, criminality and eventually murder. How could I ever be reconciled with this man's ambiguities?

I could hear at the end of the village the deep rumble of a mill wheel turning with the waters of Ramsgill Beck as it cut down to the Nidd. In harmony it seemed with my own churning thoughts.

'You one of those prying folk? We've had a lot of the likes of ye up here of late.' An old countryman, who had appeared from nowhere, swung his crook backwards and forwards threateningly beneath Bess' nose. She twitched in agitation. Rather than pull away from his challenge, I decided to dismount and meet him at eye level. 'You'll be wanting to know if this is Aram's cottage.'

'Well, is it?'

'Don't ask me. Long afore my time,' said the old man, obviously lying.

'Forgive me, but I would have taken you to be at least twenty years Eugene Aram's senior.'

'Really,' puffed the old man indignantly. 'Well, I can tell you nowt about t' gardener's son. He kept hisself to hisself working in t' schoolroom at t' big 'ouse. Stuck up, he was, with his fancy ways. But his fether, now he was a grand chap.'

'Peter Aram.'

'Aye, that was his name, Peter. He worked t' gardens nigh on thirty years previous to his son learning those gentlefolk's brats. T' son acted like gentry hisself until he got that Lofthouse lass in t' family way a second time.'

'A second time?'

'I believe so. She'd already at least one young 'un before he wed her. Things changed wi' t' next on t' way. 'Twas her brother Isaac that told t' fancy schoolmaster that he'd better make t' lass an honest woman. Shamed his own fether, shamed t' Spences who were poor but nonetheless respected in t' dale.'

'That's where I am heading, to meet Abraham Spence of Stean.'

'Ah, I know 'im well,' said the old man, a little taken aback.

'Can you direct me, sir?'

'At Low Lofthouse, turn left over t' small bridge and keep on going up t' hill.'

His direction seemed a little vague but I decided not to press him further as I had a way to go. Remounting I bid him farewell. He tipped the peak of his cap.

'I'll see ye again. I *know* I'll see ye again, sir.' With those strange words he was gone, leaving me with the impression that he knew more than he was telling. And yet he had provided me with another aspect of the man I was investigating – arrogance – Eugene Aram had not looked too arrogant standing in the Grand Jury House a few weeks ago, humble was more the adjective I would have used. I suspected that he was something of an actor though, mercurial, he could even change his handwriting to suit the occasion. Under duress, as he most certainly was when signing his deposition before Mr Thornton, I had noticed he used a large rounded *a* for aram. In more congenial circumstances his hand had retained its usual flourish *A ram*. The papers supplied to me by Vicar Collins, purporting to be from Aram's condemned cell, detailing his exaggerated pedigree, even these were executed in a beautiful cursive script. In both his documented ancestry and his deposition, he retained a tell-tale colon after the initial of his Christian name, otherwise I would have been certain one was a forgery. It was as if there were two Arams – the man was truly an enigma.

Reaching Low Lofthouse where Anna's father, Christopher Spence, once pumped his smithy bellows, the countryside turned into purple moorland. Wild and uncultivated, I swore this land had not even experienced a prehistoric plough. I checked my map and we turned left over a small bridge. We struggled up a steep incline beside a gorge. I knew this unusual geology had been eked out over the centuries by the famous tumbling water of High Stean Beck. The smooth limestone created here was known locally as Stean marble.

Taking a sharp bend in the narrow track, we were greeted with our first sight of habitation. A few dwellings stood girded tightly together as if for warmth, each was built from the local stone. The hamlet of Stean was deathly quiet. Finding a ford blocking our progress, I turned in the saddle to see a woman hanging out her washing – squawking geese at her feet – I rode back to grab her attention as I swear she was the only living soul abroad that afternoon.

'You have a gaggle of Roman watch dogs there,' I laughed, raising my hat. She did not seem to appreciate my wit, took me for an idiot, took flight towards her dwelling, washing basket in hand. 'Could you direct me to the Spence farm?' I shouted after her.

The name "Spence" seemed to hold some meaning for her. She span round, replying in such a strong dialect that I struggled to translate. From her hand gestures I realised the farm must still be further on. Discouraged, I looked up towards where I knew Great Whernside lurked beyond and Nidd Head Spring bubbled up out of its precipitous side. Had I made a mistake coming? Would the visit be worth all this time and effort?

Bess was up to her fetlocks in mud as we entered the Spences' yard. One or two chickens scraped about in thinly scattered straw. I must say I had never expected anything as bleak and dire as this.

Though the grazing was poor, I could see sheep dotted on the higher fells – nothing in this exposed location could be grown but wool – people were gradually leaving these rural farms for the towns and cities. I could see it happening everywhere. Arcadia was being left behind. The Spences must be stalwarts of the old ways. I could not help admiring them for that – someone had to attend the sheep for those who tend the clattering looms.

A lithe looking fellow, who appeared to be in his late forties, came out to greet me. He introduced himself as Abraham Spence. From my glimpses of Mrs Aram at Theakston's inquests, Abraham greatly resembled his sister. He too was dark with a rather prominent nose which had given rise to the notion that they were of Jewish blood.

'Felix Kendle,' I nodded my introduction before dismounting.

'I know,' replied Spence.

'How do you know?'

'It wasn't difficult. Nobody from around here wears boots of that quality and has such a good satchel swinging from his side. Nobody much visits us up here on horseback either,' concluded Spence, rubbing his soiled finger down his leather leggings almost in distaste.

'Well, you invited me, sir.'

'I did that. Tether t' horse over yonder from t' barn door,' he barked across at a youth who was idly forking up a pile of fodder for winter. 'Water and feed her, she's frothing from t' journey. Unfortunately, this farm's been more blessed with able-bodied lasses than lads,' he muttered as we moved towards the house.

I was forced to stoop beneath the low lintel on entering the Spences' dwelling, Abraham was not. There was a roaring fire in the parlour – which I took to be the main room – it had a snug family feel to it.

A red faced older man sat at the table. Fuller, jollier looking than Abraham.

'My elder brother, Isaac,' explained Abraham. Isaac beamed. Abraham instructed an equally mature woman rocking in a nearby chair to bring us warm milk. I took this gaunt person to be Abraham's wife though he obviously felt her unworthy of introduction.

I could see what he meant by an abundance of lasses. Several slender girls clung to the walls, coyly looking me over. Obviously Abraham's progeny but longer limbed. They reminded me of a cluster of damselflies waiting to mate.

'Come, come, find some occupation elsewhere, lasses.' Abraham clapped his hands and his daughters were instantly banished.

'I attended the trial of your brother-in-law at York,' I informed him, 'and I feel all was not explained there.'

'You are right, it wasn't,' agreed Abraham.

'No,' said Isaac.

'Isaac here wants things put right for our Anna,' explained Abraham. 'Already she is cast in a bad light for history.'

'By her husband,' I proffered.

'Aye, by 'im right enough,' replied Isaac.

'Forgive me, and do not answer if you feel my question impertinent, but there have been rumours abroad that your sister Anna could be of Hebrew descent.'

Abraham laughed at this, the previously jovial looking Isaac did not.

'I'll tell you this once, Mister, a relative of ours laid down his life for his faith at the end of the previous century and he was no Jew. John Spence died during imprisonment at York rather than deny his Quaker belief,' said Isaac.

'Fine,' I said. 'All's well,' I said.

'Just so as you should know.' Isaac spat into the hearth. This bear of a man began to frighten me.

'Now Eugene accused you of bringing some of Clark's stolen property up into the Dales, is that so?' I directed this question to Abraham.

'Yes, though I'll not admit to knowing it was stolen, and it wasn't in my possession long.'

'Why was that?'

'That Knaresborough linen draper threatened me.'

'You mean Francis Iles?'

'Mr Francis Iles,' sneered Abraham.

'How did he threaten you?'

'He said if I did not give up t' goods into his keeping, he would see that we all hanged.'

'Tell me this, this has always been a big mystery to me, how did Eugene and Richard Houseman get away with stolen goods being found in their possession back in '45? – velvets, cambrics, woollens and stockings hidden in Eugene's Church Lane garden, leather and some whips under flax in Houseman's heckling shop up the White Horse Yard.'

'Again I suspect Iles was behind Mr Norton's trumped up charge of calling Eugene to account for an unpaid debt in t' first place. By having him arrested, Iles was attempting to force him into revealing where the plate and suchlike was so he could secure it for himself.'

'But according to the constable your brother-in-law had enough money in his pocket to pay off the debt.'

'Aye, Eugene was too wily for 'em there.'

'You mean duplicitous.'

'Sir, you have to live on your wits with men like Iles around.'

'And did the linen draper achieve his goal?'

'I believe so. In my case he certainly did.'

The gaunt woman finally arrived with three pots of hot milk. Without a thank you, Abraham waved her out of the room.

'But how could the gang have hoped to get away with such an obvious fraud? The newly married Clark had to disappear.'

'As I've been told he didn't get on with his wife or at least his mother didn't get on with her. Dorothy Clark never took to t' excise man's daughter, Hannah Oldham. They fought like two cats in a bag in Daniel's little cottage, so that situation wasn't hard to leave behind.'

'But he had a successful cordwainer's business in Knaresborough.'

'Iles was married to the daughter of a wealthy landowner with estates in both Devon and Cornwall.'

'Dorothy I'ans.'

'You know her?' asked Abraham, surprised.

'No, I've just recently heard of her.'

'Well, no doubt Iles promised to set Daniel up in business down there well away from the North.'

'Are you telling me that this respectable Knaresborough merchant was in on the plot from its conception?'

Abraham shrugged and suddenly clamped up.

'Perhaps my brother is saying that Iles was t' brains behind t' whole business,' Isaac piped up. 'Take it or leave it, Mister.'

'Our lass told me it was Iles instructed Eugene to quit Knaresborough once the plot was uncovered,' added Abraham.

'Anna said that?'

'She did. Iles wanted Eugene out of the way lest he talked.'

'But what about Houseman?'

'Dickey Houseman was Iles' fool.' Abraham spat on the stone flagged floor. 'He'd rather lick his arse than offend the man.'

'And the murders?'

'Murders? We know nowt about them,' he replied quickly.

'Why didn't they just let Clark go off and set up afresh in the West Country as you've suggested?'

'Perhaps he was too windy,' declared Isaac.

'Too unreliable,' agreed Abraham.

'And the Jew?'

'What Jew?' asked Abraham.

'The body of the Jewish servant at first believed to be Clark's found on Thistle Hill.'

'Oh him, he had to be killed else he would have exposed 'em all,' said Abraham matter-of-factly.

'What was you brother-in-law really like?'

'He was a fair enough chap,' said Isaac. 'He wedded Anna and I my Jane on t' same day at Middlesmoor, fourth day of May, 1731.'

'Eugene wasn't a fair enough chap once he got our sister under his roof though,' objected Abraham.

'No?' I asked.

'No, he was like two men,' explained Abraham.

'He had a touch of Cain and Abel about 'im,' conceded Isaac.

'From what I've gathered so far he seemed to favour his daughter, Sally, above all others,' I said.

Silence – a sword through air – Abraham looked to Isaac, Isaac to Abraham. Abraham was first to speak.

'Aye, our Sally, I've not seen or heard of her in a while,' he said.

'She was found to be living with her father down in Lynn when he was arrested,' I told them.

'I believe so,' said Abraham, clearing his throat.

'Tell me, something that has been troubling me, why did Eugene try to pass Sally off as his niece in Lynn when she was his daughter?' I asked.

'I couldn't rightly say,' replied Abraham.

'Perhaps to silence wagging tongues,' conjectured the man who had shared Aram's wedding day. 'I heard tell she had a bairn down there.'

'A child? A child with whom?' I asked. Both brothers shook their heads over the question of paternity.

'Our Anna had much to contend with throughout her marriage,' replied Abraham instead. 'Yet t' world maligns her because of wicked insinuations made out against her by a depraved husband.'

'"Depraved" how?' I asked. Neither brother seemed willing to expand on the theme of Eugene's depravity either. I wondered if they had heard of the tale of him paying court to boys dressed up as women. 'So, you don't believe your sister indulged in an adulterous affair with young Daniel Clark?' I asked. Both men shook their heads again, more slowly this time. I could tell that deliberation and dilatoriness was a way of life on this hill farm.

'And if she did, who could blame her?' piped up Isaac; no doubt called in for and bent on the defence of his abused sister's reputation.

'Indeed,' I said, blowing thoughtfully on my cooling milk.

'A long while ago, I recall calling upon my sister on my way back to Stean from business in York. Anna said something bad was happening and I wasn't welcome in t' 'ouse that night,' said Isaac, shrugging his large shoulders.

'You have to understand, Mister, Eugene only ever had time for our Sally,' said Abraham. 'Sally could do this, Sally could do that, Sally could do no harm. And I believe she welcomed it. She adored her papa as much as he did her.'

All conversation dried up at that. A bitter almost unimaginable possibility hung in the parlour air – only the milk remained sweet to my tongue.

CHAPTER FIFTEEN

I declined their offer of accommodation for the night, saying I was keen to visit the Chapel of Middlesmoor. With no indication of taking offence, Abraham directed me onto the footpath which leads from Stean to the village of Middlesmoor, crossing the ravine by a narrow stone arch.

Stonebeck Up – aptly named – and there it was the high-vantage chapelry standing guard over the dale and its parishioners more like a bleak Roman garrison than a House of God. I secured Bess to a post in the yard.

Built in 1484 this house of worship had a square tower to the west end. Inside I found it to be disappointingly plain with a regulation nave, chancel and porch. But it was a font to one side that caught my attention. The font was like a cup with a short stem and it was so huge it lent itself to full immersion.

Somehow I felt this chapelry to be unnerving. It was as if I shouldn't be there and was being scrutinised. I swung round to the sound of the creaking door and the gentle padding of approaching feet.

'Anglo-Saxon,' explained the slippered priest, pointing to the font. 'Older than the chapelry.'

'Sir, might I view your register,' I asked, seizing the moment as I had done in Ripon.

'Who are you looking for?'

'I've been told an uncle of mine came from these parts.'

'What was his name?'

'Yorke,' I lied. I had noticed two 17th century sepulchral inscriptions to the Yorkes on the chancel entrance – recusants or not they were here.

'Certainly,' he replied, leading me to the registry table. 'Please, take all the time you need, sir.'

It did not take long to find: **Low Loftus** (for Lofthouse). **Isaac Spence & Jane Peart married 4th May 1731**. There was a peculiar stroke above the *P* in Peart that might have looked like an *F* for Feart but the *F* in the February above looked nothing like it. And there in the column beneath: **Ugenius** (for Eugenius) **Aram & Anna Spence** married on the same day. If he had troubled to see it, I wondered how the punctilious schoolmaster would have reacted to this careless spelling of his name. I went back to his birth in 1704 – the priest here had spelt his Christian name correctly. Just fancy, this austere place was where Aram had tied the knot with Anna Spence – a knot that was to unravel with such disastrous consequences.

1732 Low Loftus. Anna Daug: of Ugenius Aram bap: Jan. 23rd.

This didn't fully bear out what the old man had told me back in Ramsgill: Aram's daughter, Anna, was baptised nine months after his marriage but on what date exactly was she born? I would have to discuss dates of conception and gestation with my friend Doctor Hutchinson. However it did appear to have been a close-run race to the church. Baptism usually takes place within a week of birth. Little Anna would almost certainly have been purified in the magnificent Anglo-Saxon font here. But what about Sally? Was she ever baptised? – I could find no reference to her in the register. Sadly I found little Anna died four months later.

1727 9th March, bur. Christopher Spence, Longside Moor. Was this little Anna's maternal grandfather who had predeceased her by a few years, I wondered. But why Longside Moor? – Anna's father had worked at the smithy in Lofthouse. Perhaps he had become too ill or frail and was staying with relatives down the dale.

The priest had long bid me good afternoon and gone home. While pointing out the way here, Abraham had told me all about his brother's and sister's double wedding and the feast that followed. It had obviously been a memorable occasion for him. Standing in the chapelry porch, gazing down the dale, in my mind's eye I saw it all.

* * * * *

Before the clapper had struck the chapelry bell, guests were struggling up the climb – huffing and puffing and respectful. While those in the valley below, uninvited folk with folk-memory, whispered that Middlesmoor's hallowed ground had known other rites – black rites during the Age of Darkness – and no lass of theirs would be allowed to wed up there with or without child.

This sort of gossip did not deter Alice, the rosy plump dairymaid, her pilgrim eyes fixed with awe and hope on the target ahead, as she prayed someone might make an honest woman out of her too one day, though fearing those few mistakes with the local lads were her undoing. The ingenuous shepherd in rags, who had left his dozen sheep penned that morning to be present at Isaac's wedding, admired Alice's hips and followed on. And then, coming down from Middlesmoor village itself, the respectable regular congregation who equated godliness with attendance times and who looked more elevated and pious but were not.

So, as his small flock either cursed their steep ascent or descent across difficult cobbles towards mother-church, occasionally dusted by the few with good land and rich enough to ride, the parson twittered in the pulpit over his mental rehearsal, looking down now and then across the nave to see everything was in place. The twitch to one side of his lean mouth occurred before these solemn occasions not because he suspected he was wanting; nor because the ceremony was new to him; nor out of deference to those of importance whom he was about to address, because nobody could be as important as one of God's representatives on earth – no, it was just that the Middlesmoor parson had found his vocation had become a trying and wearying one, and he would rather have been at home with his feet up than here in this draughty building.

Outside the chapel, hens fluttered in clouds, pushed indiscriminately aside by horses and men alike. Clogs scraped in competition with hooves in the yard. Guests or not, everyone wanted to see the comings and goings.

He, who had always been drunk with life, was now drunk on fear. Aram had lived life to the full, passionately, inebriated against the petty, drawn-up rules of other men – now they were calling him to book – how he hated them and their pinching little community.

He was drunk at his wedding. He had to be drunk at his wedding. His bride was gravid again and his attendance that day in church wasn't of his own volition – was more her brother's doing, her mother's doing, her doing.

The first Tuesday in May – God, May, that most fertile of months – the month of fertility rites; not marriage though, and weddings. But wedding it was, a double wedding, a most uncommon affair for Middlesmoor and a good crowd was expected for the spectacle.

Aram could hardly explain, not even to himself, how he felt seeing Widow Spence crawling into a pew weakly supported by his own now bowed and enfeebled father, unless it was he sensed a premonitory sign.

'Perhaps those two will make it a triple wedding,' someone laughed.

''Twould be t' last thing they did from t' look o' yon,' roared someone else.

Aram felt numb as he turned to see his bride wobbling down the aisle towards him. Her pale face – today a lighter pale with anxiety and morning sickness.

'Dearly beloved, we are gathered here in the sight …'

Aram gulped: Isaac's Jane looked radiant in comparison to Anna. How ironical, Anna was pregnant again and by some miracle Jane had still escaped.

Little Sally stood in the front pew, hand in hand with Aram's sister, Orinda. From time to time the child sobbed for her mother. Anna stood like a blancmange, trying to ignore her. Trapped himself in this charade, Aram could spare little sympathy for the humiliation of his bride. And, anyway, hadn't Anna got what she wanted? Didn't Anna always get what she wanted?

'Therefore if any man can shew any just cause, why they may not lawfully be joined together, let him now speak, or else hereafter for ever hold his peace.'

Aram listened, hoping – no one spoke out – there was only the hollow echo of the parson's words bouncing off the white-washed walls. His eyes fell upon Anna's grey boots, her best boots, peeping from beneath her delicate dress. How he hated those boots of hers, boots of seduction. Had she nothing more special for today? How insipid their greyness looked with that dress. The woman had no idea. Couldn't she see they were not in keeping? And she looked old, too old for him, their love-making was already old, stale. Anna never had the young, almost boyish, undernourished love-body of the whore in Old Drury. When he made love to Anna, he was forever trying to win back that child-whore of missed opportunity whom he had met while working in London as a sixteen year old. Why couldn't he just learn to accept that life was full of missed opportunities?

'… that if either of you know any impediment.'

Any impediment? Could a Drury whore be regarded as an impediment?

'Wilt thou have this woman …?'

Was he required to give a response here? No, he relaxed again, Isaac and Jane were to answer first.

'Yes, yes … I do, I do.' His heart dropped; Aram let the bridal hand drop as soon as they were pronounced man and wife.

Like the fuss of hens outside the church, the squawking wedding party fell on the Spences' Lofthouse cottage expectantly. They were not to be disappointed: laid out on a long trestle-table in the yard was an assortment of fresh spring vegetables, sweetbreads, cooked joints of beef, ham and chicken, duck eggs, bread just out of the oven, and jugs of ale, plenty of ale.

'See, we'll cut our personal costs by half, Eugene, getting 'em wed together, wined and dined together.' He remembered Isaac's pre-nuptial reassurances. Well, there was to be no stinting on the wining and dining, he could see that.

'A feast,' his father whispered, tempted to risk his careful veteran diet.

It was noon. The sky was clear and the sun high and warm. Aram could not help being moved to smile by the jovial company, although, as time went on and the ale flowed with greater enthusiasm, the table manners of some of the guests began to detract from the beauty of the scene, and the charm of an Italian Last Supper soon degenerated into Bruegel's Wedding Feast.

From amid the huddle of Isaac's friends, pouring ale rapidly down their own and each other's throats, Isaac staggered up. Jane was forced to cover her pretty blushing face with her ugly rough hands, as the men cheered her husband's more lewd sentiments about the future children they would produce. It was then that Aram observed the glances of one or two of the older, more wily women across the table. They were casting a critical eye Jane's way: these women were after all experts in appraising cows suspected of being barren and prettiness never entered into their businesslike deliberations.

'As you all can see our Anna's already well-tupped,' slurred Isaac, waving a suggestive finger at his brother-in-law, before boasting of the home he would be providing for his own new wife. His friends' guffaws soon turned to yawns.

Why does the bastard always have to try and gain some advantage over me, wondered Aram tight-lipped. Why is he reminding me that I have everything to offer Anna but a roof? For the first time Aram saw Anna's second full belly as a plus. Was that it? – was Isaac actually jealous of their fertility?

'Poor dear Anna, must be t' excitement o' t' day and too much sun,' said one of the Spence aunts kindly, as the new

Mrs Aram slumped across the table, scattering plates, cups and ale alike, before vomiting into the lap of God's right-hand man.

* * * * *

I shivered. Evening seemed to be rising up from the valley floor. Again I felt something or someone was watching me. I walked round to Bess in the yard. She too seemed agitated for the off. She was pawing the ground, and there was a nervous twitch to her croup as if she was being attacked by a swarm of evening gnats but there was none to be seen. I unleashed her reins from the post, mounted, and we gently progressed down the hill from the chapelry. I had no regrets at leaving the harsh landscape of Stonebeck Up and making for the more gentle meadows of the Nidd.

I debated whether I should push on through the night. The horse beneath me had fallen from a slow trot – known as a fadge in the Yorkshire Ridings – into a tired lethargic plod, and I had no desire to make my way through those eerie tors of Brimham in darkness.

CHAPTER SIXTEEN

Bess and I retraced our course along the valley bottom back to Ramsgill. Night had fallen but still battalions of farmers were out working the land, ploughing in the harvest stubble for winter, aided by the odd lamp and the light of the moon.

My thoughts travelled back up to the Spences in Stean, sitting on their almost impossible grazing, and my heart went out to them. I could appreciate how Abraham had been drawn into the plot of easy money to be made from receiving stolen goods. Like his brother-in-law he had a wife and children to feed, unlike his brother-in-law he had no profession to follow. That for me was one of the many conundrums regarding Eugene Aram: he was a man of learning, a well-respected school teacher who had secured a position in Knaresborough society instructing the sons of wealthy merchants. Why on earth had he risked all that? Was it out of greed or was there something in his nature that enjoyed the risk, needed the thrill? I certainly suspected he deeply resented the power and wealth of those he regarded as his intellectual inferiors – the gentry who had often offered him a helping hand up the social ladder, the gentry who had the resources to do so.

I decided to put Bess into livery for the night at Ramsgill. The inn was a cross between a coaching house and shooting lodge. Judging from its clientele more the latter in the present season. I was drawn to the fragrance and heat of the peat fire burning merrily away in the drinking parlour. After warming my backside before the hearth, I took a seat and table close by in the inglenook and ordered ale and beef. I was famished after my day's travel.

I hated eating alone in public. It seemed to be a requirement of my profession when following up a story in a strange place, however I never got used to it. Sitting there amongst the shooting fraternity with all its male bonhomie, I felt odd and lonely. I watched all the strutting, backslapping and wondered if they were aware how ridiculous and immature they looked.

'Huh! Huh!' One twill carcase, blown up with pudding and hot air, knocked against the table, spilling my tankard of frothing ale without a word of apology.

I had decided to make for my bed, unwilling to witness anymore pomposity, when I experienced whispering against my right lobe.

'There ye be. Told thee I'd see thee again.' The old countryman, whom I had met earlier in the day outside Aram's cottage, was now standing at my side like a spectre.

'Sit down,' I said, desperate for company.

'Alfred Suttill, clogger.'

'Clogger?' I queried.

'Aye, I make clogs for folk in these parts.' Alfred stuck out his hand, the arm protruding below his short sleeved jacket was knotted with sinews and veins.

'What is your drink, Alfred?'

'Same as thee will do.'

I motioned to the landlord. Alfred's ale arrived after some delay. He grinned teeth and his whiskers shimmered in the candlelight like the stubble fields had done earlier. With the celebrations continuing above us, my new companion guarded his tankard with a large hand. He was not about to lose his precious drink to the raucous goings on of sporting gentlemen.

Thankfully the twills moved off nearer the counter and Alfred sat back and lit his clay pipe. He did not speak for a minute or two, sucking contentedly away like a baby on its thumb.

'So,' he slurred, pipe still in place. 'Did ye find Abraham Spence?' I nodded. 'Eugenius Aram used his sister ill, by God he did that. An old lass who has lived in t' village longer than I care to remember, told me he insisted that the Spence lass went to his sister in Ripon to have her misbegotten bairns on the quiet like.'

'So little Anna could have been born months before her baptism?'

'I believe so. November time following the wedding. T' other was born years afore.'

'Are we talking of Sally?'

'Oh, I've no idea of names. But if he treated his missus like that before they were wed, how did he treat her afterwards?' pondered Alfred.

The question seemed to hang in the air between us. If this old village woman's story was right then it was as I imagined: little Anna wasn't conceived within wedlock and possibly Sally wasn't either. Anna Spence's second pregnancy had forced Aram into marriage. I ordered Alfred and myself more ale.

'How's the clog business, Suttill?' The twill carcase that had upset my drink was staring down on us benevolently.

'I am still able to make a living, sir, in these hard times,' replied Alfred.

'Good, good. And who is your friend?' asked the carcase.

Alfred looked across at me doubtfully.

'Felix Kendle, the *Gentleman's Magazine*.' I introduced myself.

'Hiram Omerod. I am a subscriber to your magazine. Do you shoot, sir?' I shook my head. 'Do you ride, sir?' I nodded.

* * * * *

I attended church, deciding to kick my heels in Ramsgill another day as the inn there was so comfortable. I was sure that a day of rest would not go amiss for Bess either.

After breakfast, on the Monday morning, I had arranged to meet Omerod and his fellow shooters. They had offered to escort me onto the moors above the hamlet of Bouthwaite, romantically named as a township of Fountains Earth. Their assurances that the higher scenic route back over the moors above the Nidd would be different from my outward bound journey, held some appeal for me.

Hiram Omerod did not seem such a bad fellow on better acquaintance. Although my initial reservations regarding him remained.

Our party slowly progressed up an extremely steep hill. So steep I feared I would slide off the back of my saddle. Once out on open moorland, Omerod insisted we all dismount so he could show off his gleaming flintlock rifle. This was a new sport, walked up grouse shooting, not yet the sport of kings.

Bang. An explosive cloud. Within seconds a red grouse had tumbled from the sky to earth like a stone. Omerod's returned spaniel rubbed against his master's buckskin breeches, eager for praise, eager to ferret out more prey. Omerod grinned, proud of his success. As a man held our horses, we edged forward on foot. Omerod and his companions opened fire on a small low-flying flock flushed from beneath boots, buckled shoes and dogs. The birds looked to be flying north at 80 mph. This was competition, this was war. I could not help feeling sorry for the enemy, the winged victims in all this. It was time for me to move on.

The flowering heather rolled out before me in a purple carpet that seemed to go on forever. In my whole life I had never seen such beauty in such desolation. I sensed Bess' apprehension as we made our way on an indistinct path avoiding sphagnum moss bogs and entrapping ferns. Bess kicked through low bilberry bushes where the odd uneaten fruit remained like dry little black raisins. Although I had kept the sun to my right side, the south side, I feared we were lost.

Eventually we came out onto a road far above and beyond the smoking chimneys of Pateley Bridge. I believed we must be on High Bishopside; then Low Bishopside; then I finally recognised my location from my outgoing journey and with a good deal of relief we cantered down towards Brimham Rocks.

Some magic drew me to this place. I could not resist making the slightest of diversions to explore further. Approaching one huge mass of rock resting amazingly on the smallest of pedestals, Bess began to twitch uneasily beneath me. Then she snorted, snorted again, shying as a man jumped out into our path. He was dressed in an unfashionable snuff-brown coat.

'Know what this is called?' he shouted up at me, pointing to the rock. 'It's called the Idol Rock.'

'All very interesting, sir, but you are blocking our way.'

'But you're not an *idle* chap, are you?' he asked insolently. 'More a meddlesome chap is the way of it.'

'Do I know you?' I asked outraged.

Bess staggered back a pace. Her eyes rolled wild and white as the man drew out a pistol.

'No, but you are about to,' he hissed, waving the weapon above his head.

Two other men emerged from either side of the Idol Rock. One held a cudgel. I swung a hundred degrees in the saddle. I was in trouble. There was no one else about, no one else but these men to witness my end.

"My pen is my protection," I had told Dr Hutchinson, when he had offered me the loan of his French pistol. How I now rued that statement.

'Get down from the nag and tie your reins round that bush,' the original footpad in snuff-brown commanded. He had a slight lisp, making his words sound measured but all the more threatening for that. His confederates leered bad-teeth satisfaction. Things were not going well.

I did as he asked, looking from man to man. Did I recognise any of them? Could they be part of the same band of ne'er-do-wells that had attacked me in Mother Shipton's Cave? I could not be sure as my memory had failed me after being knocked insensible.

'Satchel,' he demanded.

Oh no, I thought.

He took my notebook from the satchel, flinging the satchel aside. He smiled as he read out the inscription on the notebook cover. 'Well, thank you so very much, Mr Felix Kendle. You'll not have any more need of this in Grub Street.'

'How do you know I am a correspondent?'

'Corr..es..pondent,' he drawled, trying to imitate my London accent. 'We know everything about you, squire. Where you go, who you see. Don't we boys?' His two accomplices nodded obediently like licking dogs. 'Now that looks a nice timepiece,' he said, pointing at my Millington.

Oh no, not again, I thought, with a terrible foreboding. At that moment I would have taken them all on if it had not been for the pistol.

'Who is most in need of a nice pocket watch, lads?' he asked the two other men. They both nodded again enthusiastically. 'Please be good enough to hand the watch over, Mr Felix Kendle.' Pistol man thrust his weapon into my throat, forcing my head back. I remembered the explosion from Omerod's gun as he felled that first grouse. I feared this footpad was about to blow my head off. Reluctantly I was forced to give him my pocket watch from Bella, lose my most sentimental possession once more. 'Any rings?' he demanded.

I shook my head. 'I am not married.'

'Take off your gloves.' I did as he bid. He snatched my leather gloves as I stretched out the ringless fingers of my left hand. He slapped the hand hard with my own gloves, like a schoolmaster punishing a child, before he set about beating my face with them. 'Next time, Mr Busybody Correspondent, you will not escape with your life. Turn about, turn away,' he snarled.

My legs turned to jelly. Both my hands were shaking. Bess began to paw the ground sensing my distress. By the time I dared to look back the three men had vanished.

I picked up my discarded gloves and satchel – obviously these men had no interest in leather. But how had they known I would come by the tors? Had they been following me throughout the weekend or had someone alerted them to my route? – a passing farmer perhaps? Could one of the shooters have betrayed me? Apologetically, I freed Bess from her restraining bush. This intimate encounter with my assailants had been far worse than being knocked out in Mother Shipton's Cave. It had been a degrading experience.

Heaving myself into the saddle, tears of humiliation ran down my stinging cheeks. I felt violated.

* * * * *

'What on earth has happened to you?' asked the Royal Oak's landlady, already perfectly dressed for dinner in lavender-blue silk.

'My horse threw me,' I lied.

'I am surprised,' she tittered, 'that old lass seems incapable of throwing anybody or anything.'

'Well she threw me,' I replied, stubbornly sticking to my story.

'While you were away you had a visitor. A lady,' she winked.

'Who? Did she leave her name?'

'She did not have to as she is known to me.' I was sure the landlady was tantalising me now. In my present state I was in no humour for it.

'Janet Brown?' I sighed.

'The same.'

'Did she say if she would be calling again?'

'Tomorrow, sir. She said she would try again tomorrow.'

Back in the safety of my room, I felt too exhausted and upset to eat after the incident at Brimham. I decided to miss dinner and fast until morning. I looked across at my gloves and satchel on the table. Why couldn't the footpads have taken them instead of my pocket watch and notebook? The satchel particularly was of the finest Russian leather. My head sank in my hands, how could I have allowed myself to lose possession of Bella's pocket watch a second time.

Once I had collected myself, I walked across to the table and opened William Thornton's satchel as if willing my notebook to be there. Of course it was not, I had seen the footpad run off with it with my own eyes. I felt rather like John Milton must have done having written two acts of his tragedy, *Adam Unparadiz'd*, only to misplace them forever. With my recent Knaresborough notes gone everything written regarding Aram and his case must be subject to memory.

With mild curiosity, I reached my hand down inside a pouch in the satchel's lining that I had somehow overlooked earlier. To my astonishment my fingers fixed on paper – sheets of thin explosive paper.

The King – against – Houseman
The Examination of Richard Houseman of Knaresborough Flax Dresser

Within the margin were various notes, one referred to *Observations on the Prisoner's examination – M. Pickersgill*. The notes were written in a clear and educated hand and appeared to be Houseman's solicitor's instructions on how best for counsel to conduct his case in court. I could not conceive how William Thornton had come by this original document but obviously, for some reason, he had decided to put it my way.

I began checking the document with my copy of Houseman's original statements made to Thornton. The document contained a transcript of the flax-dresser's second examination, which took place following his arrest when his path accidently crossed with the Justice of the Peace's in York. According to his conductors, Houseman showed he was concerned in the murder as far back as the village of Green Hammerton, while under escort to York's Castle prison. Having been told that Mr Thornton happened to be passing by on Micklegate, Houseman was desirous that he might be called into a house and in his presence make a more considered confession.

Houseman said that it was true that Daniel Clark was murdered by Eugene Aram late of Knaresborough. He now gives a more accurate date of Friday morning the 8th February, 1744 (1745 by the new calendar). He admitted he, along with Clark, was at Aram's house in the early hours of that morning. In this meandering laboured confession Houseman reveals that he went out of the house before Aram and Clark, went up the street before them, until they "called to him to go a little way with them and he accordingly went with them to a place called Saint Robert's Cave near Grimble Bridge". He said "Aram and Clark stopped a little and then he saw Aram strike him (Clark) several times over the breast and head and saw him fall as if he was dead". At this Houseman said he came away. He did not know if Aram used a weapon or not, nor did he know what he did with Clark's body but believed he left it in the cave mouth. Fearful for his own life, Houseman got to the bridge end and saw Aram coming out of the cave with a bundle in his hand. (It was an impossibility to see anything of the cave from

Grimble Bridge, let alone a bundle in a man's hand, as I had already proved. Even Houseman's legal representative notes in the margin: *These passages seem inconsistent and in some sort to contradict each other.*) Houseman went on to say he "made the best of his way to the town without joining Aram again or seeing him again till the next day and from that time till this he never had any private discourse with him".

Mr Pickersgill had to acknowledge that Houseman was too expressive regarding his knowledge of this melancholy affair. He instructed counsel that they would counter this with the excuse that *this honest man* made the statement while under duress. *Fearful that the examination with other oral tradition connected with the case* might result in him being charged as a principal.

Anna Aram was next to come under Mr Pickersgill's scrutiny: *Aram's wife will be called to offer some strong circumstances against Houseman* but that *we shall assign reasons* for Houseman being in the company of her husband and Clark on the night of the murder (or murders). And if she alleges that Houseman and her husband later returned to the Church Lane cottage without Clark, we will point out that she did not actually see Houseman only heard him.

You'll please to ask her if Houseman and Clark were not very intimate friends and if they did not then talk about some leather viz. – that which was pledged by him to Houseman; if they did not go out together as friends; if she dare swear that she saw Houseman afterwards that night, ask her particularly if she has not said (for we will prove it upon her) that she never saw or knew any ill by Houseman in her life. And if Houseman had not always the character of a honest sober peaceable man.

The following paragraph is more telling: *perhaps several more will be called to prove Houseman walking along with them that night, these can only be asked in general as to Houseman's behaviour, character and conduct in life.*

Philip Coates next falls beneath the spyglass. *If one Coates who is a relation of the deceased should be called upon any account pray ask him if he knew Clark's handwriting and if he has a book wherein any concerns between him and Houseman are entered. Then call for the schedule of Clark's writing in my custody of the leather given into Houseman's hands for a pledge for some money and the note of hand in my possession of £20 by way of strengthening their intimacy in dealing together and showing the improbability of the man's having any design upon a life so dear to him. These Coates has owned to me to be of Clark's writing. Lastly if you find him not bloodthirsty, ask him Houseman's character as above and whether he thinks him capable of forming any such piece of wickedness.*

There was another margin note *As to Aram's wife* – a note that was about to make my jaw drop. *I had almost forgot to observe provided anything extraordinary against Houseman arise from her testimony. If she knew all that so long since why she did not divulge it heretofore. She knows her husband to be a most wicked treacherous man and is not unacquainted with his having got her own daughter with child and knows his atheistical principles.*

I had been slow. Here it was, Abraham Spence's hint of depravity made against his brother-in-law corroborated in black and white by an attorney-at-law.

Mr Pickersgill goes on to mention a Mr Ward, a saddler. He says Houseman returned some whips to Ward, previously procured by Clark, and accidently wrapped up in some leather which had been pledged by Clark to Houseman for money owed. *This Ward himself will tell you and at the same time will give Houseman his due character and that he does not think him from his behaviour and conduct in life capable of entering into so wicked a scene. That he believes him driven into it unwittingly.*

There is another margin note which appears to be written by a different hurried hand: *Prisoners Defence – To prove the occasion of his being at the house the night before this* (illegible) *was viz. Clark's delivering.*

A child could see Houseman was obviously lying during his examinations. At Aram's trial I remembered wondering how Houseman had got away with it. After reading Pickersgill's proposal for a defence that question had an even greater sting to it. At best his defence could be described as weak. But who had paid for all this legal counsel? Aram, the schoolteacher, could not afford to be represented. He had been forced to conduct his own defence. So how had Houseman, a poor flax-dresser, met such weighty court costs? Had Francis Iles paid for Houseman's defence? Iles by 1759 was certainly prosperous enough to be able to afford it, but why should he? It was Aram and Terry who had deposed against him not Houseman. Perhaps he felt poor old Dickey could be more easily bought, and his cooperation would counter any allegations made against him by the other two men. Now, more than ever, I was sure Richard Houseman was as much a participant in the death of Daniel Clark as Aram himself.

* * * * *

I had a dream that I was an invisible presence at Aram's Church Lane breakfast table. I saw it all.

Like any patient gardener, he had watched his eldest daughter blossom from child to woman. Champing over his miserable crust and cheese, he became increasingly aware of the developing Sally's thrusting bodice opposite. He swore that chest of hers grew bigger by the day. Reluctantly his attention would be arrested by some facile comment from his scraggy overworked wife – who had recently expanded into pie-making – or he would be diverted by the food-filled, open-mouthed eating habits of other members of their rampageous brood. But his eyes always fell joyfully back to the reassurance of Sally's proud and growing breasts, the only good things to grace his morning table. Yes, and fight it as he might, the germ of desire started to quiver in his soul. He wanted to make those breasts his – hold them in his hands – feel the weight of them again.

'Is it not time you bought a respectable dress for Sally for she's almost outgrown that one?' he snapped irritably to the hovering Anna, pointing at the now rising and falling bosom of their indignant daughter.

He had tried hard to put temptation behind him. But what had he to replace it? – the flat chested hirsute Anna and her vulgar ways? He was convinced that Anna was to blame in part for the unnatural rise in his loins whenever he looked Sally's way. For all Anna's overt sexuality, she never once satisfied him in a deeper sense, and if a woman failed to give her man complete satisfaction then surely she shared some responsibility for any of his ensuing inappropriate feelings.

CHAPTER SEVENTEEN

I had only just finished attending to my toilet the next morning when there was a light knock on my door. Janet Brown stood in the passageway, her brow furrowed with anxiety.

'Come in, come in,' I bid her.

'Thank goodness, you are unharmed,' she said.

'"Unharmed", why should I be anything else?'

'The word in the street is that unless you quit Knaresborough you will leave in a coffin.'

'Is it really?'

'Yes,' she sighed. 'Perhaps it is no more than hearsay but folk are saying you have upset someone in authority and he wants you gone.'

'I can believe that. Yesterday, at Brimham Crags, I was waylaid by footpads. They took my notebook and pocket watch.'

'Not your beautiful watch again?' exclaimed Janet.

'Yes, the Millington you were wrongly accused of stealing. It had great sentimental value.'

'Is she very beautiful, Bella, the lady who gave it to you?'

'How do you know about Bella?'

'You left the watch on your bedside table at the Bell once or twice. I could not help noticing the inscription on the back while dusting.' Janet looked to the floor, adding, 'But I would never have dreamt of taking it.'

'No, I am sure you wouldn't. And no matter, Bella is dead,' I sighed.

'I am so sorry,' said Janet, reaching for my hand. 'Whatever must you think of me. I must also apologise for not thanking you earlier for obtaining the landlord's note of reference. Servant jobs are not easy to come by in this part of the world and I have been well-occupied trying to feed myself and the boy.'

'Why not come and work for me in London?' I gave the hand on mine a restrained peck.

'I couldn't possibly …' Janet looked at the hand I had kissed in disbelief.

'Consider it at least.'

'Thank you, sir, I will.'

'Now tell me who is this person of authority who keeps sending out his flunkies to chastise me?'

'Do not make light of it. I am deeply afraid for you. This man is capable of doing anything to safeguard his reputation.'

'Murder, are we talking of murder here?'

* * * * *

Thomas Hutchinson and Richard Collins were already waiting at a table in the bar come dining room of the Royal Oak that Tuesday evening. It was the 4th September and still I remained in the North. My editor had written to say he was growing impatient – where was my report on the aftermath of the Aram trial? With my notebook stolen and feeling this story was far from over, Mr Richard Cave would have to be patient and wait a little longer.

Hutchinson and Collins were arguing just as I had left them a few days ago. Though this time it was the colonial war between France, Spain and ourselves that was the cause of hostile debate. Hutchinson, still wrapped up in a cloak, was pushing back his bush wig in annoyance. Collins' shoulders were frosted with powder as he flicked the rolls above his ears, his pigeon-winged toupee dishevelled through agitation. What a couple of popinjays my companions were that evening, I could hardly contain my amusement.

'No, no, you are wrong there, Thomas. I have faith that Wolfe will eventuallỳ take Quebec,' said Collins.

'He might die trying and take many English lives with him,' snorted Hutchinson.

'Good evening gentlemen,' I interrupted. 'Now what are you drinking?'

Unbelievably, young grouse was on the menu that night. I was not sure I could face the dish after witnessing the gunning down of the species. But following my first tentative bite I realised the bird was certainly juvenile and delicate in flavour, and the bottle of claret that the doctor ordered was fine enough to help anything down.

'Whatever you think about the French, Richard, they know how to make good wine,' taunted Hutchinson.

Collins shook his head. Unwilling to be provoked as more powder fluttered down onto his coat.

I wondered if I should tell them about my confrontation with the footpads. I decided against it, asking Collins instead if he could arrange a meeting for me with Francis Iles.

He could not. I had word from him before breakfast the following morning that Iles refused to meet me. Now why was that? Nevertheless, a more positive sun shone through my window – shone across the square – that midweek Wednesday. Although I had been a fortnight in Knaresborough and still had failed to find a truth that satisfied me, my soul was filled with warm thoughts of Janet Brown.

* * * * *

'Mr Kendle, I see you will not take no for answer.'

'You have every reason to draw that conclusion, sir.'

'Indeed,' smiled Iles. But his eyes did not smile, his eyes looked as if they never smiled.

It had not been difficult to find his drapery business. There was not a person in Knaresborough who did not know Mr Iles' premises. Beyond the counter, I could see two or three men working in the backroom. They appeared to be cutting lengths of cloth with scissors as big as shears. One I recognised though he was minus his unfashionable snuff-brown coat. Today Iles' man sported brick-red. He looked up at me, looked to his boss – the scissors a threat.

'That linen has to be ready for the client before noon,' grumbled Iles. Iles' man resumed his snip-snipping. 'So what can I do for you, Mr Kendle?'

'I am curious, sir, why both Eugene Aram and Henry Terry in their original depositions accused you of availing yourself of much of your neighbours' stolen property.'

'Nonsense. I was as much a victim of the fraud as the next man.'

'I have spoken to Abraham Spence up the dale. He maintains it was you who possessed yourself of much of the plunder.'

'Well, he would wouldn't he. He is a criminal and the brother-in-law of a convicted murderer.'

'And Henry Terry?'

'Puh! His brother, Robert, on How Hill was the primary fence for the silver plate. Heard he shipped and sold it over the Scottish border.'

'You seem to know a lot about these illegal transactions, Mr Iles. Perhaps you could tell me who was the real mastermind behind the scheme to defraud the good people of Knaresborough? Wickedness, that resulted in the death of Daniel Clark and a Jewish pedlar.'

'Are you Jewish yourself, Mr Kendle?'

'What if I am?'

'If you are then that is a good reason for your interest.'

'I am a writer and interested in finding the truth.'

'But surely according to law the truth is hanging up there on the edge of Knaresborough Forest.'

'You know as well as I do, Mr Iles, that is only part of the truth.'

'Is it really?'

'Yes, other matters have come to light. Matters that are in here,' I said, knocking a forefinger against my skull. 'Matters I did not risk to my notebook.'

'Fearing libel, no doubt.'

'Is that how you kept your name out of the proceedings, Iles, with threats? Are you the sort of man who finds weaknesses in the poor souls around him and waits for the time to pounce and exploit them?'

'I warn you, Kendle, if you print one word against me I *will* sue you and your magazine for a great amount of money.'

'Is that how you kept your name out of the newspapers back in '45?'

'Conjecture, supposition, Kendle.'

'Not so. I have a document that confirms that it was you who paid Houseman's legal fees.'

'What document?' scoffed Iles.

'Do you deny it?'

'What document?' persisted Iles; a quaver to his voice.

'Fees owed to a Mr Pickersgill.'

'Kendle, I am warning you …' His voice trailed away.

'I wonder what your standing will be with the townsfolk of Knaresborough when that piece of information comes to their notice.'

Iles fell speechless. 'What do you want?' he finally choked.

'The return of my Millington pocket watch. Then and only then might I be prepared to forget what I've learnt,' I replied; guessing my notebook was already ash.

'And this alleged incriminating document you speak of,' enquired Iles.

'I will destroy it. I will destroy it in front of your man.'

'Seymour,' Iles bellowed into the backroom. Seymour slid forward in his brick-red coat. 'Do you think you might be able to help Mr Kendle here locate his missing pocket watch?'

The surly bruiser nodded his cooperation.

'Now where can we find you, Mr Kendle?' asked Iles.

'The Royal Oak. Surely you know that already, sir.'

Iles did not respond to this, saying instead, 'I trust once your watch is restored there will no longer be any need for your residency at the Oak.'

'You have the word of a gentleman, Iles. A gentleman like yourself.'

I bowed farewell. I had no intention of keeping any promise to a man like Francis Iles. I had no written link to him and Houseman's defence – it had all been bluff and guesswork but it had paid off.

* * * * *

The weather had turned that afternoon – a deluge, worthy of the ark, ran down the streets outside.

I sat by the fire in my room at the Royal Oak engrossed in the second volume of *The Adventures of Roderick Random*. I loved the bawdy earthiness of Tobias Smollett, enjoyed losing myself in his adventurous world for an hour or two. Tobias was the boldest writer of our age. His honesty in reviews and suchlike carried its own perils. He was forever in hot water with someone or other. Originally a medical man like Thomas Hutchinson – indeed I did not find the two men dissimilar – many is the time I have had the pleasure of sharing his company in the London coffee-houses of Pall Mall.

Just as I was revelling in my acquaintanceship with the author of this pocket edition that travelled with me everywhere, there was a knock on the door.

Seymour. He strode into my room in a red blur of skirted coat.

'Found at Brimham Crags,' he said. 'You must have dropped it.' He chose not to place the watch directly into my hand but placed it on the nearby table.

'Indeed, I must have. How lax of me. Just as careless as when I hit my head and fell down at the Dropping Well.'

Seymour did not respond to the goad.

'And the document that Mr Iles said you will burn?' he enquired. Placing his hand over the Millington – the Millington that was not yet mine.

'Why, here it is,' I said, taking up the bill purporting to be Pickersgill's legal costs for the defence of Houseman.

Lifting his hand from the watch, Seymour took the document from me and examined it carefully. The forgery, written in my own disguised hand, seemed to pass muster. He nodded and I threw "Mr Pickersgill's bill" into the fire.

'I hope you enjoyed your expedition with Mr Hiram Omerod's shooters, sir,' he sneered.

'Was it one of his men who alerted you to waylay me at Brimham?' I asked, with little hope of a satisfactory answer.

'Mr Iles has friends everywhere, some are highly placed respectable gentlemen.'

'I realise that.'

'You will have no need to remain with us here in Knaresborough much longer now your watch is returned,' lisped Seymour.

'Perhaps a day, two at most.'

'Good, good,' he said. 'No hard feelings, I hope.' He stuck his hand out. I refused to shake it. Withdrawing his grimy nails into frayed turned back cuff, he turned away and in a stride was gone.

Within seconds there was another knock on the door. My heart dropped a beat. With a good deal of trepidation I reached for the doorknob. Had Seymour returned? Had he decided on a parting gift? – a punching fist perhaps.

'Janet,' I gasped. I had never been so happy to see a familiar friendly face, indeed an extremely lovely face at that. 'Come in. Come in.'

Janet stared at my watch on the table, her eyes wide with disbelief.

'How?' she asked.

'The man you must have just passed on the stairway delivered it.'

'Oh, him,' she said. 'He's one of Iles' cut-throats.'

'I think he certainly would have liked to cut mine.'

'I have already warned you, sir, you must keep away from Iles and those men of his.' Janet's brow ruckled with concern.

'It is more they who have sought my company than I theirs.'

'They fear you.'

'Why?'

'You know perfectly well why. They are afraid that you already know enough to expose their master. Here, a present,' she said, pushing a new leather-bound notebook into my hand like a shy child. 'It will come in for all those big cases you will write about in London.'

'So, you want me gone too.'

'No, sir, I do not. I want you to live.'

'Well, I cannot possibly accept this,' I told her, offering the notebook back. 'How on earth could you afford it? A notebook of this quality must be worth a month's wages.'

'That's just it,' she said smiling. 'I've been given a job at the Crown and the customers there seem to like me and tip generously.'

'I bet they do.' I said this more emphatically than I had intended.

Janet looked away, looked out of the window. An embarrassed silence ensued.

'Please, sir, I wish you wouldn't stare at me like that,' she said, now directly meeting my gaze.

'Like what?'

'With such intensity.'

'Janet, in a few days I will have to leave for London.'

'Yes, I expect you will.'

'Do you like me at all?'

'Of course.' A flicker of encouragement flashed in her dark eyes.

'Please come with me, you and your boy. Knaresborough is no place in which to bring up a child.'

'A bastard child, you mean?' Encouragement disappeared like the moon behind dark historical clouds of pain.

'No, that is not what I meant.'

'Was Bella the love of your life, sir?'

'You seem very concerned about my relationship with Bella.'

'That is not an answer.'

'I will not say she is the only woman I am capable of loving, though I loved her.'

'Well, my boy's father meant everything to me.'

'What was his name?'

'Simon … Simon Ruddleston.'

'But he did not marry you.'

'He was far above my station. His family would never have accepted …' She faltered. 'A Jewess.'

'With time we can both learn to forget.'

'I hope you are right because every time I look into my boy's face I see Simon staring back at me.'

'How did you meet?'

'I was in service at a big house not far from here. Simon's people owned a quarry across the Riding. He came to sell stone for a private chapel my master wished to build in his grounds.'

'And it happened.'

'Yes, it happened. When they …' She gave a deep sigh and cleared her throat. 'When Simon's family found out that he wanted to marry a servant girl, they sent him away to the Americas. He vowed that once he had made his fortune, he would return for me. Then I learnt from a friend, who had accompanied him there, that he died only weeks after landing. The yellow fever took him just before his twentieth birthday. He never knew about our forthcoming son. But of course as soon as it became apparent to my employers that I was with child, I lost my position.'

'I'm sorry,' I said, reaching to touch her arm.

'I'll not make the same mistake again,' she said, jerking away.

'I am not asking you to,' I replied with some annoyance.

'What are you asking then?'

'I would like you to keep house for me in Clerkenwell, London. I will see your boy is educated.'

'William, he's called William.'

'I will see William is well-educated then. London prices, I will double anything you might make at the Crown.'

'But why? Why should you do this for us?'

A good question – I paused for a second. *She that hath been once beguiled by some other ought to keep herself well from the same.*

'Because I have fallen in love with you,' I finally admitted.

'I have no interest in being a city gentleman's mistress.' Her face puckered in distaste. She appeared not to have heard me.

'I love you,' I repeated.

'Stop! We would be a burden to you. You do not know me.'

'I know more about you than most men know about their wives.'

'"Wives?"' she repeated in bewilderment.

'Yes, wives, wife. I know that you are honest, compassionate and able to survive whatever hardships life throws at you. I know that you have an innate intelligence and an integrity that cannot be bought.'

'You are confusing me,' she said. The blush subtle under her dark skin.

'Janet Brown, will you do me the honour of being my wife?'

'My real name, my Hebrew name is Jael pronounced Ya'el.'

'Then that is what I will call you.'

'No, no,' she laughed. 'I prefer Janet.'

I pulled her gently towards me and I knew that the warmth generated there could not lie. I kissed her and it was no longer a flicker of moonlight but the sun burning there in her eyes.

When Janet finally left, my thoughts returned to my investigation of that extinguished life haunting me. Had it ever been like that for Aram with Anna Spence? Had it been gentle and tender or was he incapable of warmth. Had he once loved Anna as he had come to love his daughter Sally. How had Aram felt with Anna that first time.

* * * * *

Dawn broke, Saturday came. Looking out of his small chamber window across the knotted gardens of Gouthwaite Hall, Aram thought of how his family circumstances had changed. How as a respected professional man, he was now afforded a room in this great house where his poor dead mother once worked as a maid. Faith met and married his father here. It was plain to see that there had once been order down there in the gardens, but now borders were no longer clear and grasses split open the paving stones along the walks. His father – a perfectionist – would be very distressed to see the neglect since the previous Sir Thomas' time.

The new day smelt well enough to Aram despite the usual incessant Nidderdale dampness wetting the air. He leaned forward, his elbows resting on the window-sill, a slow smile of pleasure brightening his face: the final snowdrops of the season had appeared on the small lawn directly beneath, hanging white tears on lashes of grass. And his spirits were lifted even higher when he saw from a blue break in the sky that there was every chance the early morning hours would give way to a lovely March day.

It was a good mile from the Spences' cottage to the village of Stean and the track underfoot stony. Showing off, Isaac Spence and Aram strolled arrogantly ahead of the girls.

Aram's prediction had been correct: the day was indeed a grand one. The whole party had an air of cheer about it: the girls were happy because their mothers had given them the rare freedom from the usual daily drudgery; Isaac was happy because he found he was able to match Aram stride for stride; Aram was happy because the day was indeed fine and he had decided to come rather than sit brooding over his studies.

The track became steeper and the men waited for the girls to catch up for the final ascent to Stean village. Aram kept the lead now with young Rebecca Spence at his side; Isaac followed with his fiancée Jane Peart and his sister Anna, one girl on each arm.

'A country gentleman if ever I did see one,' Aram heard Jane snigger. Drunken-slow the three behind stumbled and giggled after the more intense Aram and his companion ahead.

'Was Abraham unable to join us today?' Aram decided to address the taciturn Rebecca.

'One of Uncle's bulls is poorly.'

'What is exactly wrong with the bull?'

'Dying,' replied Rebecca, with a hint of annoyance at having to elucidate further.

Isaac had already informed Aram that the multitudinous Spence family farmed much of the acreage of Upper Nidderdale and that now both he and Abraham had decided to follow suit. But times were hard for all the farming families in the dale and the loss of a good breeding bull before its time could prove to be disastrous.

'How old are you, Rebecca?' Aram asked her.

'Seventeen,' she said, still without smiling.

Seventeen … how Aram would have smiled if he had only been seventeen.

They started to climb towards the top of the gorge hacked out by How Stean Beck. Wood smoke curled after them from valley chimneys. Springs bubbled up in the fields on either side of them. They were as impressed as any fine party might be walking through a rich man's garden spouting artificial fountains.

And all the while the beck gurgled and crashed down the mossy greenness – soft water grazing the hard land making it smooth. And Aram thought of Anna behind: Anna dressed in her green Sunday best; Anna's smooth breasts. And his throat went dry, and he stooped to his knees where the water was dammed and eddied – a whirlpool like his emotions – and he saw desire reflected back at him, and he slaked his thirst until the others caught them up.

Coming to one particularly dramatic fall, they decided to sit and take a little repast there. Anna opened out the rush basket of food she had prepared and Isaac had gallantly carried for the last mile. Speechless, between mouthfuls of bread and chicken wings, they watched the hypnotic cascade – down and down to a place of unseen fate, much like their own.

Jane Peart looked down on her scouring-raw hands, knowing her lot would be eased by marriage to the adoring Isaac. Her light-blue Norse eyes lifted flirtatiously to Isaac. She sucked and played on his brown serious gaze because she knew he would succeed in farming, in life. Simpering she leapt to her feet, her skirts flouncing about her, and ran to hide provocatively in a thicket knowing Isaac would follow.

Aram and Anna became stiff and uncomfortable at the concealed pairing they sensed was going on behind them. There was the occasional rustle of leaves – or was it fabric? – coming from the trees. Rebecca, running a straw between her teeth, was so locked in her own reveries she appeared to be unaware of Jane's and her brother's absence.

'Be so good as to fill this from the stream down there, Rebecca love.' Anna handed her dreaming sister an empty jug.

This left Aram more confused than ever: surely sending Rebecca off like that could only add to their mutual disquiet. He cleared his throat.

'Abraham is attending a sick bull, Rebecca was telling me.' A bland enough opening he thought.

A whimper from the foliage at their backs.

Anna gave Aram a shy little nod; her only gesture towards overriding the event in the trees.

Moans and groans now came from behind them.

And surprisingly with them, Anna's own coyness seemed to evaporate – a mocking little smile pursed her lips – she was reproaching Aram for his modesty.

'I …' he stopped. He felt a warm pressure on his knee – Anna's hand on his knee – a shuddering sigh next from the trees.

'See, Mr Aram, youth is soon spent,' laughed Anna, tossing back her head.

Rebecca returned with the jug of water. Adjusting their clothes, Jane and Isaac reappeared. Anna had called Aram's bluff.

Spring was moving fast into summer and although the sky was heavy with clouds the air was muggy-warm the next time he asked Miss Spence to join him on a walk. This time they were alone.

It cost him little to abandon his cloak for a seat. She smiled up at him. Her dress – the same green dress as before – vivid against the cloak's blackness. He hesitated, unable to decide what to do next. He thought her some exotic bird he would like to wrap up and take away.

'Stop fidgeting and come and join me here,' she said, patting the cloak. There it was – the subtle change in her again – something more knowing and confident.

He flushed, taken aback as he had been at How Stean Beck. A curtain had gone up on real life and Anna Spence was playing herself once more. His long ungainly legs collapsed beneath him as he sank to the cloak. Anna looked at the respectable space between them as if it was an insult. He said how much he admired the vista over Masey Edge towards Lofthouse. Did she not agree that it was beautiful? She said nothing. He turned to look at her. She was not smiling.

'Why art tha so nervous, Mr Aram?' she asked.

He did not correct her on her address or assumption. Watching the white knuckles of his clenched fist as if his life depended on it, he suddenly appreciated an increase in body-heat. The space between them was no more, and he knew it was not of his doing. He kept pretending to admire the view; kept looking ahead, down, anywhere away from her searching eyes.

'Don't be so distracted, my dear.' Her coaxing voice was as soothing as her body was close. Her hand began to caress his thigh, the inside of his thigh. Her touch was butterfly-light, gliding and playing its own game.

He shuddered with want. The sensations came from a source outside himself. He sighed out loud. He was not really sure he liked this arousal manufactured by another's hands and out of his control.

'Please, Miss Spence … Anna, I mean, you must stop … stop this, p … please.' How ridiculous he sounded: a man in his late twenties reduced to a stuttering wreck by a mere country woman. But it had nearly all gone so terribly wrong before, during his final transaction with the boyish whore in Old Drury. She had been menstruating and she hadn't told him. The fastidious Aram had been traumatised by the bloody rag flung to the ground. Since then he had kept himself away from it – clean – away from the risk of contamination.

Anna appeared not to hear him – heed the warning in his voice – he was losing control and darkness was closing in.

'Please.' He made a last desperate appeal.

She stopped and he, blinking, looked her fully in the eyes for the first time.

Bewitched – this vulgar creature was bewitching him. Anna adult-locked her mouth to his – her hands setting about their wicked work again – her will became his power.

His hands pressed and cajoled the cushioned breasts, plunged deep between her bloomerless thighs. He could not stop himself.

You are not the first, nor could he rid himself of the insinuation.

He hated the smell of sex – there was something impure about a womanly body – he hated himself for doing what he was doing but it had been so long.

You are not the first, repeated the imaginary voice.

A scream and then silence, silence on Cockle Hill.

Then he took Anna Spence a second time, and a second time she screamed but did not bleed. How he wanted her to bleed as he spiritually bled – taste her blood – not waste blood but virgin blood.

* * * * *

Before we left Knaresborough I knew for my own peace of mind that I would be forced to run the gauntlet of Richard Houseman's fluttering raven again – his feathered sentry – alerting his master to all unwelcomed visitors, and for the heckler I was sure all visitors were unwelcomed. And there I found the man himself – the only living witness to what actually happened in St Robert's Cave some fourteen years before. Houseman was skulking amongst his piles of flax almost in exactly the same position as I had left him days before.

'What do you want?' he grunted.

'I have one or two more questions for you. One or two final pieces to put into place.'

'Thought you weren't one to give up easily,' he smirked.

'Your friend Iles acknowledged as much about me yesterday.'

'Iles, what business had you with him?' The same look of alarm crossed Houseman's face as it had done before at the mention of the linen draper's name.

'Why did you give such damning evidence against your one time friend, Eugene Aram, particularly during your second examination with William Thornton?'

'I thought he was safely away. I didn't think they would catch up with him.'

'When the constables were dispatched to Lynn to arrest him, was it you who sent that intercepted note saying "Fly for your life, you are pursued"?'

'I cannot say who sent that note.'

'Cannot or will not?' I asked. Houseman shook his head. 'Did you both intend to murder Clark?'

'I did nothing, it was Aram.'

'Why did Aram murder Clark?'

'Dan began taunting him.'

'Taunting him about what?'

'You can't uphold your marriage vows, that sort of thing. Eugene believed that he was thick with his wife.'

'"Thick"?'

'He believed Anna was cuckolding him with poor pock-broken Dan.'

'Did you know this to be true?'

'I can't say,' Houseman shrugged. 'But Eugene had little cause to call the kettle black.'

'What do you mean?'

Houseman hesitated, looked uncomfortable. 'I mean he had his own peculiar tastes. Anyone who dresses a young lad up in lasses' apparel and pays court to him, and worse, isn't entirely manly.'

'But wasn't that just to make his wife jealous?'

'Who told you that,' sneered Houseman.

'Tell me, what was the last thing Clark said to Aram before he hit him?'

Again Houseman hesitated, shuffling from one foot to the other.

'You prefer your daughter in bed to your wife,' he finally blurted out; his eyes seeking the ground as if the shame was his.

But could I believe him? Could I believe anything this man said?

'Mr Houseman,' I finally found my voice, 'to have heard Clark's allegation you can't have been any distance from the murder in Saint Robert's Cave.'

'So, what are you going to do about it, Mister?'

'Write about it.'

Houseman's shoulders rounded more, appeared bowed beneath some great weight. 'Then I will sue you for libel,' he told me.

'You too.'

'How do you mean?'

'Again, your friend Mr Iles threatened me with the same.'

'Iles is friend to no man,' said Houseman, swiping at the line of sweat that had formed above his top lip.

'If that is true, who paid your legal fees, Mr Houseman?'

'Now, that would be telling.'

'Who paid for your solicitor and counsel?' I persisted. All colour drained from Houseman's face and he looked to the ground again, a habit with him.

'Please leave,' he finally mumbled. 'And leave alone.'

'What are you talking about?'

'That new barmaid working at the Crown, there's gossip abroad that you might be taking her with you.'

'Word is not long getting about Knaresborough, is it? But what of it?'

'It's best to leave without her, Iles takes a special if distant interest in that Brown lass.'

'Does he indeed. He seems to be a man who takes a distant interest in everything.'

'You can take this as a piece of friendly warning or not,' snapped Houseman. 'It's up to you.'

'What interest could a middle-aged man like Iles have in Janet Brown?' I asked, believing I already knew the answer. Houseman's wig shook from side to side. He was like a horse refusing a fence. I could see I would get no more out of him.

Whether it was the physically stronger Dickey Houseman or effete Eugene Aram who struck the fatal blows that brought down both Daniel Clark and the forgotten Jew, on that snowy February night in 1745, would be open to conjecture for years to come. Did it matter? Both were accomplices in these horrendous crimes. Although I strongly suspected that someone regarded as their social superior had been above them pulling their strings – someone deeply implicated but who, like Houseman, walked free.

The bird squawked its farewell, I was put in mind of Shakespeare's famous words *the raven chides blackness*. Houseman was truly in a dark place.

* * * * *

Thomas Hutchinson offered to ride Bess back to her stable in Harrogate for me. Janet, William and I were to take a carrier to York and then catch the stagecoach outside the Black Swan in Coney Street. Young William was excited by the prospect of a long journey to London, which should take about four days in clement weather. Despite all the threats and unpleasantness, Knaresborough was the town in which Janet and I met, and though looking forward to a happy future together our leaving would be flavoured with a dash of regret.

I never mentioned my conversation with Houseman to Janet regarding Francis Iles. My Jewish bride to be – although not practising, Jewish she truly was through her maternal line – had enough to do packing her trunk without any further emotional distraction. Her mother was long since dead. She had no kin but William, so her leave taking was free of complication or so I thought.

Thomas Hutchinson and Richard Collins hugged us all warmly before we mounted the carriage outside the Crown on that cool Saturday morning. True friends, I acknowledged. Had anyone come to hug Eugene Aram on his day of departure, I wondered. It was then that I saw Francis Iles standing in his shop doorway. He half raised his hand in acknowledgement before dropping it to his side. He was letting us go.

CHAPTER EIGHTEEN

After Clark's disappearance, after his first taste of imprisonment, Aram had secured a teaching post in London through letters and good references from some of his old and influential friends who were ignorant of his troubles in Knaresborough. On the long journey south he was happy to stop at Nottingham and spend a few respite days with some dull and undemanding relatives. April, 1745, found him back in the commercial hunting ground of his youth. He began teaching both Latin and writing in Piccadilly for the Reverend Mr Painblanc. In return, along with a salary, Mr Painblanc taught him the French language, about France and more importantly perhaps about the French themselves. Aram toyed with the idea that if things became too difficult for him, he would cross the water to lose himself in the land of England's historical enemy. He felt something of an outcast in his own country anyway.

But that day never came.

He began learning other languages, ancient languages, and slowly started making friends with men who shared his interests. Aram was smiling: Knaresborough felt more than two hundred miles away now things were going so well. Unlike the days of his youth, he had money to spend from his share of the booty and could afford to dress in the manner of a gentleman. In London he had time to himself to read Turneforte, Ray, Miller and Linnaeus, and as of old he relished this protected time.

A lone wolf skirting the flock – seldom in need of other people's company – made him increasingly more attractive and desirable to ecclesiastical society.

'Tell me, Eugenius, the Reverend Painblanc says you are about to embark on the study of Arabic and the Chaldee?' asked a senior cleric one evening over an oyster supper. Aram gave a polite but bored nod of confirmation: unlike these men he preferred to educate himself rather than to talk about it. 'Well,' continued the cleric, draining his oyster in one, 'I'll be only too pleased to lend my Erpenius and Chapelhow to assist you. How about supper with me next Wednesday say?'

Although the books they lent him were useful, the dinners and suppers became tedious and endless. In the interests of peace, solitude and a rise in salary, he next went to Hays in the capacity of writing-master to a gentlewoman there. Once he had happily taught this good lady and her family the rudiments of a good writing hand, he moved on to the household of another reverend gentleman. He continued here for about another three to four years – still enjoying the civilized manners and landscape of the south of England to the harsh realities of his native Yorkshire.

He found great pleasure and freedom dabbling among the exotic plants in the Botanic Gardens at Chelsea. On many occasions he was accompanied to the Gardens by one of his few true friends, a man who could rival both his passion and expertise in the study of flora. The Reverend Anthony Hinton would later robustly defend him against all his critics with the memorable words that "such was Eugene's nature, he would carefully avoid a worm that might chance in his path" (let alone kill a man).

During his period of exile everyone failed to grasp the true mettle of Aram, perhaps he even did himself: he could trace pleasure through a thousand fields whereas he could find little in his fellow man.

Eventually his command of the pen gained him employment in the City transcribing the Acts of Parliament to be registered in Chancery. His life was about to take fire.

* * * * *

Janet and I are several years happily married and living in a spacious London town house just off Red Lion Square, but a stone's throw from Westminster where Aram worked. We have two children of our own, Simon and Bella, and so much love we feel able to embrace our ghosts. William is doing well as a scholar at the nearby St. Paul's School, and I have taught Janet to read. A quick and receptive pupil, my wife's poetry reading evenings have become popular with our friends.

Through the most roundabout circumstances I was again reminded of Aram, reminded that I had done nothing to put his story to rest for once and for all. With my mind cluttered with domestic issues, who should I meet one day walking down the Strand but my old friend Tobias Smollett whose work I had been reading back in Knaresborough. I had heard shortly after returning from the North that Smollett was to serve three months in the King's Bench Prison for questioning the courage of Admiral Sir Charles Knowles. Three years on and this was the first time I had set eyes upon him.

'Worst of it was, Kendle, not the bloody hundred pound fine but having to relinquish my editorship of *The Critical Review*.'

'A shame,' I sympathised.

'Shame indeed,' snarled Tobias.

'Why don't we give this new coffee house a try?' I suggested, pulling him into the Turk's Head.

As I supped on my coffee and Smollett supped on something stronger, he asked me what I had been doing these past years. I told him how I had met and married a Knaresborough lass and all about our children, and was surprised to learn that he shared my interest in Eugene Aram.

'He was the dupe, Kendle. He was sacrificed. Surely a man like him was entitled to a little mercy. Despite his lowly birth …'

'I don't think Aram would appreciate your referring to that, he spent most of his life trying to ennoble himself.'

'A pompous arse he might have been but the man was a genius.'

'You really think so?' I asked surprised.

'Course,' spluttered Tobias. 'Despite straitened circumstances he mastered mathematics, philosophy, learnt ancient and modern languages, and executed part of a Celtic dictionary that had he been able to finish it might have thrown essential light upon the origin and obscurities of European History.'

'I would never have believed you to be an Aram devotee, Tobias.'

'I am not saying he was innocent of dispatching the cobbler. I am saying he should not have been the only one to swing for it.'

'Well, yet another opinion.'

'Come, come, Kendle, don't say you haven't thought the same.'

'There are many aspects to this man's character some of which appear to be most unsavoury.'

'"Unsavoury", how unsavoury? I love unsavoury.' Tobias smacked his booze lubricated lips.

'Alas, I know you do as one of your regular readers,' I teased. 'Forgive me though, at present I have not enough evidence to divulge all regarding Aram's lack of conventional morality. Though I do agree with you, he was not the sole perpetrator of the crime imputed to him.'

'Before his own trial, did you know he nearly became embroiled in one down here?'

'Is that so?' This was news to me.

'Ever heard of a chap called William Guthrie?' Tobias asked.

'Wasn't he a writer on *The Gentleman's* along with Samuel Johnson?'

'A little before your time, Kendle. An interesting character though, Guthrie. A Scot, like me, he was politically pragmatic but essentially a Jacobite. He was accused of making a toast before witnesses to "the bonny prince across the water". Your friend Aram happened to be one of those witnesses. Whether some rival of Guthrie's had coerced Aram to depose against him, I do not know. Regrettably, I have heard rumours that it was a fellow writer who first brought the accusation against Guthrie for supporting the House of Stuart. However it happened, your Knaresborough man must have soon realised he could not afford to draw attention to himself in court while still under suspicion of murder.'

It was through Tobias Smollett, plain-spoken raconteur of our age, that I first got wind of the Guthrie affair. My old editor always told me to double check my sources: I confirmed the author's information regarding the deposition given to one William Hammond on 4th November, 1756, by Eugenius Aram of Air Street, Piccadilly, through State Papers – George II Bundle 136, No 18. I found no evidence that this sedition case ever came to trial but I suspected that Wee Willy Guthrie might have made some powerful enemies – as indeed Smollett had himself.

* * * * *

London was the political capital of Georgian England at a critical time and Eugene Aram was an inquisitive man. Despite knowing his father had hated them dearly, he was curious about the Jacobites – curious, too, when he found himself standing in a friend's parlour late one Wednesday evening, 20th October, 1756, holding a glass bearing the Jacobite flower.

'Here is a health to your love and mine, Prince Charles Stewart, on the other side of the water,' spluttered Guthrie, slobbering his sentiments and port wine freely all over the boards of his Putney home.

And there Aram was, fascinated, glad of a glass and only too pleased to keep his mouth shut for it.

'Here is a health to Prince Charles Stewart, the rightful King of Great Britain, and destruction to that usurper of his crown, King George, and all the Hanoverian family, particularly to that royal ass the Duke of Cumberland.' Guthrie raised his finger aloft like a wand to make it happen, to bring Bonny Prince Charlie bouncing back from over the sea. And all of this shouted at the top of Guthrie's voice; shouted before his poor wife; shouted before his two sons,

Henry and James, who looked somewhat abashed at their staggering father's rendering; and, more alarmingly, shouted before their humourless boarder, William Rawlins.

'A gentleman's been enquiring after ye, Mr Aram,' Mr Cranes, his landlord, had told him a few days later on his return from Chancery to his lodgings in Piccadilly.

'Oh, what was he like?'

Mr Cranes, a dealer in coals, shrugged. 'An aggressive little chap, trouble I'd say.'

Mr William Hammond JP called the very next evening to find his quarry at home. Mr Hammond wanted Aram to act as Judas against one William Guthrie of Putney.

'Too many papist bastards still abroad in London,' snarled the little man; his eyeglass slipping down the moist bridge of his nose.

'And who might I ask, sir, has informed on Guthrie?' Aram tried to keep his voice level, reasonable.

'I'm not at liberty to tell you that,' retorted puffed up Hammond belligerently.

'And if I refuse to do as you wish, sir?' tested Aram, sensing his arm was already figuratively pinned behind his back.

'Then you might find yourself under arrest for complicity,' warned Hammond. 'By the way, of what persuasion are you?'

Aram made no answer, only shuddered.

Under arrest again … Already a fugitive from Knaresborough, he had no choice but to sign the statement then and there betraying Guthrie. But here was a second dilemma for him: he would never be able to back up his Guthrie statement by risking an appearance in court against him.

Damn Guthrie. And damn his treacherous boarder, that rat Bill Rawlins. Aram had often noticed how Rawlins' lecherous appetite feasted upon Mrs Guthrie's plate. Wasn't the boarder's intention all too plain? – to warm his landlady's bed once he had got her husband out of the way. Why hadn't he anticipated the danger earlier, kept away? He could have remained hidden in the dull protective fabric of Westminster forever.

Unaware of Aram's own dubious background, position and decision to leave, Guthrie arrived first thing the following morning and thought fit to add his own ingredient of threat should Aram decide to stand and testify against him. His threat had something to do with emasculation, Aram later recalled.

'Not me, not me, you should turn your attention nearer home. What about Bill Rawlins?'

'William Rawlins,' sneered Guthrie. 'I doubt the State would take much heed of anything said by the likes of him.'

'And your wife?' Aram spurted out maliciously. He never saw a man's expression run such a gamut of emotions – fear to anger to crushing hurt – as Guthrie's did that day.

* * * * *

'On this bleak arena alone the Rosemary tree flourishes,' Thomas Weatherhead reassured Aram: Aram who had been forced to uproot himself yet again following the Guthrie affair back in London.

'Why, sir, the climate of this county is as hard as her flint churches.' The pedagogue shivered; his cup of tea chattered in its saucer. He had not been subjected to such biting winds since leaving Yorkshire and wondered whether he had fled in the right direction. The Reverend could never convince him that Ingoldisthorpe was warmer than places inland. 'No wonder,' Aram continued, 'poor Princess Pocahontas of the Americas died within a year of her arrival here.'

'Liked that story did ye?'

'Sparing her death, sir.'

'Death! Death! 'Tis nothing. We all meet that challenge sooner or later.' The pragmatic, good-natured Weatherhead laughed heartily on that raw afternoon.

The marriage of the late colonist John Rolfe of Heacham, Weatherhead's present parish, to an Algonquin princess and the friendly alliance that followed between Indian and Englishman was, Aram guessed, Weatherhead's favourite story for all newcomers over afternoon tea – but then newcomers cannot have been too frequent at the Rectory of Ingoldisthorpe.

Despite this, Christmas Day, 1757, found Eugene Aram amicably arm in arm with his new employer on their way to being entertained by another Ingoldisthorpe wit, John Davy of Mount Amelia.

'John's been a dear friend for years,' the Reverend explained on first receiving the invitation. 'You're invited too, Eugenius.'

Davy's red bricked house was impressive with its tall chimneys, pillars and screaming garden peacocks. As they walked up the drive amid the strutting dowager birds, Aram was reminded of Newby Hall and his happy childhood there. Looking down the long dining table glittering with wealthy guests, he began to wonder if his luck had taken a turn for the better here too. Daniel Clark was forgotten; Houseman and Iles forgotten; his estranged wife and children back in

Knaresborough forgotten. He was going to enjoy his smug little position among these people for as long as it lasted.

Eels, oysters and fish of all sorts, plovers' eggs, duck eggs, bedecked roasted birds were reflected along the polished table surface.

'There's no finer or more tender bird could ever have graced this life,' said his employer's wife, Mrs Frances Weatherhead, singing the praises of the goose.

'No, my dear, you are wrong,' remarked her florid husband further down the table. 'There's never a goose that's graced this life better than thee.' The Reverend was pleased with himself. Why shouldn't he drink and jest with the best of 'em? – only a few hours earlier his Christmas Day sermon had been applauded as a great success by the entire parish.

There was some polite behind-the-hand giggles at this witty exchange between husband and wife from the other guests, giving Aram his first opportunity to observe, unobserved, the head of the table. John Davy appeared to be some half-dozen years his junior. He used his knife and fork with an almost feminine delicacy – his fingers themselves delicate tools – there was something of the dilettante about John Davy.

After the syllabub and various sweet puddings had been devoured, the bloated company separated. The men remained seated at the table while the ladies retired to the drawing-room.

'Mr Aram.' Looking up, Davy caught Aram still scrutinizing him.

'Mr Davy,' Aram nodded.

'I fear we are the only bachelors here today,' Davy quipped, making a point of singling out his new guest.

'Aye,' lied Aram, enjoying the fictitious freedom others had created for him and fancying in some way it restored his lost youth. '"Fear" though? Is it not the married state that is to be feared, sir?'

Davy's eyes wrinkled, smiled and Aram knew he was winning over another influential friend.

'Would I be right in thinking that there is a hint of the North in your speech?' asked Davy.

'Aye, sir, I originated from Nottingham way a long time ago.' Aram took an uncomfortable sip at his port-wine.

'Do you like Norfolk though, Aram?' Davy must have sensed his unease and, being the skilled conversationalist that he undoubtedly was, attempted to pull back onto safer ground.

'Aye, 'tis a fine county.'

'Then perhaps you will settle here.'

'As I think you know, sir, my position with the Reverend Weatherhead is a temporary one, tutoring his two boys for the holiday period only. I must move where work calls me.'

'So there is no point in me trying to make a match for you with a lady of the parish as Mrs Weatherhead would have me do?' laughed Davy.

'You already have my opinion on wedlock, sir.'

'I have heard you are a man of great education, nevertheless. Surely there must be plenty of employment for an able fellow like yourself in Norfolk, nay in Lynn alone.' Davy's open-boy-face suddenly aged beneath a frown. 'Why, I myself have a relative over at Mileham with a whole brood to teach. His three boys go to the grammar school with the Weatherheads in Lynn, but there are others left at home. Girls, I believe.'

'Please do not trouble yourself on my account, sir.'

'No, no, I will make enquiry on your behalf of Edward,' he insisted. 'Then my step-brother William's sons will soon be of an age to learn to read and write. See, that is William over there just returning to the room.'

* * * * *

'Call me Thomas,' invited Weatherhead one day.

There was so much laughter and informality and goodwill generated by the family within the Rectory's four cold walls, such a warm core to a cold shell, that Aram began to dread his imminent leaving. And again, Ingoldisthorpe had enough woods and a rivulet to explore whenever he wished to escape from the pandemonium of a parson's house … and there was always the garden.

Above all other advantages the Rectory garden proved to be Aram's mainstay: on the coldest of days Thomas and he would dig away at it to keep warm. And when the Weatherhead boys returned to school in Lynn after the Christmas holiday, Thomas kindly offered to keep his friend, Eugene, on until the whole garden was turned and sown for spring.

One afternoon, in early February, Aram's luck took a further twist as he and Weatherhead worked silently side by side thrusting their blunted spades against the resistant earth. They both were so engrossed in this labour, this frustration, neither heard the crunch of hooves on the lane outside. When they finally looked up, they let out a guffaw in unison on seeing a fashionable tricorne hat gliding above the Rectory hedge.

'Whoa,' cried John Davy, pulling his horse to a halt. 'I did not see you there at first.' Smiling as always he peered down over the hedge to their soil bed. 'Reverend Weatherhead, Mr Aram.' The tricorne hat tilted higher above the hedge.

Was there a supercilious note in the gesture? Looking down on his blistered hands, Aram felt a flash of hatred. How could such a dandy, employing a whole string of gardeners, appreciate that some men chip at frozen soil out of love?

'My, must say I'm most impressed, such industry on a day when all other living creatures are huddled by their fires,' tittered Davy, until he saw the resentment of both men at his intrusion.

'But you're not indoors, John,' noted Weatherhead sharply.

'No, because I've learnt something this morning that might interest you,' he said, getting down to business quickly. 'But perhaps more so Mr Aram.'

'In that case do you care to take tea with us?' Weatherhead asked him, still an edge to his voice.

'No, no, wouldn't dream … we can talk well enough as we are. I can see you are both busy.' Davy shuffled his narrow rump in the saddle.

Aram rubbed the sweat from his nose and wished he looked more respectable.

'The master of the grammar school at Lynn,' continued Davy, lowering his voice as if imparting a great confidence, 'is to dismiss his usher, Birkes.'

'John Birkes, but why?' asked Weatherhead.

'Something to do with him being found in the master's bedchamber during the night. Knox woke up and suspected him of trying to rob the boys' term fees.'

'Rob the fees?' repeated Weatherhead.

'Don't worry, Thomas, the fees are untouched,' reassured Davy. 'But Birkes' reputation is in question and Knox says he will no longer have him at the school. So there, I think, is an end to him and an opening for you, Aram.'

'Yes, that would be a step up right enough, Eugene, usher and then perhaps master of Lynn Grammar School,' enthused Weatherhead.

'A more stable appointment than casual tutor, Aram,' emphasised Davy for good measure.

Aram picked up his spade and stabbed at the ground randomly, telling them he did not want to profit from another man's misfortune.

'Nay, Aram,' exclaimed Davy. 'Birkes has brought this trouble on himself. Thomas and I will supply you with good references, won't we, Thomas?' Weatherhead nodded his accord with a hint of regret which Aram gratefully registered. 'I'll even take you into Lynn and introduce you to John Knox personally,' offered Davy.

'You're very kind, sir,' Aram told him, examining his blistered hands more charitably this time.

'My respects to your good lady, Thomas,' said Davy, raising his hat again before kicking his horse on. 'Think it over, Aram, and let me know,' he shouted back.

The fourteenth day of February was fair and a mild south-west wind blew across the land as John Knox informed the Lynn Assembly by hand that he had dismissed John Birkes, usher, and had appointed as his successor Eugenius Aram.

CHAPTER NINETEEN

Over the next decade I received occasional letters from my dear friend, Thomas Hutchinson. He told me he was well on his way to assembling his museum. He talked little of personal matters but complained much of the weather and his ailments. I believed him to be still a bachelor.

Knaresborough, 20ᵗʰ February 1769.

My Dear Felix,

I thought you might be interested to know that last month Ann, the wife of Richard Houseman died. Since you left, his stepdaughter, Nancy, has been forced to cut him down from the family apple tree on several occasions after he attempted to hang himself. Living or dead, I think poor Dickey is beyond being saved.

Judging from the physical results of his latest attempt, I fear the next time will be his last – the cord of guilt is proving too tight for the flax-dresser.
Your humble servant,
Thomas Hutchinson

* * * * *

In the March of 1785 my present editor, David Henry, sent me to East Anglia to cover a murder trial that had caught his imagination. Little did he know that I was more than a willing traveller to this area as it held significant interest for me. The years had passed by and still I had not embarked on what I considered to be my life's work. I resolved that as soon as the Norfolk trial was over I would move up to King's Lynn. I was curious to visit the scene of Aram's arrest, and equally intrigued about the fateful encounter that had led to his apprehension on this remote limb of our isle. Perhaps one day, when business and family commitments slackened, I would be able to give voice to the conundrum that was Aram.

Still, I first had an obligation to my editor to file this present day story. My initial visit was to St Mary's Church, Hunstanton, where two victims of the smuggling trade rested in peace.

I zigzagged the graveyard, unable to repress the smile on my face, looking for the unfortunate principals in my coming report. Smile? – Yes, because the only newsworthy item I had ever heard regarding Hunstanton happened a century or two back. The story goes that the parson of this same venerable house, before which I stood, was accused of a dalliance with a married woman witnessed by her husband. The sin of adultery: perhaps a misconduct not as unusual as one might think in rural communities, if it wasn't for the fact that the two participants, the Reverend Charles Crotch and Mistress Jolles, were names worthy of Smollett himself. The Reverend Crotch seemed to have ridden out the tirade against him and remained "frocked" for the next few years. One can only speculate on the destiny of Mistress Jolles and her husband.

My smile soon vanished on coming across Private William Webb's gravestone.

In Memory of
William Webb
late of the 15th Lt. D'ns
who was shot from
his Horse by a Party of Smugglers
on 26 of Sep 1784
Aged 26 years.
I am not dead but sleepeth here
And when the Trumpet Sound I will appear.
Four balls thro' me Pearced there way.
Hard it was I'd no time to pray.
This stone that here you Do see
My comerades Erected for the sake of me.

Though ungrammatical the inscription wasn't without feeling. William Green's was likewise.

Here be
the mangled remains of
poor William Green
an Honest Officer of Government
who in the faithful discharge of his duty
was inhumanly murdered
by a gang of Smugglers in this Parish

On the night of 26th and early hours of 27th September, 1784, a group of smugglers found some customs officers and a party of General Elliot's Light Horse Dragoons lying in wait for them. Attempting to reclaim their contraband that the officers of the Crown had seized the smugglers shot thirty-seven year old William Green, a customs officer, and Private William Webb of the Light Dragoons from their horses in the ensuing exchange of fire. Subsequently Captain William Kimbell and two of his crew, namely Andrew Gunton and Thomas Williams, were arrested for murder and taken to be gaoled in Norwich Castle. At their first trial the men had been acquitted, but the prosecution insisted they be re-tried on the grounds that it was improbable a Norfolk jury would find any smuggler guilty. Unlike the Knaresborough schoolmaster, Aram, I was to see Kimbell, Gunton and Williams walk out of a Thetford court free men a second time. It was at such times that I began to question the inequality in our justice system.

So on to King's Lynn by rattling stage, where I was told that Sally Aram had long since quit the town. This did not dismay me unduly as I harboured no expectation of finding her there. Rumours about her were rife at the time of her father's trial. I had heard from one source that a suicidal Sally begged a York publisher to give her money following publication of the court proceedings. William Bristow, editor of *The Genuine Account of the Trial of Eugene Aram for the Murder of Daniel Clark*, said he met Sally around the year of 1767. She was married to a London innkeeper on the Surrey side of Westminster Bridge and had two or three children. With "double check your sources" ringing in my head and little hope in my heart, I decided to search the parish register in St Nicholas's Chapel to see if there was any record of this marriage. It was while searching down the columns for a reference to the surname Aram that I came across the following under the date 28th July, 1768.

Barnaby Fox, single, married Ann Aram, single, before Mark Burn, Curate, in the presence of witnesses, Thomas Fox and Mary Pike.

I couldn't catch my breath, my heart fluttered. History will ultimately be my judge but was this Ann the living proof of Aram's incest with Sally, his daughter? I would imagine that Anna Aram – peeping from her pie shop on that warm July night to see the body of the murderer, Tom Lee, being housed in the Blue Bell Inn on his way back to Grassington to meet the same gibbet fate as her husband – would have had no idea that down in Lynn, Sally's daughter, her granddaughter, was preparing to wed one Barnaby Fox.

* * * * *

Aram's knowledge of Lynn or Lynn Regis evolved like a slow love affair. Like York the town was walled, like York it stood on a river Ouse, and, although closer to the sea, like York it had been a prominent port which was now slowly losing prestige. He felt comforted by Lynn's familiarity to his old county town while being enthralled by its individuality. The town had originally developed round the Benedictine Priory and Church of St Margaret, the priory having been founded in 1101 by Herbert de Losinga, Bishop of Norwich. It had then been called Lenne Episcopi or Bishop's Lynn and in time began to take in lands eastwards and then north of the Ouse's tributary – the Purfleet. The Parish of St Nicholas with its Tuesday market and fair eventually joined that of St Margaret's with its Saturday Market Place. By the time

Aram arrived in Lynn, only the newly built Custom House standing over the Purfleet served as a reminder of that once ancient boundary.

All went better than expected: he enjoyed his new teaching position free of the expense and responsibility of running his own establishment. The grammar school was housed in the old Charnel Chapel adjoining the north side of St Margaret's Church. The lower storey was used as a depository for human bones which had been disturbed from time to time in the precincts of the church, while above, studiedly ignoring below, Mr Knox and his usher would enlighten their little charges on piety, letters, manners and finally order.

Aram lived at Mr Knox's house which also acted as a dormitory for some of the school's boarders. The Master's House stood at the corner of Skynner's Row and Codling Street and was but a minute or two's walk from the grammar school. The close situation of house and work suited him well as he had to be up to take morning prayers at half-past six.

'Master Burney, late again,' Aram admonished the organist's son, who had travelled from the High Street. 'Playing along with sister Fanny, no doubt.' The six year old day-boy hung his head as others sniggered. Although young James was often last to arrive and first to leave, Aram found him to be bright and engaging, a taking child rather like another little boy, George Horner, had been back at Gouthwaite Hall all those years before.

It fell to Aram to instruct these smaller boys until eleven o' clock and then from one to five, Mr Knox having arranged to teach the easier older boys and enjoy a shorter working day in keeping with his position. But at least during his first term at the grammar school, Aram escaped the added duty of Librarian to St Margaret's which had been normally allocated to ushers in the past. A man called Charles Phelpes now fulfilled the post, and it did not take Aram long to cultivate this man for books to aid his research for his comparative lexicon.

He spent most of his leisure time in the church next door which led to one of the most uplifting experiences of his life when he chanced upon Dr Charles Burney, young James' father, practising Purcell on the new Snetzler organ.

'Master Burney,' he hailed James through the chalk air of a noon lit classroom. 'An hour ago it was my privilege to sit with closed eyes in a St Margaret's pew and listen to your father making music. Be proud of him, boy, for he is a man of remarkable talent.'

Whether or not the little boy fully appreciated the depth of Aram's feeling, it was hard to tell, but from that day on James gave greater attention to his lessons.

Sometimes when Aram took an evening stroll in the fields adjoining Lynn, muffled in his horseman's greatcoat with a large flapped hat pulled over his eyes, he would spy some of the school's more daring pupils behind him. These lads rarely giggled or vented their spleen on their eccentric teacher but merely followed – whatever else, he seemed to command a distant form of respect and curiosity from even the most rebellious of them.

This need for solitude was, as in London, not always to be – was to suffer greater incursions than pursuing boys – again his bookish presence was sought by clerics, gentry and the deprived educated classes of Norfolk alike. Although he had to admit he did enjoy the company of John Davy, Thomas Weatherhead, and sometimes on Sunday evenings he was invited to dine with the convivial Samuel Steadman, Rector of Gaywood.

Through such contacts, he began tutoring extra pupils out of school hours to supplement his income. Two of whom were the daughters of Dr Thomas Lidderdale: Susana and Mary George. He found it especially flattering to be entrusted with the Lidderdale girls' education as their father was a man respected in his own right throughout Lynn for his scholarship. And, oh, what pretty little things Susana and Mary George were – bright as two silver buttons just as Sally once had been.

Bending over their books with them, head to head with them, Aram felt those old wicked thoughts starting up again, thoughts that had lain dormant for over a decade. The man's (not the tutor's) blood boiled again with a dangerous passion.

Sally – he must send for her soon – or he would not be answerable for his actions towards one or both of these perfect creatures. Purity and perfection were the two ideals Aram most revered.

'It's so good for us all to be united again, Father,' said Sally, taking off her bonnet and placing it carefully on the window-seat as she looked around at her new surroundings with obvious gratitude.

She had reason to be glad for, as she reluctantly confessed to her father, the last months in London had been hard ones. Aram had not realised that his infrequent payments had hardly kept the child fed and shod let alone Sally herself: London, it seemed, was becoming the most expensive place on earth to live.

He coloured at the memory of John Davy's sumptuous table, and how only the other day he had put forward his unorthodox opinions to amuse Samuel Steadman with all the assurance of a full belly.

'We realised your forgetting, Father, was due to your mind being on higher things.'

Trust Sally to think the best of him.

'You do both still love me though?' he asked.

'Yes, of course, Father,' exclaimed Sally, somewhat surprised. 'We both love you dearly, don't we, Ann?' She looked to the plain pubescent Ann for substantiation but there was none to be found in the girl's sulky face. Ann withdrew to the fireless hearth.

'Ann has grown up within months but her expression remains the same,' observed Aram coldly.

'She is merely fatigued with the journey and adjusting to change,' excused her mother; having no wish for another unpleasant confrontation over Ann when they had only just arrived in Lynn.

Aram took up Sally's tattered bonnet and began fingering it in annoyance. The drab attire of the two females had not escaped him. Could it be that Sally was becoming a slattern like her mother? Had Anna's ghost followed him all the way from Knaresborough to manifest itself in this surprising way? This reconciliation was not living up to expectations, he was disappointed. He suddenly caught the sharp searching eyes of Sally upon him. She looked away to where his pale-blue greatcoat was flung carelessly over a chair arm exposing its rich white lining; she looked down to her own dress that had seen better days years ago. Nothing was said but Aram knew she had read his thoughts as easily as if they were her own – again to his shame.

Damn me, he thought. This is still my beloved Sally even if she doesn't dress as finely as Miss Susana Lidderdale.

'Here,' he said, pushing three guineas onto the window-seat next to the bonnet. 'Have new dresses made for you and the child, beautiful dresses.'

Little Ann shuddered in the fireless hearth as her mother scraped up the money.

'Why don't you tell Grandfather that we cannot eat dresses?' she scolded bitterly.

Sally stared at her daughter who was so often sickly but spoke with a frightening wisdom way beyond her years. How like Eugene the child was, and how they hated each other.

'With three guineas there will be money enough for both dresses and food,' Sally reassured her.

'Grandfather only wants us dressed in frippery lest we are seen abroad with him, Mamma.'

Here the child was wrong: "Grandfather" had no intention of risking his newly acquired respectability in Lynn by being seen abroad with either of them. He must avoid at all costs any whiff of scandal regarding his relationship to the two females above the baker's shop. Lynn was not London: he would remain living at the Master's House; he would visit Sally and Ann secretly, and they would be wearing the pretty dresses indoors for his pleasure alone.

The novelty of Aram's ushership soon palled. Teaching the rudiments of grammar to disinterested little boys became tedious, and after long working hours he would wearily turn to Sally for supper.

'If I did not think it will be but a short time before Knox retires and I replace him, then I doubt I would stay a moment longer,' he told her after one particularly harassing day.

They had renewed their habit of working together on the Celtic Dictionary, sometimes late into the night, and at first this shared occasional labour brought them some emotional harmony. But Aram became more and more intolerant of his endless days of teaching and was often bored by "clever" society. Emotionally, he began to live solely for the room above the baker's shop – this in itself created a problem.

Frequently, regularly now, the suppers she made for him turned cold as, unbeknown to her, her father walked the streets of Lynn in the company of his old dilemma. Thank goodness his tutoring of Susana and Mary George Lidderdale was concluded.

Standing in Cold-hirne Street he would watch the drunken whalers falling out of the Greenland Fishery Tavern, a whore on each arm. These men brought the oil that glowed in the lamps around St Margaret's Church, and implanted the pox to fester in the recesses of Lynn womanhood. He turned away in disgust, he would not risk the dangers at his age of spending his lust between the legs of a Lynn harlot. He had noticed the older he got, the less risks he was willing to take, the more important self-preservation had become.

Walking into Saturday Market Place, he looked up to the chequered splendour of the Guild Hall and wondered what move he should make. Creeping down St Margaret's Lane he was still accompanied by the Devil, couldn't lose him. He passed under the shadows of the empty and neglected Hanseatic Warehouses as if he was walking through the valley of the shadow of death, the claggy hand of temptation there on his shoulder all the time.

Love is a state of mind – incest has additional ties.

Sitting on a step by the mud bank of the river Ouse, he watched the swans on the night water, white on black. He wondered what justice awaited a man who was in love with his own daughter, a man poised at the gates of hell. Still, he did not believe in heaven or hell. He contemplated throwing himself into the merciful relief of all consuming water. He stayed an hour, fixed and cold, mentally acting out the scene – his suicide – which he knew he had no real will to execute.

Dragging himself up, he made his way to the Maid's Head Inn like a wooden man in search of spiritual uplift. He found it in a warming tot of rum and then another and another.

Maid's Head, maidenhead … he thought back to the first time they had made love, how he had broken his virginal daughter's maidenhead. Where had been the harm? He truly loved her, did he not? The act between father and daughter was not against the law, only the subject of silly ecclesiastical censure and that only nominally. Anyway, he had no real proof that Sally was of his blood. There had always been that doubt. He had never found out the truth of it from Anna. Perhaps the slut had never known who Sally's father actually was. Aram threw back his head and thrust the last tot of hot liquor down his throat for courage.

A bell rang out one o' clock as he climbed the stairs to the room above the baker's shop. If his emotions could have been measured on the face of the moon clock outside St Margaret's Church, the dragon hand, which told Lynn merchants when their ships would sail in, would have pointed to high tide. It was several minutes before his loud knocking roused the sleeping Sally.

She knew straight away what he wanted of her. In the space of one missed breath, one nervous roll of his tongue across parchment lips, his strange inconsistency over the weeks was explained to her. Her bosom rose and fell beneath the fashionless night-gown – she hardly felt its billowy cloth against her skin – already she felt naked in his grasping hands. Unseen by her father a tear rolled out.

CHAPTER TWENTY

Nothing much passes the attention of schoolboys, and during the latter part of that Lynn term before the summer vacation, Aram was sure they must have sometimes heard him stealing down the creaking staircase in the early hours – or were their smothered dormitory giggles just part of his culpable imagination? He had decided to make his calls on the baker's shop at that unorthodox time because little Ann would be asleep on his arrival, and he would be gone to open up the school at six before she awoke.

'Thought I heard the street door close well before daybreak this morning,' queried John Knox, during a quiet period between classes. 'But when I checked the dormitory all the boys were safely abed.'

'I do not always sleep well. The nights have been so close of late. Now and then I take a walk,' lied Aram.

Mr Knox was not fooled for a moment. Although the senior pedagogue much preferred the robust and less dangerous company of his boys and other men, he was not blind to the fact that some fellows would go to any lengths to enjoy the acquired taste of female charms.

That evening, over supper and claret, Aram heard Knox comment to their host John Davy, 'Damn me, if Eugenius hasn't got himself a woman'.

'Good for him,' guffawed Davy, well in his cups. 'What's her name, eh?'

What's her name? – his Sally, his daughter Sally – what's *in* a name? Aram had done his best to reassure her that their regular union was blessed by the gods. Did not love of this special nature happen all the time in the Greek books they read together? Sisters had commerce with brothers; mothers with sons; fathers with … No, it could not be wrong when the greatest civilization ever to exist had indulged itself in the same. Had he not fed his daughter since childhood on the higher principles of the ancients to escape the low reality of contemporary English life? Had he not spread Electra on the coarse grained bread that Anna had stuffed into her mouth daily?

However as the weeks went by he was not at peace, knew he was doing wrong, whatever Greek excuses he postulated. But like a laudanum addict he could not stop himself, was forced to return, could not break the habit, he needed her so much. Sally never had the benefit of doubting she was of his seed, yet it was to this slim hope that Aram's conscience increasingly clung, clung more and more like a drowning man. Perhaps he wasn't her real father, perhaps.

He gained some transitory relief from this ongoing conflict when he was invited away at weekends to this or that great house to give the children there extra tuition. One of his pupils at the grammar school was young William Davy, Mr Knox having the responsibility of teaching his two older brothers, Edward and John. The three boys were the relatives John Davy had vaguely mentioned to him at Mount Amelia, and were the sons of Edward and Mary Davy of Mileham. Through the kind offices of John Davy and Mr Knox, Aram had been entrusted with the occasional elementary teaching of the Mileham Davys' daughters.

The three little girls regarded their lessons in the drawing-room as a treat, and were very receptive unlike most of the boys back in Lynn who had been forced away to school and to listen. There was Mary aged twelve, Elizabeth aged six, who was William's twin, and little Anne aged four. Baby Lydia, who was just one year old, only took instruction on her attractive mother's knee. No opportunities ever occurred here for Aram to stray into inappropriate gropes with his three Davy charges as their mother and Lydia were always present, and, to be absolutely truthful, in some way Aram found Mary Davy's deterring presence comforting.

Ambitious and climbing, he made a point of winning over their father too. After only a few weeks of subtle campaigning, Edward Davy began inviting him to stay overnight more in the capacity of confidant than tutor.

Mileham was a one street village, rather as Skelton on the Newby estate had been during his early childhood. Although, unlike Skelton, Mileham possessed the ruins of an old moated castle which immediately captured his interest. But what Aram loved most were the trees and parkland round Edward Davy's hall, and, ironically, it was this parkland that turned out to be the setting for his undoing.

It happened one warm Saturday afternoon in June, after he and his host decided to walk off the effects of a full and hot dinner – such an everyday thing to do – they were deeply engaged in a discussion on the latest methods of husbandry when Edward Davy stopped in mid-stride.

'What the deuce?'

'Begging your pardon, sir.' The man emerging from the trees doffed his cap. A large stallion dwarfed him.

'This is private land,' bellowed Edward.

The man continued on his steady approach, stopping a yard or two before them.

'Sorry, sir, but one o' yon lads back at t' stables says I am to speak wi' thee personal like. 'Tis about this 'orse that comes of the finest stock ... Irish breeding stock.'

'Irish, you say?' Edward looked more interested, appraising the stallion's rump with raised brow.

'Yes, sir,' reaffirmed the man somewhat edgily.

'You have secured my attention, pray get to the point, man.'

'Well, Your Lordship.'

Edward winked across at Aram regarding his sudden rise in station. The man now cast a professional eye Aram's way too, in case this friend of the gentry might be swayed into taking his part as to the quality of horseflesh on offer.

'He would serve all Your Lordship's mares well. He is a stallion and a half,' continued the horse-dealer optimistically.

'"A stallion and a half" indeed. Hear that, Eugenius, the beast must have three balls,' ridiculed Edward coarsely.

The stallion's ears pricked up at Edward's laughter and the man's pricked up at the name Eugenius.

'Do I know thee, sir?' he asked Aram.

'No, I think not,' replied Aram, turning sharply and walking a little way up the path but remaining within earshot.

'I could have sworn I know that gentleman,' the man confided in Edward Davy awkwardly.

'Perhaps you have seen him in Lynn, Eugenius is the usher at the grammar school there,' responded Edward with little interest.

'No, no, begging your pardon, Your Lordship,' refuted the man in bewilderment. 'It has come to me now, there was a chap who resided in Knaresborough some years back who was his very image, a Yorkshireman like missen.'

Fortunately, Aram could see Edward thought the man a fool and was making too much of the matter. He told him he could not help him further and that the stable had already arranged a stallion for the Davy mares and so they could do no business. The man appeared unmoved by this, was used to being snubbed by the gentry. But as he passed by Aram with his horse in tow, he nodded again intimately – impertinently – the new usher of the grammar school turned away in disgust.

'Eugenius, eh,' he heard the man muttering up the path.

Instinctively Aram knew he had made a mistake here: dismissed by the gentry was one thing but to be ignored by a man whom, back in Knaresborough, the horse-dealer would regard as little above his own station was not a slight he was likely to forget.

* * * * *

The Lynn schoolroom above the old Charnel Chapel was empty, only the hum of vendors on Saturday Market Place filled the silence. The noise of slate pencils screeching on slate boards had long vanished like irritating ghosts.

Aram stood at an oak bookcase, a dusting cloth in hand, bathed in sunlight. Taking one book at a time off the shelf, he gently blew away the chalk dust from its gilding. He knew it would be more efficient to use the cloth but it was end of term and he was enjoying watching the chalk clouds rising into the air. He even laughed to see chalk had fallen like flour across the front of his waistcoat. Freedom – like a holidaying schoolboy he was experiencing what was for him a moment of rare happiness – that was until Mr Knox burst in, burst in on his mood and changed it irrevocably.

Knox's shoulders were slumped, his voice tense as he asked Aram to withdraw with him into the withdrawing room.

Aram took in the whole scene at once: the men, their stone faces, the ominous silence. Sir John Turner, whom Aram knew only by sight but was well-aware of his power in the town, dominated everything. Other men, men who were complete strangers to him, stood respectfully behind, and behind them all cowered poor John Knox squeaking that there must be some mistake. Raising his ringed hand imperiously to silence Knox, Sir John was first to speak.

'Do you know Knaresborough, Aram?' he asked.

'No,' replied the usher, flinching like a bird.

'Have you ever had any acquaintance with one Daniel Clark?' enquired one of the strangers.

Aram was sensible enough to recognise the hard clipped accent. The name Daniel Clark made him shudder, had not been mentioned to him for years, and sounded as bleak and far off as the Yorkshire moors which had bred them both.

God! He thought in disbelief. That I should have to go back and answer now.

'I never knew …' he hesitated, he could not bear to use Clark's name. 'I never knew such a man.'

At this the whole assembly fell stiff and tight-lipped. The noise and smells of everyday life rose and wafted through the open window of the withdrawing room, a room normally used by either Knox or his usher to relax away from the boys. But there was no relaxation to be had now.

Amazing how certain people can change the entire character of a room, acknowledged Aram to himself, amazed at his own sense of dissociation in the circumstances.

Sir John Turner moved to the window and, with a theatrical flourish, waved down to someone who must have been standing vigilantly waiting on Saturday Market Place among the stalls of fruit and leather.

Aram waited, his shirt cold and clinging against his back. They all waited as the thud of a man's boots started to pound the stairs. Aram desperately sniffed up the warm street smells in the hope of gaining some comfort from their ordinariness, his faculties trying to filter out the portent of what was actually happening.

The sound of boots stopped. The door was slowly opened with care. A familiar face confronted him across the threshold and he felt something giving way within.

'How do you do, Mr Aram?' John Barker asked, trying hard with his best king's English before the Lynn dignitaries.

'How do you do, sir? I don't know you,' Aram retorted quickly, too quickly, struggling to collect his wits.

'What?' cried Barker. 'Don't you know me? Don't you remember that Daniel Clark and you always had a spite against me when you lived at Knaresborough?'

God! – not Clark again.

'Yes, I think I do recollect you now,' Aram reluctantly admitted, realising Barker was sure to win this opening parry and would only be enjoying its prolonged duration.

'And Knaresborough?'

'Yes, there too,' he sighed, wanting this thing to be over, wanting to retreat back into his shell like a poked snail.

'Do you know Saint Robert's Cave?'

'Yes,' he whispered sadly, suspecting this jumped-up constable must have rehearsed his lines many times over, knowing there was no dress-rehearsal for him.

'Aye, to your sorrow,' hissed Barker.

⋆ ⋆ ⋆ ⋆ ⋆

The horses refused at the crossroads. In the carriage behind, the three men lurched up and down on the hard wooden seats each rudely jerked out of his personal fantasy. Aram, dressed in frills and with the bearing of a gentleman, looked to the other two for an explanation.

Were they about to be robbed? Continuing to rock in the sprung chaise, his shabby companions ignored his silent enquiry. Their expressions remained grim and fixed. Left to himself, Aram noticed that the air outside was thick with insects. He stiffened, braced and leaned forward off his seat. To his horror a pair of naked blackened feet swung into view above the window glass.

'Watch him!'

Alerted, a rough hand shot forward to push him back into his seat. Not fast enough, not far enough, not until he had seen the blue and green iridescent flies seething and gathering and licking across the flesh of the man dangling in chains from the crossroads' gibbet. Bluebottles, metallic greenbottles, golden throated cluster-flies – *Calliphora vomitoria, Lucilia caesar, Pollenia rudis* – flashed sinister messages through their see-through wings. Blow-flies, flesh-flies, hovered and settled and tried to suck out the remains of that August day. Hoping, no doubt, to leave some of their larval future in exchange. Other flies, more tentative flies, came in, joined in, tried their luck at the table. They hummed, buzzed and fussed, programmed to keep trying in and out of the hanging cage.

'Why have we stopped here?' demanded Aram tersely.

No answer: only the buzz, buzz, from the flies, the creaking coach, the squeaking gibbet post, the voice of jangling chains.

The flies appeared to realise that they also had been duped at the crossroads. The corpse's vesture of canvas and pitch, designed to ward off inclement weather and the most adaptable of appetites, seemed to be working. Angry now, the flies swarmed about the spoilt feast in clouds of bellicose indignation.

The unfortunate felon outside looked like a chimney-sweep hanging there. He looked smutty and unreal as sweeps often do. Death was already taking over. Where the canvas and pitch had been too meanly applied, once healthy flesh was turning purple and blistered. It wouldn't be long before the most persistent flies found that here was a site for their love after all. The man's mouth, which once must have opened on kisses and smiles itself, now curled back in a fixed jungle snarl. And his eyes, desperate eyes, the bulging eyes of a drowning swimmer.

'A pretty sight, eh, Eugenius?' chuckled Constable Barker; his elbow pressing into Aram's ribs. The thick dirty finger on his other hand making its point on the breath steamed window.

A barbaric sight, Aram was moved to reply but shook his head instead. He refused to supply Barker with further satisfaction. Barker's lips were already too thin, too cruel, too smug in his new elevated role.

'Saw a monkey once, at Bradford fair it was, jigging about on a string like he,' mumbled Constable Francis Moor opposite them, pointing to the gibbet. 'Only the monkey was alive.'

Aram realised that this was said without humour, not even sadness, merely poor Moor's resolute acceptance of a world he was unable to change. He turned his attention outside again, away from his own helplessness. The nails, beaten into the gibbet to discourage relic hunters, only they glinted sun and any hope for him. The stench of decomposition penetrated the chaise. He wriggled his hands – the gyves having begun to chafe his wrists.

'God, why can't we move on now?' he pleaded.

Barker merely chuckled again.

'Cannot our driver make out t' way 'ome or what?' complained Moor too.

'Postilion's just plain morbid,' sniggered Barker; smothering his nose deep into the arm of his greatcoat.

'Barker, you do not fool me,' Aram decided to challenge head-on. 'You alone are the author of this escapade.'

'Me?' Barker feigned hurt. 'What reason would I have for doing such a thing?'

The whip cracked above them – the metaphoric clock struck twelve – the old drab Cinderella frock was reinstated – warped time fell true again – and the terrible presentiment of Aram's own possible fate was swapped for the almost equally daunting prospect of returning home.

As the chaise lurched away from the crossroads that oldest of inventions, the wheel, ground away at his imagination. Try as he might the stink and portent of the man on the gibbet would not leave him. Nor, paradoxically, did it seem to ride easily with his fellow travellers, not even Barker. Indeed, the two auxiliary constables hired to escort him back to Yorkshire had little to say after Lynn, seemed to have little in common with each other either. All three men then were left to their own morbid preoccupations, right until the Norfolk/Lincolnshire boundary when Constable Barker's goading voice suddenly vented into life.

'You had a pallor back there at the Lynn crossroads, Eugenius.'

'Who was he?' Aram chilled at the memory of the man's dancing limbs, uncoordinated sticks drying and blown by the last warm winds of summer.

'No idea.' Barker shrugged indifference. 'Didn't notice the gibbet on our way in, did we, Francis?'

'You might have but not I.' Moor rubbed his nose through soft fabric fingers, his loose-skinned hatter fingers. 'Wonder how long t' poor devil's been a hanging there?'

Barker shuffled from one fat buttock to the other. He perked up, interested. He was an amateur who enjoyed the odd speculation: a flutterer over the gaming-table; an occasional visit to the cockpit.

'I'll wager a week, maybe two.' But above all the constable was a man of practical matters; he was a man who felt uncomfortable with the abstract, with feelings, emotions, that sort of thing.

Yes, that's Barker right enough, recalled Aram. A most peculiar man.

'Summer does her work quicker than winter or spring.' Barker loved this game of fact. He was not a clever man, he was a very ignorant man, and he tried to cover his ignorance by stating the obvious. 'What are you smirking at?' he asked, dragging on Aram's gyves.

'Me? Nothing.'

'A man in your position has nothing to smirk at.'

New and better pike roads were rare in Norfolk and Lincolnshire. The furrowed track they now travelled was gut busting, jarred them together. Despite this, Barker seemed determined to keep up his impersonal, almost comic air of officialdom over his prisoner.

'How are all my old neighbours in the town?' Aram asked him, quickly switching to a more ingratiating approach. Thirteen years had passed since Knaresborough, unlucky thirteen, and in those thirteen years he had learned to be a more political animal.

'They are much enraged against you for the loss of their goods.' There was no softening Barker.

'Isn't it possible to make up the matter?'

'You might save yourself, if you can restore to them what is lost.'

'That is impossible, but I could perhaps find them an equivalent,' offered Aram, seizing at any sign of a chink in Barker's millstone profile.

Barker shook his head and turned back to the window. Aram, in turn, turned yet again to the relative safety of his own window glass. If only it were possible to blow solid troubles through such polished illusion. But it was not possible, magic was never there when you needed it most, the genie was always away. And Aram knew all about genies from Antoine Galland's translation of the *Arabian Nights*. Aram's friend, Painblanc, back in London, had helped him with Galland's more difficult French passages. Anyway, he had learnt that genies, especially Arabian ones, lived mainly on mountain tops, and there were no mountains here to speak of – only the ones we made for ourselves.

MY ADDITIONAL NOTES TAKEN AT THE TRIAL

(Including a re-enactment of Eugene Aram's famous defence taken from his manuscript book with all its factual and grammatical inaccuracies.)

I was late to take my seat at the assizes. I was forced to wait for the line of prisoners crossing my path out in the yard. After months of incarceration in stone and straw, they looked like winter beasts being led out of the byre. It was only a few yards from the Castle Prison to the Grand Jury House's cells but some of the prisoners in the line seemed to have difficulty coping with even that short distance. And there he was right enough, one of the principals in that day's capital case. I had heard he was a natural walker, if there was hesitation in Aram's stride too I guessed it was from almost a year's inactivity, then again perhaps it was more out of fear than fatigue.

Beasts indeed – the robed judge ran a professional and dispassionate eye over each of them as a farmer would judging stock.

Aram looked pale amongst the assorted felonry crowded at the bar. But his eyes were alert to every movement about him. His nose was more Roman than Greek; no powdered wig for him, his natural hair was left receding into the grey backwater of his head, left free-flowing down his neck and round his ears; his cheeks were no longer full and innocent; only his jowls sagged into an extra wave, which was to be expected of a man in his fifty-fifth year. And what of that tell-tale – the mouth – the schoolteacher's mouth remained surprisingly generous in light of its present constraints.

Mr Justice Noel plumped up his yellow wig and yawned. He feared he was destined to see out his days watching other men endure.

Aram began to sway between Houseman and Terry like a willow between oak. The prisoners behind them pressed forward to hear what was going on. From where I sat I could smell the clawing stench of prison mingling with the scents of the fashionable arranged on the public benches. The court appeared to be bulging with persons of quality that day. The bookseller, Mr Christopher Etherington, at the sign of the Pope's Head in Coney Street, York, had warned me that this case was to be a cause célèbre. I could see Etherington had not exaggerated. It seemed every gentleman in the county was interested in *Rex v. Houseman, Aram and Terry,* yet not one of them had been willing to come forward and speak up on Aram's behalf. Aram's chin sank to his chest, not for the crime they accused him of but because he was wearing the same waistcoat, breeches, now tattered shirt, he had been arrested in a year ago.

Indeed all three of the Knaresborough men stood before the court like tawdry puppets. I wondered if the somebody who had possibly been pulling their strings was present in court that day – in our society there is usually a puppet master to benefit most and lose least.

The Clerk of Arraigns stood to address them. 'Prisoners at the bar, hear what is said to you. These good men you shall see called are those who shall pass between our Sovereign Lord and King and you upon your lives and deaths.'

It was Houseman's turn to shake. This York court had none of the amateur informality of John Theakston's courts back in Knaresborough, and the flax-dresser had not enjoyed them very much either.

'Therefore, if you would challenge them, or any of them, you must challenge them as they come to the book to be sworn, before they are sworn, and you shall be heard,' droned the clerk mechanically.

The accused seemed to lose interest as Thomas Sutton, Robert Skelton, Robert Kitchin and nine other meaningless names were sworn in. Not one prisoner raised his voice to challenge the right of those twelve elected men to pass judgement on him. They remained silent, unwilling to stand out from the herd in this new and dangerous country.

But then on what grounds could you challenge a stranger? Surely you had to have a better reason than not taking to his face. There were at least five sullen countenances that I would have rejected on that score.

Next the clerk called on all and sundry to inform 'my lords the King's justices, the King's Sergeant, or the King's Attorney General of any treasons, murders, felonies, or misdemeanours, done or committed by any of the prisoners.' The witnesses were then called to come forth and give their evidence 'for the prisoners stand now at the bar upon their deliverance.'

A weed of a man, George Mason, was instructed to step forward to the bar. Aram and his fellow prisoners were hustled back down to the hold below. Longer to wait – their trial deferred.

'Houseman, Aram and Terry.' After only minutes, an officious voice summoned them to return to the courtroom.

'For the sake of two paltry pecks of malt costing one shilling and sixpence, they've burnt me hand,' moaned a bloodless-faced George Mason as he staggered past them down the steps. Mason was weeping. It was their turn now.

Mr Justice Noel rubbed his own unblemished palms together. Good, the cause célèbre, things were moving along quite nicely this morning.

Mason's case had been a waste of time. And, anyway, William Noel hated the smell of burnt flesh. The public bubbled and heaved once more in anticipation, adjusting their food swollen bellies to a more comfortable position on the hard wooden benches. I watched as Aram looked anxiously round the room. He frowned: there was no sign of his wife, no sign of a smile of encouragement from a familiar face.

The court was told the Crown had no evidence against Terry. The case against him was dismissed. I later heard he left York in triumph with a cockade in his hat.

'Richard Houseman.' Next the heckler was put to the bar. His lawyer gave him a nod of encouragement as his supposed wrongdoings were read out to the jury. In the seconds that followed a dropping pin would have sounded like a successful Gunpowder Plot. Houseman's matted wig flopped over his deep brow. He clumsily pushed it back and waited like a penned bull for the gate to open.

The court rustled as Noel looked quizzically across to where the Crown lawyers were seated. Fletcher Norton, known in legal circles as Sir Bull-Face Double-Fee, rose from the gaggle. It was not surprising that Noel's full attention now locked onto Norton: the KC was renowned for being the bane of every judge's life. Ignorant, unread and having suffered great hardship in early life, Norton would, given free rein, intimidate defendants and witnesses alike.

'Well?' asked Noel firmly; no doubt determined to have none of Norton's verdict getting tactics at the expense of justice in his court. 'Mr Norton,' he prompted again with a hint of exasperation.

Fletcher Norton cleared his throat. A consummate actor, he knew perfect timing created maximum effect. Houseman rubbed the back of his hand across his nose.

'We ask for a verdict of not guilty be brought in favour of this man, your lordship, if the court be willing,' the KC announced dramatically.

The public benches gave a volcanic rumble and then exploded. For once our press benches did not react. We were stunned. This was not expected. I had attended John Theakston's Coroner's Court myself where the evidence of Houseman's involvement in fraud and murder had been overwhelming.

'For shame!' Some gentlemen were moved to cry.

'Silence!' screamed Noel, quick to react before all hell broke loose. 'It is entirely a matter for counsel's discretion.' He gestured helpless appeasement towards the public. 'And I direct the jury to find a verdict of not guilty against Richard Houseman.'

Mutinous feet – the rabble stormed again.

'Silence or I'll clear the court.' An apoplectic Noel's authority told a second time, and the rather confused jury obediently and expediently returned the verdict directed by him.

An uncomfortable silence fell across the court as Houseman took a step back from the bar. His lawyer smiled but he knew his client was far from free yet: acquitted as a principal, he could still be indicted as an accessory before or after the fact. The shambling Houseman would have to tread carefully between truth and lies a little longer. But for the moment, before leaving centre stage, he had one more bizarre act to perform.

'God save the King and honourable court,' he bawled, sagging to his knees. The utterance was given full body and well above his usual range. His lawyer must have primed him on what would be expected, and however foolish he looked Houseman was only too thankful to oblige on this occasion.

'Eugene Aram, hold up thy hand. Gentlemen of the jury, look upon the prisoner. He stands indicted by the name of Eugene Aram, late of Knaresborough, in the county of York, schoolmaster, otherwise called Eugenius Aram.' The Clerk of Arraigns began to list Aram's so called crimes before the citizens of York and the country gentlemen from every corner of the kingdom.

'One of his greatest crimes was trying to run with the likes of them,' muttered Etherington, nodding to the quality stuffed together on the public benches.

' … with a certain offensive weapon.'

Such hostility. Aram looked naked, foetally rolled within himself.

' … which he in his right hand then and there held.'

I tried to concentrate on the proceedings but I was unable to take my eyes off the man standing alone and accused. I could not fully grasp how the cases against his co-accused had so simply and easily evaporated.

'He is also indicted upon the Coroner's Inquisition. Your charge, therefore, is to inquire whether he be guilty of the felony and murder whereof he stands indicted or not guilty. If you find him guilty you shall inquire what goods or chattels, lands or tenements he had at the time of the felony and murder committed or at any time since, and if you find him not guilty you shall inquire whether he fled for the same; and if you find he did fly for the same you shall inquire of his goods and chattels as if you had found him guilty; and that he did not fly for the same, say so and no more, and hear your evidence.'

They seemed to have Aram either way. Would the clerk's threatening flat voice ever cease? Would Anna Aram appear in court to give moral support to her husband?

A slim, young junior counsel jumped up for the Crown. He repeated the indictment briefly, much to everyone's relief, and slid youthfully back into his seat. The curtain had risen on act one. Fletcher Norton was next to bob up again and address the jury. The judge – a more sophisticated member of the cast – lifted his eyebrows from time to time at some of the leading counsel's more verbose rhetoric but, frustratingly, Noel could find nothing substantial to censure Norton with yet. Fletcher Norton resumed his seat, safe, hands gripping his gown's lapels, a smirk of satisfaction playing upon his moon face.

To me, Aram appeared to be disassociated from all this – this performance – he was a man happier with scholarship than theatre.

A more humble Stanhope followed. Like the junior counsel before him, he took up a much smaller space than the rotund Norton. Stanhope looked to be about fifty-six and long out of Gray's Inn. I was struck by the fact that this must be an important trial for the local man, coming so late in his legal career, but then it was an important trial for them all. Stanhope called Houseman to the witness box and the fickle perfumed ghouls, who had become restless again with the laborious preliminaries, settled.

'Some of the wealthiest folk in the county, nay in the country, are in this room,' noted Etherington.

'Pity they've nothing better to do with their time than gloat over Yorkshire business,' shrugged a man working for the *York Courant*.

'"Business", is that what it's called?' retorted Etherington.

Between these two difficult men, I began to feel morbidly lonely. Lonely like Aram. Houseman looked downcast too. He studiedly avoided looking Aram's way.

'Mr Houseman, when were you last at the house of Eugene Aram?' Stanhope launched himself gently into the waters of history.

'About Candlemas, 1744,' muttered Houseman, without lifting his eyes.

'That's by the old method of reckoning, is it not, Mr Houseman?'

'Aye, sir,' agreed Houseman diffidently, but he could see no trick to the question.

'So what occasioned you to be at Aram's house in February, 1744,45?'

Houseman's nerve abruptly appeared to fail him. He fell into a well of embarrassed silence from which he was either unable or afraid to climb.

'Mr Houseman?'

Nothing – no reply. The court cleared its throat, embarrassed too.

'Mr Houseman?' Stanhope's voice finally reached down to the heckler like a ladder.

'To receive some leather of him,' choked Houseman. His monotone continued on and on justifying his own actions while sulkily damning Aram.

'Would you like to cross-examine this witness?' Noel turned to Aram. The prisoner appeared too stunned to voice a full or concise reply but bowing respectfully he declined. 'Very well then.' Noel dismissed Houseman with ill-disguised regret.

As he left the box, Houseman brushed past Philip Coates. The heckler's eyes were now very much fixed on the feet of other men.

Daniel Clark's servant, Peter Moor, was called. I wondered what enlightenment this flinching nervous man could offer.

Hastily removing his cap at the usher's request, Moor began his account of overhearing a conversation between Aram and Clark some fourteen years before.

'You can remember exactly what was said, word for word, after so much time has elapsed?' queried Noel doubtfully.

'That's the honest truth, your honour.'

'My lord,' the usher reminded him. The court brayed its approval.

Next a certain Thomas Barnett, displaying his best leather leggings, squeaked into the box. He eyed the court with a roving suspicion: they weren't going to make a fool out of him.

'They're now setting the wild hordes of Knaresborough against Aram,' observed Etherington.

The dyer gave his testimony, in an almost unintelligible dialect, that he had seen a hooded Houseman coming out of Aram's cottage on the night in question.

'What? I did not quite get that,' complained Noel, hand to ear. 'What is the witness trying to tell us?'

'Mr Barnett says he saw Houseman come out of Aram's cottage in the early hours of Friday, eighth February, 1744, 45,' explained Stanhope.

'On account of the leather transaction,' muttered Houseman's counsel, looking a little unnerved by the translation of Barnett's testimony.

'On account of the leather transaction,' Stanhope obligingly repeated the prompt.

The heckler's experienced legal team sat back once more, after all their client was no longer deemed to be on trial.

'Mr Beckwith,' Stanhope announced the next witness, rubbing his hands together.

The aggrieved shopkeeper glowered across the court at Aram. Beckwith told how he had been swindled out of yards of cambric by Daniel Clark. And how he had later gone, with other men, to dig up Eugene Aram's Church Lane garden where he had recovered his buried cloth.

'William Tuton.' Tuton was called but failed to materialise. 'William Tuton!' repeated the usher more forcefully.

Finally arriving, Tuton slipped going into the witness box.

'Let's hope the mason doesn't trip over his tongue,' stage-whispered Fletcher Norton into Stanhope's ear.

With little interruption, Tuton wheezed and rambled on about seeing Aram and Houseman in Clark's company in the early hours of Friday 8th February, and about his missing pick which he seemed to think the three men had appropriated. Aram leaned forward on his elbows trying to catch his every faltering word, unable to conceal his scorn at the frightened mason's obvious half-truths.

'Do you wish to question *this* witness, Aram?' Noel almost begged him. Aram shook his head. What would be the point? Again it would only be his word against the mason's, and the mason wasn't standing accused at the bar.

Along with Noel, the rest of the court was beginning to wonder what on earth Aram's defence could be. Soon we would all know.

Stephen Latham next told of the great amount of money Eugene Aram had on him at the time of Clark's disappearance.

'Perhaps you could *profitably* question this witness, Aram,' suggested Noel drolly. The judge had made a joke. The court laughed politely in a low key. Noel remained inscrutable.

A year after Aram's arrest, a long year at that, arresting constables Francis Moor and John Barker were falling over each other to gain superiority following their newly acquired fame. Who had actually "done and seen what" had become contentious. Their evidence wasn't running in harmony.

The court liked this – they like a little controversy – livened up the proceedings.

'What?' croaked Noel.

'Constable Barker says he arrested Aram in the grammar school down in Lynn,' Stanhope was ever helpful.

Aram cleared his dry throat.

'Forgive me,' he interrupted, 'but it is to the best of my knowledge that it was not in the school but in the room adjoining the school that Sir John Turner and the witnesses first saw me.'

You could see that Aram did not really know why he had made this interjection. Just something to please Noel, I suspected. Just something, anything, to say.

Noel abruptly dismissed Barker and sat back. From the judge's slumped posture it appeared that he considered Aram well beyond help.

Like in some macabre fairground show, Aaron Locock, barber-surgeon, at the behest of Mr Stanhope, produced a human skull to the horror, delight and amazement of the court with the telling exception of Noel of course. Noel appeared to adopt the attitude of skulls, skulls, he had seen plenty of them before, so what was so special about this one.

'Let us be clear. What skull is this?' he asked Locock.

'Why, the one found in Saint Robert's Cave, your lordship. See, here is a fracture to the left made by some blunt instrument.'

'Blunt instrument, did you say?' Noel brightened.

'Aye, your lordship. A piece were beaten inwards.' Lifting the grisly specimen Hamlet high, Locock removed a section and inserted his fingers through the gaping hole. 'See it cannot be replaced but from within.'

'Could not such a breach proceed from natural decay?' Noel was obviously enjoying probing this somewhat inarticulate barber-surgeon. 'Or indeed from the instrument with which it was dug up?' he pressed.

'No, your lordship, begging your pardon. There is no sign of decay elsewhere in t' skeleton and t' break seems to be of many years standing,' replied Locock, trying hard to sound scientifically convincing.

'Tell me, Mr Norton,' asked Noel, abruptly turning to the King's Counsel, 'was Tuton's pick a blunt instrument?'

Fletcher Norton opened his mouth and for once nothing came out. Raising his hands he shrugged vacantly.

'Pray continue,' Noel instructed Stanhope, who showed he was eager to reclaim his cross-examination of Locock. A hint of satisfaction – or was it victory? – now marked the judge's lips.

The last witness was the plumed and preened William Thornton, who after the death of young Armytage over in France had been re-elected the previous December to represent York in Parliament. To a mature Parliament-man like Thornton, who had experienced forty-eight years of county life, no occasion was too outfacing for him and he casually confirmed that he had originally examined both Aram and Houseman. He showed no sign of constraint or repentance as the depositions, with all their spelling errors and erasures, were taken from his hand and shown to the smirking gentlemen jurors. Mr Thornton was a squire of the old kind, who believed in "no shilly-shallying with presentation, just get the thing done".

With the flowing exit of William Thornton, the case for the Crown closed. On the whole, Fletcher Norton and his three colleagues looked pleased with the black on black case they felt they had painted against the defendant. Now we all waited with seasoned eyes to see how Eugene Aram would attempt to brush himself in sunshine. No mean task for a skilled advocate, let alone an unworldly academic. To the travelling legal circus this was just another job of work, for Aram it was about to be the labour of his life – for his life.

* * * * *

There would be no adjournment until a verdict was reached. Looking across at Noel fumbling the few notes he had troubled to take, I wondered if the judge had any of the customary weakness befitting a man of his years, and, if so, how his lordship's bladder would cope with a long trial such as this.

Aram too appeared to be inspecting the judge's expression for signs of irritability. He flinched, suddenly aware that the court's attention was fixed on him. He did his best to appear composed, while realising how he must be perceived: a large, dark crane fly draped across the bar – a crane fly caught in this judicial spider's web – a crane fly awaiting the bite.

'What have you to urge on your behalf to these serious charges made against you, Eugene Aram?' Noel snapped the court back to business.

'I beg, my lord, that I might be indulged in reading my defence.' The court gaped and chortled as Aram fingered his, as yet, unused weapon in this war of accusation – his manuscript book. A book I was later loaned to transcribe through the kind auspices of my friend Etherington.

Noel's hand sliced the air for him to start and the court to be axed into silence.

'My lord, I know not whether it is of right, or through some indulgence of your lordship, that I am allowed the liberty at this bar, and at this time to attempt a defence; incapable and uninstructed as I am to speak.' Pausing for effect, Aram ran his eyes slowly over the court. 'Since, while I see so many eyes upon me, so numerous and awful a concourse, fixed with attention, and filled with I know not what expectancy, I labour, not with guilt, my lord, but with perplexity. For having never seen a court but this, being wholly unacquainted with law, the customs of the bar, and all judiciary proceedings, I fear I shall be so little capable of speaking with propriety in this place, that it exceeds my hope if I shall be able to speak at all.'

'Get on with it, man,' roared Fletcher Norton in exasperation; too loudly this time for the judge not to hear.

'Another outburst like that, Mr Norton, and I'll have you removed from the court,' Noel warned him. 'Let me remind counsel that I alone am in charge of the progression of this case.'

Fletcher Norton scowled, bowed, was for once put neatly in his place.

'Mr Aram,' Noel addressed the prisoner more gently, 'from the very eloquence of your opening address you do not strike me as a fellow incapable of putting a sentence or two together. Pray proceed forthwith.'

Was this encouragement or sarcasm from the judge, I wondered. Guffaws came from the public.

'I have heard, my lord, the indictment read, wherein I find myself charged with the highest crime, with an enormity I am altogether incapable of; a fact, to the commission of which there goes far more insensibility of heart, more profligacy of morals, than ever fell to my lot.' At this Aram hung his head. Perhaps he was not without theatricality after all. 'And nothing possibly could have admitted a presumption of this nature, but a depravity not inferior to that imputed to me. However, as I stand indicted at your lordship's bar, and have heard what is called evidence in support of such a charge, I very humbly solicit your lordship's patience, and beg the hearing of this respectable audience, while I, single and unskilful, destitute of friends, and unassisted by counsel, say something, perhaps like argument, in my defence.' Again the magical pause to see what effect his words were having on "this respectable audience".

One or two faces twitched back something like a little sympathy. Fletcher Norton sported a sarcastic grin. I suspected that Aram would have loved to smash his fist into the man's smug fat face under any other circumstances. Instead, he saw Noel nodding for him to get on with it.

'I shall consume but little of your lordship's time: what I have to say will be short, and this brevity probably will be the best part of it: However, it is offered with all possible regard, and the greatest submission to your lordship's consideration, and that of this honourable court.'

Good, he will speak with brevity, acknowledged Noel enthusiastically; who had actually begun to experience the first sensations of wanting to make water.

'First, my lord, the whole tenor of my conduct in life contradicts every particular in this indictment.'

Aram went on to explain that he had no connection with fraud or violence.

'My days were honestly laborious, my nights intensely studious.'

He then questioned how after his sober and blameless life he could have been so easily judged to have plunged "into the very depth of profligacy".

'Mankind are never corrupted at once; villainy is always progressive, and declines from right, step after step, till every regard of probity is lost, and every sense of all moral obligations totally perishes.'

Someone in the public clapped. Noel sent the usher to chastise the offender. I could not see who it was but this "someone" had entirely missed the point – this was the most succinct, yet latent, insight into a man's decline into criminality I had ever heard.

'Again, my lord, a suspicion of this kind, which nothing but malevolence could entertain, and ignorance propagate, is violently opposed by my very situation at that time, with respect to health: For, but a little space before, I had been confined to my bed, and suffered under a very long and severe disorder, and was not able, for half a year together, so much as walk. This distemper left me indeed, yet slowly and in part; but so macerated, so enfeebled, that I was reduced to crutches; and was so far from being well about the time I am charged with this fact, that I never to this day perfectly recovered. Could then a person in this condition take any thing into his head so unlikely, so extravagant? I past the vigour of my age, feeble and valetudinary, with no inducement to engage, no ability to accomplish, no weapon wherewith to perpetrate such a fact; without interest, without power, without motive, without means.'

There was a movement to Aram's left. Houseman was squirming in his seat and whispering something to his lawyer.

'A witness to prove your indisposition at that time might be helpful here,' suggested Noel in a quiet aside.

Aram shook his head: he had no witness, no one was willing to speak up for him in defence of his life.

'Makes you want to wipe a tear from your eye, does it not?' Fletcher Norton muttered to young Yates, his junior.

'I can see Noel is nearly crying,' quipped back the junior counsel.

Fletcher Norton laughed. Yates was a sharp lad, he liked him.

Suddenly becoming aware of the prosecution's indistinct mumbling again, Noel raised his forefinger peevishly towards them in further censure.

'Besides,' continued Aram warmed and undaunted, leaning conspiratorially over the bar towards the main body of the court. 'It must needs occur to every one, that an action of this atrocious nature is never heard of, but when it's springs are laid open, it appears that it was to support some indolence, or supply some luxury, to satisfy some avarice, or urged by some malice, to prevent some real or some imaginary want: Yet I lay not under the influence of any one of these. Surely, my lord, I may, consistent with both truth and modesty, affirm thus much; and none who have any veracity, and: knew me, will ever question this.'

'But he's not presented one character ...'

'Mr Norton, I'll not warn you again about these outbursts,' asserted Noel manfully.

'In the second place,' Aram raised his voice to match the judge's. A warder placed a restraining hand on his shoulder. 'The disappearance of Clark,' he continued 'is suggested as an argument of his being dead. But, the uncertainty of such an inference from that, and the fallibility of all conclusions of such a sort, from such a circumstance, are too obvious, and too notorious to require instance: yet, superseding many; permit me to produce a very recent one, and that afforded by this castle.'

The court waited – Noel waited – wondering what cleverness the defendant was up to now.

'In June, 1757, William Thompson, amidst all the vigilance of this place, in open day-light, and double-ironed, made his escape; and, notwithstanding an immediate inquiry set on foot, the strictest search, and all advertisements, was never seen or heard of since. If then Thompson got off unseen, through all these difficulties, how very easy was it for Clark, when none of them opposed him? But, what would be thought of a prosecution commenced against anyone last seen with Thompson?'

'Proof of *corpus delicti*, eh.' The Crown's table visibly juddered with the adjustment of knees and interest.

'I take it, my lord, the prisoner does not mean this is the same Thompson who found the bones on Thistle Hill?' Stanhope was on his feet again.

Noel looked to Aram, who nodded confirmation that he believed it was not the same man before quickly continuing with his argument.

'Permit me next, my lord, to observe a little upon the bones which have been discovered.'

'In Saint Robert's Cave, I hope,' put in Noel irascibly. Aram nodded.

'It is said, which is perhaps saying very far, that these are the skeleton of a man. It is possible indeed it may; but, is there any certain known criterion, which incontestibly distinguishes the sex in human bones? Let it be considered, my lord, whether the ascertaining of this point ought not to precede any attempt to identify them.' A lapse, a glance round the court, with all those hours alone in his cell Aram was well-practised. Noel appeared to be regarding him with some concord: he had himself been dissatisfied with the barber-surgeon's evidence. 'The place of their depositum too, claims much more attention than is commonly bestowed upon it. For, of all places in the world, none could have mentioned any one, wherein there was greater certainty of finding human bones, than an hermitage, except he should point out a church-yard. Hermitages, in time past, being not only places of religious retirement, but of burial too: And, it has scarce or never been heard of, but that every cell, now known, contains or contained, these relics of humanity; some mutilated, and some entire.'

'The schoolmaster's giving us all a bloody history lesson now,' sneered Fletcher Norton to his table.

The public heard and laughed; Noel heard and his frown deepened.

'A final warning this, Mr Norton,' he snarled. 'Kindly refrain from making obscene and obstructive comments or I'll hold you in contempt of this court.'

'Fletcher Norton is giving Noel something to chop his jaws on,' sniggered the man from the *Courant*.

He was right: Noel's mood was darkening by the minute. Even Aram could not help being impressed by the senior counsel's relentless cheek. Norton lolled back on his great haunches smiling benignly up at the judge.

'I do not inform,' rebutted Aram, trying not to be affected by Norton's professional laissez-faire attitude, 'but give me leave to remind your lordship, that here sat solitary sanctity, and here the hermit, or the anchoress hoped that repose for their bones, when dead, they here enjoyed when living. All this while, my lord, I am sensible this is known to your lordship, and many in this court, better than I. But, it seems necessary to my case, that others, who have not at all perhaps, adverted to things of this nature, and may have concern in my trial, should be made acquainted with it. Suffer me then, my lord, to produce a few of many evidences, that these cells were used as repositories of the dead, and to enumerate a few in which human bones have been found, as it happened in this question; lest, to some, that accident might seem extraordinary, and consequently occasion prejudice.

1. The bones, as were supposed, of the saxon St. Dubritius, were discovered buried in his cell at Guiscliffe, near Warwick, as appears from the authority of sir William Dugdale.'

'Bardsey Island! St. Dubritius was first buried at Bardsey Island and not in his cave.'

There was a sudden furore in the public. A reverend gentleman leaped up from the bench as another, holding onto his gown, tried to restrain him.

'Silence!' screamed Noel. 'Or I'll clear the court now.'

'He was then reburied at Llandaff Cathedral.' The Reverend's voice trailed away as his friend managed to tug him back to safety and out of contempt. This was all Aram needed: a religious scholar in the audience – a hostile and objectionable one at that.

'2. (Keep going Eugene, he chivvied himself on) The bones, thought to be those of the anchoress Rosia, were but lately discovered in a cell at Royston, entire, fair, and undecayed, though they must have lain interred for several centuries, as is proved by Dr. Stukeley.

3. But our own country, nay, almost this neighbourhood, supplies another instance: for in January, 1747, was found by a Mr. Stovin, accompanied by a reverend gentleman, the bones in part of some recluse, in the cell at Lindholmn, near Hatfield. They were believed to be those of William Lindholmn, a hermit, who had long made this cave his habitation.'

'I've heard enough,' piped up the Reverend again. 'He's wrong about the date and is scant on detail.'

'Hush!' whispered the friend, struggling to rein him in once more. 'It is not our place to comment here.'

Are these two in Fletcher Norton's pay, I could not help but wonder, or is the reverend gentleman simply unable to repress his hostility to Aram's scholarly interpretation.

Whichever, Aram appeared – to my surprise – to milk the situation for all it was worth: academic debate was home territory for him when all was said and done. Rightly or wrongly, he saw the Reverend as the man in court to focus on, to convince.

'4. In February, 1744, part of Woburn-abbey being pulled down, a large portion of a corpse appeared, even with the flesh on, and which bore cutting with a knife; though it is certain this had lain above 200 years, and how much longer is doubtful, for this abbey was founded in 1145, and dissolved in 1538 or 9.'

'The fellow's obsessed with corpses,' whispered Fletcher Norton, shuffling from one fat buttock to the other to express his distaste.

'Have you a question to put directly to the defendant, Mr Norton?' asked Noel.

'A man so knowledgeable on ounces of flesh, needs no help from me, my lord.'

'For once we are in agreement, Mr Norton,' flashed back the judge.

'What would have been said, what believed, if this had been an accident to the bones in question?' asked Aram. 'Farther, my lord, it is yet not out of living memory, that, at little distance from Knaresbrough, in a field, part of the manor of the worthy and patriotic baronet, who does that borough the honor to represent it in parliament, were found, in digging for gravel, not one human skeleton only, but five or six, deposited side by side, with each an urn at its head, as your lordship knows was usual in ancient interments. About the same time, and in another field almost close to this borough, was discovered also in searching for gravel, another human skeleton; but, the piety of the same worthy gentleman ordered both pits to be filled up again, commendably unwilling to disturb the dead. Is the invention of these bones forgotten, then, or industriously concealed, that the discovery of those in question may appear the more singular and extraordinary? Whereas, in fact, there is nothing extraordinary in it. My lord, almost every place conceals such remains. In fields, in hills, in highway sides, and on commons, lie frequent and unsuspected bones.'

'But could Richard Houseman, a simple tradesman, my lord, tell us where to find them?' Norton again; Norton interrupting again.

'I see you are determined that your own peerless intellect is not to be out dazzled here, Mr Norton. You will have your say later,' Noel waved Norton's objection aside with obvious relish.

'And our present allotments for rest for the departed, are but of some centuries,' threw in Aram to impress.

'The bugger grows more confident by the minute,' said Norton to Yates, no longer able to contain himself.

'Another particular seems not to claim a little of your lordship's notice, and that of the gentlemen of the jury,' ploughed on Aram undaunted. 'Which is, that perhaps no example occurs of more than *one* skeleton being found in one cell: and in the cell in question was found but *one*; agreeable, in this, to the peculiarity of every other known cell in Britain. Not the invention of one skeleton, then, but of two would have appeared suspicious and uncommon.'

Noel looked pleased with this argument.

'But then, my lord, to attempt to identify these, when even to identify living men sometimes has proved difficult, as in the case of Perkin Warbeck, and Lambert Symnel at home, and of Don Sebastian abroad, will be looked upon perhaps, as an attempt to determine what is undeterminable. And I hope too it will not pass unconsidered here, where gentlemen believe with caution, think with reason, and decide with humanity, what interest the endeavour to do this is calculated to serve, in assigning proper personality to those bones, whose particular appropriation can only appear to eternal Omniscience.'

Noel looked to the Crown's table to see how Norton was taking all this. Sir Bull-Face Double-Fee was being upstaged on his own stage. The outraged intellectual reverend had been left behind and was forgotten. Noel and the defendant and the defendant's brilliant defence were allied against Fletcher Norton finally and wonderfully.

'Permit me, my lord, also very humbly to remonstrate, that, as human bones appear to have been the inseparable adjuncts of every cell, even any person's naming such a place at random, as containing them, in this case, shows them rather unfortunate than conscious prescient, and that these attendants on every hermitage only accidentally concurred with this conjecture. A mere casual coincidence of words and things.'

Applause from the perfumed benches.

'But it seems another skeleton has been discovered by some labourer, which was full as confidently averred to be Clark's as this.'

'Fair point,' applauded someone else from the benches.

'Proceed,' Noel instructed Aram, choosing to ignore this further example of vulgar ribaldry.

'My lord, must some of the living, if it promotes some interest, be made answerable for all those bones the earth hath concealed, and chance exposed? And might not a place where bones lay be mentioned by a person by chance, as well as found by a labourer by chance? Or, is it more criminal accidentally to name where bones lie, than accidentally to find where they lie? Here too is a human skull produced, which is fractured; but, was this the cause, or was it the consequence of death; was it owing to violence or was it the effect of natural decay? If it was violence, was that violence before or after death? My lord, in May, 1732, the remains of William, lord archbishop of this province, were taken up by permission, in this cathedral, and the bones of the skull were found broken; yet, certainly he died by no violence offered to him alive, that could occasion that fracture there.' Aram glared across at Houseman. His lawyer was fidgeting, rearranging papers, while Houseman himself remained impassive; his large head cupped in his large hands.

'Feeling uncomfortable, Dickey?' someone shouted from the back of the court.

'Guilty!' someone else mocked.

At Noel's direction the usher was on the move again.

'Let it be considered, my lord, that upon the dissolution of religious houses, and the commencement of the reformation, the ravages of those times both affected the living and the dead. In search after imaginary treasures, coffins were broken up, graves and vaults dug open, monuments ransacked, and shrines demolished; your lordship knows that these violations proceeded so far as to occasion parliamentary authority to restrain them; and it did, about the beginning of the reign of queen Elizabeth. I entreat your lordship suffer not the violence, the depredations, and the iniquities of those times, to be imputed to this.' Aram theatrically drew his prison-thin arm across his brow, glanced up at Noel, before returning to his script. 'Moreover, what gentleman here is ignorant that Knaresbrough had a castle, which, though now a ruin, was once considerable both for it's strength and garrison. All know it was vigorously besieged by the arms of the parliament. At which siege, in sallies, conflicts, fights, and pursuits, many fell in all the places around it; and where they fell were buried; for every place, my lord, is burial earth in war; and many, questionless, of these rest yet unknown, whose bones futurity shall discover. I hope, with all imaginable submission, that what has been said will not be thought impertinent to this indictment; and that it will be far from the wisdom, the learning, and the integrity of this place to impute to the living what zeal in its fury may have done; what nature may have taken off, and piety interred; or what war alone may have destroyed – alone deposited.'

Some of the public cheered, a few brutes jeered, again Noel was forced to call order.

'As to the circumstances that have been raked together, I have nothing to observe; but, that all circumstances whatsoever are precarious, and have been too frequently found lamentably fallible; even the strongest have failed. They may rise to the utmost degree of probability; yet are but probability still. Why need I name to your lordship the two Harrisons, recorded in Dr. Howell, who both suffered upon circumstances, because of the sudden disappearance of their lodger, who was in credit, had contracted debts, borrowed money, and went off unseen, and returned again a great many years after their execution.'

'My lord, I must protest, I know that case well,' cried Fletcher Norton, flushed with indignation. 'It was a John Perry who had accused his brother, Richard, and mother,

Joan, of murdering one William Harrison, and he, himself, of abetting them. All three were executed and some years later the "deceased" Harrison reappeared claiming he had been kidnapped and sold into slavery.'

'I am only quoting from my source, my lord, an eminent one at that,' appealed Aram.

'Nevertheless, you should know the facts better.' Noel mentally knuckle rapped him for the first time. 'Even though through his objection Mr Norton has gone some way towards arguing your case for you,' he added, smirking across to the now deeply crimson KC.

'Why name the intricate affair of Jaques de Moulin, under King Charles II, related by a gentleman who was council for the Crown.' Aram was persistent, and his French pronunciation of "Jaques de Moulin" perfect. 'And why the unhappy Coleman, who suffered innocent, though convicted upon positive evidence, and whose children perished for want, because the world uncharitably believed the father guilty. Why mention the perjury of Smith, incautiously admitted king's evidence: who, to screen himself, equally accused Fainloth and Loveday of the murder of Dunn; the first of whom, in 1749, was executed at Winchester; and Loveday was about to suffer at Reading, had not Smith been proved perjured, to the satisfaction of the court, by the surgeon at the Gosport hospital.'

'We object, my lord.' The court had been hushed and attentive, now it was the turn of Houseman's barrister to become waspish over the citation of Smith.

'Have no fear, friend,' chuckled Fletcher Norton. 'Let him have his head, the schoolmaster will hang himself with his own ingenuity.'

'Do try and keep to the relevant points,' Noel reminded Aram: a hint of anguish in the request.

Lifting a hand, Aram indicated he was almost done.

'Now, my lord, having endeavoured to show that the whole of this process is altogether repugnant to every part of my life; that it is inconsistent with my condition of health about that time: that no rational inference can be drawn that a person is dead who suddenly disappears; that hermitages were the constant repositories of the bones of the recluse; that the proofs of these are well authenticated; that the revolutions in religion, and the fortune of war, have mangled or buried the dead; the conclusion remains, perhaps no less reasonably than impatiently wished for. I, last, after a year's confinement, equal to either fortune, put myself upon the candor, the justice, and the humanity of your lordship, and upon your's, my countrymen, gentlemen of the jury.'

The court held its great lung and then exhaled.

'What do you think of his case,?' asked Etherington quietly.

'Well thought out for someone who's not a legal man,' I replied. 'Indeed, quite brilliant in part. Might pull a verdict his way, don't you think?'

'No, no,' scoffed the man from the *Courant*, eager to pour cold water on any idea of an acquittal. 'Clever, too clever by half, too much dry teacher's chalk. Would have gone down better in a classroom of dons.'

'Or poets,' acknowledged Etherington.

'From his prepared address he had little idea that Houseman would turn against him.' A telling comment from the veteran reporter on *The London Magazine*.

'Yes,' agreed the man from the *Courant*. 'He made no attempt to explain how Houseman knew that body's head was turned to the right in the mouth of Saint Robert's Cave.'

'And how did Houseman know the exact position of those bones if he had no part in the murder?' added Etherington.

As the court mumbled its opinion on the merits of his defence, Aram looked across to where Etherington and I were seated, obviously trying to gauge from our expressions how he had fared. Etherington smiled reassuringly at him. Aram fell back exhausted and took very little notice of the official bobbing up and down that followed. I imagined the baker on the jury was beginning to wish he was back at his simple kneading; the butcher wishing he was back dressing a pig's head for his window; all wishing to be elsewhere than this place where they were about to pass a life or death judgement on one of their own.

'Although Aram claimed to be on crutches at the time of the alleged offence, he had, by his own admission in his deposition to Mr William Thornton JP, visited Saint Robert's Cave or been in close proximity to the cave on two concurrent nights,' Noel began his summing-up.

Crutches, mobility, the cave – he had overlooked that. Aram appeared deaf to most of the rest of Noel's clinical assessment. Instead his eyes flickered across the courtroom, the scene was a lip-biting blur. Had he missed anything else out? Had he done it well enough? Had he done enough to live?

'You must not give too much weight to matters of prejudice introduced by the witness Barker,' Noel was saying. Aram appeared pleased to hear that: Noel was more than balancing the scales of justice with his criticism of that conceited bastard Barker.

I noticed the beads of sweat on Noel's brow and the glisten on the faces of the jurymen as he asked them to consider their verdict. The day had grown hot. Strangely, I felt cold.

The jury leaned together whispering. They did not retire. They were talking about Aram like schoolchildren. Soon – was it too soon? – they indicated that they had reached a verdict.

'Eugene Aram, hold up thy hand. Gentlemen of the jury look upon the prisoner …'

POSTSCRIPT

So how do you find, readers, "guilty" or "not guilty"?

I feel I have delved into another man's life beyond the realms of decency. I have conjured up terrible images of what I imagined transpired on that cold winter's night back in February, 1745. The centuries will be my judge, hindsight my arbiter. The weakness of Eugene Aram's defence was his refusal to question the evidence given against him by Houseman. Whatever kind of man he was – whatever he had done – with his ferocious attack on the fallibility of circumstantial evidence, Aram helped to shape legal history in that musty August courtroom.

Plurality of murder has always lurked on the periphery of this case. I repeat the troubling quote in the *Whitehall Evening Post*: "It fell to the lot of one Clark to borrow, who met with the wished for success; at that time a Jew and his man were in the town, they sent for him, offered him the goods and sold them to him and received the money, when done, they murdered both the Jew and his man, and buried them". One body was found on Thistle Hill and another unearthed in St Robert's Cave. At the time of writing, the body of possibly a third man, perhaps a Jew, has not been discovered but that does not mean it will always be so. I feel the lack of interest regarding the fate of one or conceivably two Hebrew victims is further indication of the deplorable prejudices that still taint our society.

At the age of sixteen, Aram had first worked in Sir Edward Blackett's son's London counting house. After only a year or two in the capital, he had contracted smallpox and had been forced to return to Yorkshire giving up his post with Christopher Blackett. But for that how different history might have been.

During his second period in the South of England, he had rubbed shoulders with and taught many great men of our age. He had re-established himself as a man of good character until the Guthrie affair forced him to Norfolk. But like the good chameleon of old, he was in the process of change and reinventing himself yet again when ...

'Mr Aram! Mr Aram!' Little James Burney's distressed voice was said to have rung out as his teacher was being taken away by two stern-faced men across the playground of the Master's House.

'Jink! Jink!' The shackled Aram did not look back. He dared not chalk up the boy's future compared with his own, his own end of term future. After the distressful experience of witnessing his beloved teacher being dragged off towards the gallows, another harrowing experience was in store for little James in later life. As Rear-Admiral Burney, he accompanied Cook on his second and third voyage and was to witness the great sea explorer's terrible death at the hands of natives on the Sandwich Islands.

I believe Eugene Aram was loved by many and hated by a few. I also believe there was a Eugene and Eugenius battling away within the same man. One ordinary and reserved, the other flamboyant and ambitious; one studious and humble, the other having a simmering hatred towards those with position but without intellect. Unfortunately, the fecund

Anna Aram encapsulated all that had brought him low. He felt she alone had been his barrier to success and he blamed her, not himself, for his ultimate downfall. While teaching in Netherdale he tells us: "I married, unfortunately enough for me: For, the misconduct of the wife which that place afforded me, has procured me this place, this prosecution, this infamy, and this sentence". The word "misconduct" here fascinates me: is he referring to his belief that Anna kept bad company or had an adulterous affair with Clark say, or others? – or is he referring to happenings in higher Netherdale before his marriage? – the unregistered birth of Sally perhaps or the delayed registration of his daughter Anna.

Aram was a man who liked to be in control, the sexual control of his daughter was easy, the same control of an "inferior" wife earning her own bread and keep more difficult. During his final hours on earth, he attempted to regain control with a suicide attempt. Fate conspired against him even in this, his choice of death, as he was trundled along in a weakened state to the humiliation of York's Tyburn Tree.

Despite Aram's own rationalisation "As for any indignities offered to my body, or silly reflections on my faith and morals, they are (as they always were) things indifferent to me", what humiliation for the scholar and schoolteacher to be hanged before a pitying crowd, then hung in chains before curious children and ridiculed by his Knaresborough enemies. To be seen shrinking and mummifying in the winds; decaying in the rain; stripped to naked bone before tumbling to earth to be gathered up by ghoulish collectors.

Why was I not surprised to learn from my original source – Dr Thomas Short of Sheffield – before his own death in

1772, that after all that had passed between them it was Anna who diligently rescued most of her husband's bones from the trophy hunters. But not his skull – Eugene Aram's skull was destined to go elsewhere.

Years later the radical young publisher, William Effingham Wilson, cousin to my erstwhile friend the late Thomas Hutchinson, told me that the Knaresborough physician had mounted the gibbet post one dark and stormy night and removed Aram's skull with difficulty from its iron restraints. This did not greatly perplex me, as far back as my original acquaintanceship with him, I had realised Thomas was coveting Aram's skull for his museum.

Francis Iles died on the 1st November, 1776. His name is commemorated in stone close to the altar in Knaresborough Parish Church. Towards the end of his life he built himself a fine new house called Fish Hall, in York Place, on the outskirts of the town. An adjoining lane bears his name. It is rumoured that many luxury goods were found stored in Fish Hall after Iles' death.

I heard that the publisher and bookseller who had sat next to me throughout Aram's trial, Christopher Etherington, went bankrupt in the January of 1777. Alas, how risky our trade in the printed word.

Richard Houseman, despite all expectation, died in his bed two months later on 16th March, 1777. Fearing his body would be torn to pieces by the mob, it was removed on a cart in the dead of night to be buried in the village of his birth, Marton.

Was it Houseman or Aram who murdered Clark during the plot to defraud their neighbours? Does it really matter who physically struck the deadly blow? – they were both culpable, and perhaps others too. What does matter is that the undefended schoolmaster paid the price alone.

Aram had mentioned as part of his defence that one, William Thompson, had escaped York's Castle Prison in double leg irons in 1757. So if it were possible for Thompson to disappear despite the "vigilance of this place" why not Clark from Knaresborough? There is an interesting reversal to this story in that according to William Bristow, bookseller of London, the skeleton of Thompson was found on Saturday, the 8th July, 1780, behind the Old Court House, in the Castle of York, near the foundation. It is suspected that the criminal got on the top of the Court House building with the help of a ladder which was kept there, but somehow had fallen down the wall to his death. As nothing but nettles and weeds grew beneath, his skeleton had lain there undiscovered for twenty-three years.

Through Thomas Hutchinson's correspondence with me, I gleaned he had mellowed late in life. The word "wholesome" entered his vocabulary after Jane Walker made an honest man out of him on the 17th May, 1781, at Rothwell, near Leeds. Two years later he was granted an M.D. by Marischal College, Aberdeen. And there, I had accepted him as a bona fide physician all along.

In the following years, his infrequent letters dried up completely. In the spring of 1797, I had a letter from Jane, now his widow, telling me her husband had died some months before. Thomas had left his eldest son, William, his museum and his youngest son, George, a set of the *Gentleman's Magazine.*

ACKNOWLEDGEMENTS

We live in a world of coincidences. The man who first published *The Genuine Account of the Trial of Eugene Aram for the Murder of Daniel Clark Late of Knaresborough* was a Mr Christopher Etherington, a York publisher and bookseller originally at the sign of the Pope's Head in Coney Street. The printer of that book was Ann Ward, also of Coney Street, widow of the publisher of the *York Courant.* Later Etherington owned his own press in Coppergate and started in 1772 the *York Chronicle* in opposition to the *Courant*, but unfortunately his newspaper was short lived. History has turned full circle. Etherington, who I believe will have attended Eugene Aram's trial, had his book printed by a local press two hundred and fifty-eight years ago. This the most recent work to date again has been produced in that same city by York Publishing Services. A big thank you goes to the team at YPS.

Paul, my husband, has accompanied me every step of this long journey. Without his support and editorial input this work might never have seen the light of day.

Praise goes to Professor Miranda Aldhouse-Green of Cardiff University for her guidelines on authenticating Celtic carved heads.

I am grateful to Professor Frank Felsenstein of Ball State University for taking the time, in a busy academic schedule, to give his expert appraisal of my original manuscript.

I am indebted to Professor John Goodridge of Nottingham Trent University for supplying so much information about Eugene Aram's ancestry.

Tom Richardson's assistance at the Northallerton County Record Office was commendable in wading through a labyrinth of documents, as was the help from all the staff at the West Yorkshire Archives when located at Sheepscar, Leeds. The archivists at King's Lynn Library were wonderfully cooperative in helping me to turn up vital information regarding Aram's stay in their town. I thought I was on a film set while researching under the big reading lamps in the round room of the old Public Record Office in Chancery Lane. After 2003 the PRO was merged with other departments to form the National Archives – the reading room became the Maughan Library, part of King's College London – which only goes to show how long I have been absorbed with Mr Aram.

In more recent times Mr Crossland was the knowledgeable gatekeeper to a very enjoyable afternoon exploring Mother Shipton's Cave.

I found facsimiles of old newspaper articles invaluable in my research. As were the works of the printer William Bristow, barristers Norrisson Scatcherd and E R Watson. The A to Z of Knaresborough, by the late Dr Arnold Kellett revised by Paul Chrystal, gave me a quick and accurate insight into the town where Aram spent most of his life teaching and rearing his own children. Dr Kellett was a prolific writer on many diverse subjects. He was awarded a PhD from Leeds University for his thesis on Eugene Aram, which I believe is still housed in the library there. I chose not to visit Dr Kellett's work, not out of any disrespect for his obvious scholarship, but simply because I wanted to make up my own mind as to what actually happened.

I have travelled the length and breadth of England visiting countless religious houses, offices, officials and interviewing people with folk memories that were well worth exploring – all of whom I thank profoundly – in an attempt to find out how this terrible crime evolved on that snowy February night back in eighteenth century Yorkshire.

If the result is an enjoyable, enlightening and rewarding reading experience then it has all been worthwhile.

AUTHOR'S PROFILE

Educated in Leeds, Amanda Taylor did some magazine work and won a National Poetry Prize. She played squash for Yorkshire for nine years. Despite living in the middle of a grouse moor, about as far away as you can get from the sea, Amanda completed a successful relay swim of the English Channel and maintains that working out her plots helps the tedium of all those training miles. Her previous published historical crime novels are *Dangerous Waves, Mortimer Blakely is Missing* and *The Vigil of Rain* which form the Cairn Mystery Trilogy.

Visit her website: www.amandataylorauthor.com